Educational Thoughts of Rabindranath Tagore

Educational Thoughts of Rabindranath Tagore

Dr. Sudharma Joshi

CRESCENT
PUBLISHING CORPORATION

[The responsibility for the facts stated, conclusions reached and plagiarism, if any, in this book is entirely that of the Author. And the Publisher bears no responsibility for them, whatsoever.]

Educational Thoughts of Rabindranath Tagore

Edition 2026

ISBN 978-81-8342-161-4

Published By :
CRESCENT PUBLISHING CORPORATION
4806/24, Mathur Lane,
Ansari Road, Darya Ganj,
New Delhi - 110002
Mob. : +91-9711991838, 9999021668
Ph. : 011-23244131
e-mail : crescentbook@gmail.com

Website : www.crescentpublishingcorp.weebly.com

Laser Typesetting by :
Adee Computers

Printed at :
Balaji Digital
Delhi

Preface

Rabindranath Tagore is often remembered today for his written composition of the Indian National Anthem, as well as for being the first Indian recipient of the Novel Prize for literature. This paragon of Indian culture and aesthetics, however, encompassed an astonishing range of talents as a playwright, poet, novelist, painter, musician, and philosopher, that he is often rightly described as true Indian Renaissance Man. It is within the range of his aesthetic as well as artistic ideologies that arose his unique brand of educational philosophy, which differed markedly from his predecessors, contemporaries as well successors in its insistence on a natural, inquisitiveness-based learning through self-discovery rather tan rate learning via books.

This book on the educational philosophies of famous Indian analyses the educational ideology of Rabindranath Tagore, contexualising his beliefs in his age, as well as assessing its relevance in the present times. The book undertakes a look at his role as one of the earliest educators in terms of globalisation, and his beliefs which are aptly centred for education within multi-racial, multi-lingual and multi-cultural situations, and explores his tryst with Santiniketan, his educational establishment which run along the lines his beliefs. It also contrasts his ideology with his contemporaries, and analyses its present relevance.

It is hoped that the book's erudition and content serve well for educationists.

Dr. Sudharma Joshi

Contents

1

Introduction

Rabindranath Tagore also known by the sobriquet Gurudev, was a Bengali poet, Brahmo Samaj philosopher, visual artist, playwright, novelist, and composer whose works reshaped Bengali literature and music in the late 19th and early 20th centuries. He became Asia's first Nobel laureate when he won the 1913 Nobel Prize in Literature.

A Pirali Bengali Brahmin from Calcutta, Tagore first wrote poems at age eight. He published his first substantial poetry-under the pseudonym Bhanushingho ("Sun Lion")-and wrote his first short stories and dramas in 1877, at age sixteen. His home schooling, life in Shilaidaha, and travels made Tagore a nonconformist and pragmatist. Tagore strongly protested against the British Raj and gave his support to the Indian Independence Movement and Mahatma Gandhi. Tagore's life was tragic-he lost virtually his entire family and was devastated to witness Bengal's decline-but his life's work endured, in the form of his poetry and the institution he founded, Visva-Bharati University.

Tagore's works included numerous novels, short-stories, collection of songs, dance-drama, political and personal essays. Some prominent examples are Gitanjali (Song Offerings), Gora (Fair-Faced), and Ghare-Baire (The Home and the World). His verse, short stories, and novels-many defined by rhythmic lyricism, colloquial language, meditative naturalism, and philosophical contemplation-received worldwide acclaim. Tagore was also a cultural reformer and polymath who modernised Bengali art by rejecting strictures binding it to classical Indian forms. Two songs from his rabindrasangeet canon are now the national anthems of Bangladesh and India: the Amar Shonar Bangla and the Jana Gana Mana.

Early Life (1861-1901)

Tagore (nicknamed "Rabi") was born the thirteenth of fourteen children in the Jorasanko mansion in Calcutta (now Kolkata, India) of parents Debendranath Tagore and Sarada Devi. After undergoing his upanayan (the sacred thread ceremony, a coming-of-age rite) at age eleven, Tagore and his father left Calcutta on 14 February 1873 to tour India for several months, visiting his father's Santiniketan estate and Amritsar before reaching the Himalayan hill station of Dalhousie.

There, Tagore read biographies, studied history, astronomy, modern science, and Sanskrit, and examined the classical poetry of Kalidasa. In 1877, he rose to notability when he composed several works, including a long poem set in the Maithili style pioneered by Vidyapati. As a joke, he maintained that these were the lost works of Bhanusi?ha, a newly discovered 17th-century Vai??ava poet. He also wrote "Bhikharini" (1877; "The Beggar Woman"-the Bengali language's first short story) and Sandhya Sangit (1882) -including the famous poem "Nirjharer Swapnabhanga" ("The Rousing of the Waterfall").

Seeking to become a barrister, Tagore enrolled at a public school in Brighton, England in 1878; later, he studied at University College London, but returned to Bengal in 1880 without a degree. On 9 December 1883 he married Mrinalini Devi (born Bhabatarini, 1873-1902); they had five children, two of whom later died before reaching full adulthood. In 1890, Tagore (joined in 1898 by his wife and children) began managing his family's estates in Shilaidaha, a region now in Bangladesh known as "Zamindar Babu", Tagore traveled across the vast estate while living out of the family's luxurious barge, the Padma, to collect (mostly token) rents and bless villagers; in exchange, he had feasts held in his honour. During these years, Tagore's Sadhana period (1891-1895; named for one of Tagore's magazines) was among his most fecund, with more than half the stories of the three-volume and eighty-four-story Galpaguchchha written. With irony and emotional weight, they depicted a wide range of Bengali lifestyles, particularly village life.

Santiniketan (1901-1932)

In 1901, Tagore left Shilaidaha and moved to Santiniketan (West Bengal) to found an ashram, which would grow to include a marble-floored prayer hall ("The Mandir"), an experimental school, groves of trees, gardens, and a library. There, Tagore's wife and two of his children died. His father also died on 19 January 1905, and he began receiving monthly payments as part of his inheritance; he also received income from the Maharaja of Tripura, sales of his family's jewelery, his seaside bungalow in Puri, and mediocre royalties (Rs. 2,000) from his works.

These works gained him a large following among Bengali and foreign readers alike, and he published such works as Naivedya (1901) and Kheya (1906) while translating his poems into free verse. On 14 November 1913, Tagore learned that he had won the 1913 Nobel Prize in Literature. According to the Swedish Academy, it was given due to the idealistic and-for Western readers-accessible nature of a small body of his translated material, including the 1912 Gitanjali: Song Offerings. In

1915, Tagore also accepted knighthood from the British Crown.

In 1921, Tagore and agricultural economist Leonard Elmhirst set up the Institute for Rural Reconstruction (which Tagore later renamed Shriniketan-"Abode of Peace") in Surul, a village near the ashram at Santiniketan. Through it, Tagore sought to provide an alternative to Gandhi's symbol- and protest-based Swaraj movement, which he denounced. He recruited scholars, donors, and officials from many countries to help the Institute use schooling to "free village[s] from the shackles of helplessness and ignorance" by "vitaliz[ing] knowledge". In the early 1930s, he also grew more concerned about India's "abnormal caste consciousness" and Untouchability, lecturing on its evils, writing poems and dramas with Untouchable protagonists, and appealing to authorities at Kerala's Guruvayoor Temple to admit Dalits.

Twilight years (1932-1941)

In his last decade, Tagore remained in the public limelight, publicly upbraiding Gandhi for stating that a massive 15 January 1934 earthquake in Bihar constituted divine retribution for the subjugation of Dalits. He also mourned the incipient socioeconomic decline of Bengal and the endemic poverty of Calcutta; he detailed the latter in an unrhymed hundred-line poem whose technique of searing double-vision would foreshadow Satyajit Ray's film Apur Sansar.

Tagore also compiled fifteen volumes of writings, including the prose-poems works Punashcha (1932), Shes Saptak (1935), and Patraput (1936). He continued his experimentations by developing prose-songs and dance-dramas, including Chitrangada (1914), Shyama (1939), and Chandalika (1938), and wrote the novels Dui Bon

(1933), Malancha (1934), and Char Adhyay (1934). Tagore took an interest in science in his last years, writing Visva-Parichay (a collection of essays) in 1937. He explored biology, physics, and astronomy; meanwhile, his poetry-containing extensive naturalism-underscored his respect for scientific laws. He also wove the process of science (including narratives of scientists) into many stories contained in such volumes as Se (1937), Tin Sangi (1940), and Galpasalpa (1941).

Tagore's last four years were marked by chronic pain and two long periods of illness. These began when Tagore lost consciousness in late 1937; he remained comatose and near death for an extended period. This was followed three years later in late 1940 by a similar spell, from which he never recovered. The poetry Tagore wrote in these years is among his finest, and is distinctive for its preoccupation with death. After extended suffering, Tagore died on 7 August 1941 (22 Shravan 1348) in an upstairs room of the Jorasanko mansion in which he was raised; his death anniversary is still mourned in public functions held across the Bengali-speaking world.

Travels

Owing to his notable wanderlust, between 1878 and 1932, Tagore visited more than thirty countries on five continents; many of these trips were crucial in familiarising non-Indian audiences to his works and spreading his political ideas. For example, in 1912, he took a sheaf of his translated works to England, where they impressed missionary and Gandhi protégé Charles F. Andrews, Anglo-Irish poet William Butler Yeats, Ezra Pound, Robert Bridges, Ernest Rhys, Thomas Sturge Moore, and others. Indeed, Yeats wrote the preface to the English translation of Gitanjali, while Andrews joined Tagore at Santiniketan.

On 10 November 1912, Tagore toured the United States and the United Kingdom, staying in Butterton, Staffordshire with Andrews' clergymen friends. From 3 May 1916 until April 1917, Tagore went on lecturing circuits in Japan and the United States, during which he denounced nationalism-particularly that of the Japanese and Americans. He also wrote the essay "Nationalism in India", attracting both derision and praise (the latter from pacifists, including Romain Rolland). Shortly after returning to India, the 63-year-old Tagore visited Peru at the invitation of the Peruvian government, and took the opportunity to visit Mexico as well.

Both governments pledged donations of $100,000 to the school at Shantiniketan (Visva-Bharati) in commemoration of his visits. A week after his November 6, 1924 arrival in Buenos Aires, Argentina, an ill Tagore moved into the Villa Miralrío at the behest of Victoria Ocampo. He left for India in January 1925. On 30 May 1926, Tagore reached Naples, Italy; he met fascist dictator Benito Mussolini in Rome the next day. Their initially warm rapport lasted until Tagore spoke out against Mussolini on 20 July 1926.

On 14 July 1927, Tagore and two companions went on a four-month tour of Southeast Asia-visiting Bali, Java, Kuala Lumpur, Malacca, Penang, Siam, and Singapore. The travelogues from this tour were collected into the work "Jatri". In early 1930 he left Bengal for a nearly year-long tour of Europe and the U.S. On his return to the UK, while his paintings were being exhibited in Paris and London, he stayed at a Friends settlement in Birmingham. There, he wrote his Hibbert Lectures for the University of Oxford (which dealt with the "idea of the humanity of our God, or the divinity of Man the Eternal") and spoke at London's annual Quaker gathering. There (addressing relations between the British and Indians, a topic he would grapple with over the next two years), Tagore spoke of a "dark chasm of aloofness".

He later visited Aga Khan III, stayed at Dartington Hall, then toured Denmark, Switzerland, and Germany from June to mid-September 1930, then the Soviet Union. Lastly, in April 1932, Tagore-who was acquainted with the legends and works of the Persian mystic Hafez-was invited as a personal guest of Shah Reza Shah Pahlavi of Iran. Such extensive travels allowed Tagore to interact with many notable contemporaries, including Henri Bergson, Albert Einstein, Robert Frost, Thomas Mann, George Bernard Shaw, H.G. Wells and Romain Rolland. Tagore's last travels abroad, including visits to Persia and Iraq (in 1932) and Ceylon in 1933, only sharpened his opinions regarding human divisions and nationalism.

Works

Tagore's literary reputation is disproportionately influenced by regard for his poetry; however, he also wrote novels, essays, short stories, travelogues, dramas, and thousands of songs. Of Tagore's prose, his short stories are perhaps most highly regarded; indeed, he is credited with originating the Bengali-language version of the genre. His works are frequently noted for their rhythmic, optimistic, and lyrical nature. However, such stories mostly borrow from deceptively simple subject matter-the lives of ordinary people.

Novels and non-fiction

Tagore wrote eight novels and four novellas, including Chaturanga, Shesher Kobita, Char Odhay, and Noukadubi. Ghare Baire (The Home and the World)-through the lens of the idealistic zamindar protagonist Nikhil-excoriates rising Indian nationalism, terrorism, and religious zeal in the Swadeshi movement; a frank expression of Tagore's conflicted sentiments, it emerged out of a 1914 bout of depression. Indeed, the novel bleakly ends with Hindu-Muslim sectarian violence and Nikhil's being (probably mortally) wounded.

In some sense, Gora shares the same theme, raising controversial questions regarding the Indian identity. As with Ghore Baire, matters of self-identity (jati), personal freedom, and religion are developed in the context of a family story and love triangle. Another powerful story is Yogayog (Nexus), where the heroine Kumudini-bound by the ideals of Shiva-Sati, exemplified by Dakshayani-is torn between her pity for the sinking fortunes of her progressive and compassionate elder brother and his foil: her exploitative, rakish, and patriarchical husband. In it, Tagore demonstrates his feminist leanings, using pathos to depict the plight and ultimate demise of Bengali women trapped by pregnancy, duty, and family honour; simultaneously, he treats the decline of Bengal's landed oligarchy.

Other novels were more uplifting: Shesher Kobita (translated twice-Last Poem and Farewell Song) is his most lyrical novel, with poems and rhythmic passages written by the main character (a poet). It also contains elements of satire and postmodernism, whereby stock characters gleefully attack the reputation of an old, outmoded, oppressively renowned poet who, incidentally, goes by the name of Rabindranath Tagore. Though his novels remain among the least-appreciated of his works, they have been given renewed attention via film adaptations by such directors as Satyajit Ray; these include Chokher Bali and Ghare Baire; many have soundtracks featuring selections from Tagore's own rabindrasangit. Tagore wrote many non-fiction books, writing on topics ranging from Indian history to linguistics. Aside from autobiographical works, his travelogues, essays, and lectures were compiled into several volumes, including Iurop Jatrir Patro (Letters from Europe) and Manusher Dhormo (The Religion of Man).

Tagore was an accomplished musician and painter, writing around 2,230 songs. They compose rabindrasangit, now an integral part of Bengali culture. Tagore's music is inseparable from his literature, most of which-poems or parts of novels, stories, or plays alike-became lyrics for his songs. Primarily influenced by the thumri style of Hindustani classical music, they ran the entire gamut of human emotion, ranging from his early dirge-like Brahmo devotional hymns to quasi-erotic compositions. They emulated the tonal color of classical ragas to varying extents; while at times his songs mimicked a given raga's melody and rhythm faithfully, he also blended elements of different ragas to create innovative works.

For Bengalis, their appeal-stemming from the combination of emotive strength and beauty described as surpassing even Tagore's poetry-was such that the Modern Review observed that "[t]here is in Bengal no cultured home where Rabindranath's songs are not sung or at least attempted to be sung ... Even illiterate villagers sing his songs". Music critic Arther Strangeways of The Observer first introduced non-Bengalis to rabindrasangit with his book The Music of Hindostan, which described it as a "vehicle of a personality ... [that] go behind this or that system of music to that beauty of sound which all systems put out their hands to seize." Among them are Bangladesh's national anthem Amar Sonaar Baanglaa and India's national anthem Jana Gana Mana; Tagore thus became the only person ever to have written the national anthems of two nations. In turn, rabindrasangit influenced the styles of such musicians as sitar maestro Vilayat Khan, and the sarodiyas Buddhadev Dasgupta and Amjad Ali Khan.

At age sixty, Tagore took up drawing and painting; successful exhibitions of his many works-which made a debut appearance in Paris upon encouragement by artists he met in the south of France-were held throughout Europe. Tagore-who likely exhibited protanopia ("color blindness"), or partial lack of (red-green, in Tagore's case) colour discernment-painted in a style characterised by peculiarities in aesthetics and colouring schemes.

Nevertheless, Tagore took to emulating numerous styles, including that of craftwork by the Malanggan people of northern New Ireland, Haida carvings from the west coast of Canada (British Columbia), and woodcuts by Max Pechstein. Tagore also had an artist's eye for his own handwriting, embellishing the scribbles, cross-outs, and word layouts in his manuscripts with simple artistic leitmotifs, including simple rhythmic designs.

Theatrical pieces

Tagore's experience in theatre began at age sixteen, when he played the lead role in his brother Jyotirindranath's adaptation of Molière's Le Bourgeois Gentilhomme. At age twenty, he wrote his first drama-opera-Valmiki Pratibha (The Genius of Valmiki)-which describes how the bandit Valmiki reforms his ethos, is blessed by Saraswati, and composes the Ramayana. Through it, Tagore vigorously explores a wide range of dramatic styles and emotions, including usage of revamped kirtans and adaptation of traditional English and Irish folk melodies as drinking songs.

Another notable play, Dak Ghar (The Post Office), describes how a child-striving to escape his stuffy confines-ultimately "fall[s] asleep" (which suggests his physical death). A story with worldwide appeal (it received rave reviews in Europe), Dak Ghar dealt with death as, in Tagore's words, "spiritual freedom" from "the world of hoarded wealth and certified creeds".

His other works-emphasizing fusion of lyrical flow and emotional rhythm tightly focused on a core idea-were unlike previous Bengali dramas. His works sought to articulate, in Tagore's words, "the play of feeling and not of action". In 1890 he wrote Visarjan (Sacrifice), regarded as his finest drama. The Bengali-language originals included intricate subplots and extended monologues. Later, his dramas probed more philosophical and allegorical themes; these included Dak Ghar.

Another is Tagore's Chandalika (Untouchable Girl), which was modeled on an ancient Buddhist legend describing how Ananda-the Gautama Buddha's disciple-asks water of an Adivasi ("untouchable") girl. Lastly, among his most famous dramas is Raktakaravi (Red Oleanders), which tells of a kleptocratic king who enriches himself by forcing his subjects to mine. The heroine, Nandini, eventually rallies the common people to destroy these symbols of subjugation. Tagore's other plays include Chitrangada, Raja, and Mayar Khela. Dance dramas based on Tagore's plays are commonly referred to as rabindra nritya natyas.

Short stories

Tagore's "Sadhana" period, comprising the four years from 1891 to 1895, was named for one of Tagore's magazines. This period was among Tagore 's most fecund, yielding more than half the stories contained in the three-volume Galpaguchchha, which itself is a collection of eighty-four stories. Such stories usually showcase Tagore's reflections upon his surroundings, on modern and fashionable ideas, and on interesting mind puzzles (which Tagore was fond of testing his intellect with).

Tagore typically associated his earliest stories (such as those of the "Sadhana" period) with an exuberance of vitality and spontaneity; these characteristics were intimately connected with Tagore's life in the common villages of, among others, Patisar, Shajadpur, and Shilaida while managing the Tagore family's vast landholdings. There, he beheld the lives of India's poor and common people; Tagore thereby took to examining their lives with a penetrative depth and feeling that was singular in Indian literature up to that point.

In "The Fruitseller from Kabul", Tagore speaks in first person as town-dweller and novelist who chances upon the Afghani seller. He attempts to distil the sense of longing felt by those long trapped in the mundane and hardscrabble confines of Indian urban life, giving play to dreams of a different existence in the distant and wild mountains: "There were autumn mornings, the time of year when kings of old went forth to conquest; and I, never stirring from my little corner in Calcutta, would let my mind wander over the whole world.

At the very name of another country, my heart would go out to it ... I would fall to weaving a network of dreams: the mountains, the glens, the forest .... ". Many of the other Galpaguchchha stories were written in Tagore's Sabuj Patra period (1914-1917; also named for one of Tagore's magazines).

Tagore's Golpoguchchho (Bunch of Stories) remains among Bengali literature's most popular fictional works, providing subject matter for many successful films and theatrical plays. Satyajit Ray's film Charulata was based upon Tagore's controversial novella, Nastanirh (The Broken Nest). In Atithi (also made into a film), the young Brahmin boy Tarapada shares a boat ride with a village zamindar. The boy reveals that he has run away from home, only to wander around ever since. Taking pity, the zamindar adopts him and ultimately arranges his marriage to the zamindar's own daughter. However, the night before the wedding, Tarapada runs off-again. Strir Patra (The Letter from the Wife) is among Bengali literature's earliest depictions of the bold emancipation of women.

The heroine Mrinal, the wife of a typical patriarchical Bengali middle class man, writes a letter while she is traveling (which constitutes the whole story). It details the pettiness of her life and struggles; she finally declares that she will not return to her husband's home with the statement Amio bachbo. Ei bachlum ("And I shall live. Here, I live").

In Haimanti, Tagore takes on the institution of Hindu marriage, describing the dismal lifelessness of married Bengali women, hypocrisies plaguing the Indian middle classes, and how Haimanti, a sensitive young woman, must-due to her sensitiveness and free spirit-sacrifice her life. In the last passage, Tagore directly attacks the Hindu custom of glorifying Sita's attempted self-immolation as a means of appeasing her husband Rama's doubts.

Tagore also examines Hindu-Muslim tensions in Musalmani Didi, which in many ways embodies the essence of Tagore's humanism. On the other hand, Darpaharan exhibits Tagore's self-consciousness, describing a young man harboring literary ambitions. Though he loves his wife, he wishes to stifle her own literary career, deeming it unfeminine.

Tagore himself, in his youth, seems to have harbored similar ideas about women. Darpaharan depicts the final humbling of the man via his acceptance of his wife's talents. As many other Tagore stories, Jibito o Mrito provides the Bengalis with one of their more widely used epigrams: Kadombini moriya proman korilo she more nai ("Kadombini died, thereby proved that she hadn't").

Poetry

Tagore's poetry-which varied in style from classical formalism to the comic, visionary, and ecstatic-proceeds out a lineage established by 15th- and 16th-century Vai??ava poets. Tagore was also influenced by the mysticism of the rishi-authors who-including Vyasa-wrote the Upanishads, the Bhakta-Sufi mystic Kabir, and Ramprasad.

Yet Tagore's poetry became most innovative and mature after his exposure to rural Bengal's folk music, which included ballads sung by Baul folk singers-especially the bard Lalan Sah. These-which were rediscovered and popularised by Tagore-resemble 19th-century Kartabhaja hymns that emphasize inward divinity and rebellion against religious and social orthodoxy.

During his Shilaidaha years, his poems took on a lyrical quality, speaking via the maner manus (the Bauls' "man within the heart") or meditating upon the jivan devata ("living God within"). This figure thus sought connection with divinity through appeal to nature and the emotional interplay of human drama. Tagore used such techniques in his Bhanusi?ha poems (which chronicle the romanticism between Radha and Krishna), which he repeatedly revised over the course of seventy years.

Later, Tagore responded to the (mostly) crude emergence of modernism and realism in Bengali literature by writing experimental works in the 1930s. Examples works include Africa and Camalia, which are among the better known of his latter poems. He also occasionally wrote poems using Shadhu Bhasha (a Sanskritised dialect of Bengali); later, he began using Cholti Bhasha (a more popular dialect). Other notable works include Manasi,

Sonar Tori (Golden Boat), Balaka (Wild Geese-the title being a metaphor for migrating souls), and Purobi.

Political views

Marked complexities characterise Tagore's political views. Though he criticised European imperialism and supported Indian nationalists, he also lampooned the Swadeshi movement, denouncing it in "The Cult of the Charka", an acrid 1925 essay. Instead, he emphasized self-help and intellectual uplift of the masses, stating that British imperialism was not a primary evil, but instead a "political symptom of our social disease", urging Indians to accept that "there can be no question of blind revolution, but of steady and purposeful education".

Such views inevitably enraged many, placing his life in danger: during his stay in a San Francisco hotel in late 1916, Tagore narrowly escaped assassination by Indian expatriates-the plot failed only because the would-be assassins fell into argument. Yet Tagore wrote songs lionizing the Indian independence movement and renounced his knighthood in protest against the 1919 Jallianwala Bagh Massacre.

Two of Tagore's more politically charged compositions, "Chitto Jetha Bhayshunyo" ("Where the Mind is Without Fear") and "Ekla Chalo Re" ("If They Answer Not to Thy Call, Walk Alone"), gained mass appeal, with the latter favoured by Gandhi. Despite his tumultuous relations with Gandhi, Tagore was also key in resolving a Gandhi-Ambedkar dispute involving separate electorates for untouchables, ending a fast "unto death" by Gandhi.

Tagore also criticised orthodox (rote-oriented) education, lampooning it in the short story "The Parrot's Training", where a bird-which ultimately dies-is caged by tutors and force-fed pages torn from books. These views led Tagore-while visiting Santa Barbara, California on 11 October 1917-to conceive of a new type of university, desiring to "make [his ashram at] Santiniketan the connecting thread between India and the world ... [and] a world center for the study of humanity ... somewhere beyond the limits of nation and geography."

The school-which he named Visva-Bharati-had its foundation stone laid on 22 December 1918; it was later inaugurated on 22 December 1921. Here, Tagore implemented a brahmacharya pedagogical structure employing gurus to provide individualised guidance for pupils. Tagore worked hard to fundraise for and staff the school, even contributing all of his Nobel Prize monies. Tagore's duties as steward and mentor at Santiniketan kept him busy; he taught classes in mornings and wrote the students' textbooks in afternoons and evenings. Tagore also fundraised extensively for the school in Europe and the U.S. between 1919 and 1921.

Impact and legacy

Tagore's post-death impact can be felt through the many festivals held worldwide in his honour-examples include the annual Bengali festival/celebration of Kabipranam (Tagore's birthday anniversary), the annual Tagore Festival held in Urbana, Illinois in the United States, the Rabindra Path Parikrama walking pilgrimages leading from Calcutta to Shantiniketan, and ceremonial recitals of Tagore's poetry held on important anniversaries. This legacy is most palpable in Bengali culture, ranging from language and arts to history and politics; indeed, Nobel laureate Amartya Sen noted that even for modern Bengalis, Tagore was a "towering figure", being a "deeply relevant and many-sided contemporary thinker".

Tagore's collected Bengali-language writings-the 1939 Rabindra Racanavali-is also canonized as one of Bengal's greatest cultural treasures, while Tagore himself has been proclaimed "the greatest poet India has produced". He was also famed throughout much of Europe, North America, and East Asia. He was key in founding Dartington Hall School, a progressive coeducational institution; in Japan, he influenced such figures as Nobel laureate Yasunari Kawabata.

Tagore's works were widely translated into many European languages-a process that began with Czech indologist Vincent Slesny and French Nobel laureate André Gide-including Russian, English, Dutch, German, Spanish, and others. In the United States, Tagore's popular lecturing circuits (especially those between 1916-1917) were widely attended and acclaimed. Nevertheless, several controversies[?] involving Tagore resulted in a decline in his popularity in Japan and North America after the late 1920s, contributing to his "near total eclipse" outside of Bengal.

Tagore, through Spanish translations of his works, also influenced leading figures of Spanish literature, including Chileans Pablo Neruda and Gabriela Mistral, Mexican writer Octavio Paz, and Spaniards José Ortega y Gasset, Zenobia Camprubí, and Juan Ramón Jiménez. Between 1914 and 1922, the Jiménez-Camprubí spouses translated no less than twenty-two of Tagore's books from English into Spanish. Jiménez, as part of this work, also extensively revised and adapted such works as Tagore's The Crescent Moon.

Indeed, during this time, Jiménez developed the now-heralded innovation of "naked poetry" (Spanish: «poesia desnuda»). Meanwhile, Ortega y Gasset wrote that "Tagore's wide appeal [may stem from the fact that] he speaks of longings for perfection that we all have ... Tagore awakens a dormant sense of childish wonder, and he saturates the air with all kinds of enchanting promises for the reader, who ... pays little attention to the deeper import of Oriental mysticism".

Indeed, Tagore's works were-alongside works by Dante Alighieri, Miguel de Cervantes, Johann Wolfgang von Goethe, Plato, and Leo Tolstoy-published in free editions around 1920. Tagore's talents came to be regarded as over rated by a few westerners like Graham Greene who in 1937 remarked that "I cannot believe that anyone but Mr. Yeats can still take his poems very seriously."Modern remnants of a once widespread Latin American reverence of Tagore were discovered, for example, by an astonished Salman Rushdie during a trip to Nicaragua.

2

Family Life and Early Influences

Rabindranath Tagore was born on 7 May 1861. At some time towards the end of the seventeenth century, his forefathers had migrated from their native lands to Govindpur, one of the three villages which later came to constitute Calcutta. In the course of time, the family came to acquire property and considerable business interests through the pursuit of commercial and banking activities. They had particularly benefited from the growing power of the British East India Company. Rabindranath's grandfather, Dwarkanath Tagore, lived lavishly and broke the Hindu religious ban of those times by travelling to Europe, just like his contemporary, Rammohan Roy, the nineteenth century social and religious reformer.

Roy started a religious reform movement in 1828 that came to be known as the Brahma Samaj Movement. Rabindranath's grandfather supported Roy in his attempts at reforming Hindu society. Dwarkanath's son, Devendranath Tagore, also became a staunch supporter of the Brahma Samaj Movement. In order to encourage its spread, in 1863 he established a meditation centre and guest house on some land about 100 miles from Calcutta at a place called 'Santiniketan', the Abode of Peace.

Although deeply steeped in Hindu and Islamic traditions, Tagore's family contributed large sums of money for the introduction of Western education, including colleges for the study of science and medicine. This peculiar situation explains the combination of tradition and experiment that came to characterise Rabindranath Tagore's attitude to life.

Rabindranath's father was one of the leading figures of the newly awakened phase of Bengali society. He had been educated at one stage in Rammohan Roy's Anglo-Hindu school and had been greatly influenced by Roy's character, ideals and religious devotion. Devendranath Tagore was well versed in European philosophy and, though deeply religious, did not accept all aspects of Hinduism. He was to have a profound influence on his son's mental and practical attitudes.

Rabindranath was the fourteenth child of his parents. His brothers and sisters were poets, musicians, playwrights and novelists and the Tagore home was thus filled with musical, literary and dramatic pursuits. The family was also involved with diverse activities at the national level.

Important changes were taking place in Bengal at the time Rabindranath was born. Iswar Chandra Vidyasagar had been attempting to reform the position of women in society. Schools using English as the language of teaching were being established, alongside the traditional Sanskrit schools. Vidyasagar had established Bengali-medium schools at different places in Bengal with little or limited government support. He had also established a centre to train teachers for these schools. Rabindranath attended this school and, as he says himself, owed his love of Bengali language and literature to it. He was also sent to a number of English-speaking schools, but he did not like theirteaching style and had no wish to be taught in a foreign language.

He gradually withdrew from formal schooling when he was around 14 years old. The remainder of his education was carried out at home through his own personal efforts and with the help of tutors in various subjects. He also had lessons from professionals in wrestling, music and drawing. The manner of his early schooling was to leave a deep impression on him.

When Rabindranath was 12, his father took him to Santiniketan, the meditation centre established in 1863. During their brief stay there, Devendranath gave his son lessons in Sanskrit, astronomy and the scriptures that formed the basis of his reformed religion. After these lessons were over, Rabindranath was free to roam among the fields and forests. This routine continued when father and son journeyed on and stayed at Dalhousie in the Himalayan foothills. After lessons in Sanskrit, English literature and religion, the would-be poet explored the mountains and forests. Life in close proximity to nature was unknown to him in the urban surroundings of Calcutta.

The close and affectionate contact between teacher and pupil that he felt when his father taught him was also completely absent in Calcutta. It was this childhood experience of the willing pupil enthusiastically following lessons given by his father in the manner of a noble teacher among agreeable surroundings that guided Rabindranath in establishing a school at Santiniketan in 1901.

In 1878, when he was 17, he was sent to London by his father to qualify for the Indian Civil Service or as a lawyer. He took his matriculation examination and then joined University College, London. He came to like his lessons in English literature, and became exposed to British social life and Western music, both of which he enjoyed. But he returned home suddenly after some eighteen months without completing his education.

However, he did gain the impression that human nature was perhaps the same everywhere.

Back in India he continued with his personal education and his creative writing and music. His Sandhya Sangeet [Evening songs], a volume of Bengali verse, came out in 1882. It was at about this time that he had a kind of mystical experience that led him to appreciate the unity of all that exists and himself as an integral part of it. In the same year, he wrote his famous poem Nirjharer Swapna Bhanga [The awakening of the fountain]. He became aware of his unusual talent as a poet. Between 1884 and 1890 various volumes of his poems appeared, together with a profuse output of prose articles, criticism, plays and novels.

Tagore married when he was 23. At this stage, beyond his literary pursuits, he had begun sharing his father's religious responsibilities. In 1890 he made a second trip to the United Kingdom, but came back after a month to look after the family estates.

This responsibility opened up new vistas of inspiration for him. Whereas his previous literary work had been primarily based on imagination, he now came to acquire a direct and intimate experience of the wretched life led by the poor Bengali peasants. This new experience led to the composition of Galpaguccha [A bunch of stories] (1900), and the many letters he wrote to his niece, subsequently published as Chhinnapatra [Torn letters] and Chhinnapatravali [A collection of torn letters], considered to be landmarks in the writing of Bengali prose and in describing the countryside of Bengal.

Tagore was overwhelmed by the economic, social and political misery in which the peasants lived. He gave a description of them at a later date:

> Our so-called responsible classes live in comfort because the common man has not yet understood his situation.

> That is why the landlord beats him. The money-lender holds him in his clutches; the foreman abuses him; the policeman fleeces him; the priest exploits him; and the magistrate picks his pocket.

These conditions, he thought, cannot be changed by appealing to the religious sentiments of the landlord, policeman or money-lender. In human society, necessity is a greater force than charity. The first requirement therefore is that people should discover the bond that holds them together asa society. If there is one path likely to achieve this, it is education.

Tagore realised from his own experience of the farmers' attitudes and their social behaviour that strength can be generated only in a self-reliant village society developing its own locus of power and its own momentum of growth. He turned again and again in various contexts to this theme of local self-reliance, local initiatives, local leadership and local self-government centring on co-operative ways of life. This could be the basis for reorganising India's fragmented rural society, and could serve as an instrument of welfare.

Tagore realised that education and village councils or panchayats were the only available instruments of economic and social change, and that the villagers should obtain various forms of expert help from outside to accomplish this change. As he says: 'Poverty springs from disunity and wealth from co-operation. From all points of view this is the fundamental truth of human civilization.'

As a young landlord managing his family's rural estates, Tagore came to realise the possibilities of introducing education and co-operation to transform rural life. Thus he began to turn his thoughts towards the problems of education. He spoke publicly on 'The Vicissitudes of Education'in which he made a strong plea for the use of the mother-tongue. His first experiments in teaching also date from this period. He started his own school in Seliadah, the headquarters of his estate, to which he sent his own children to be taught by teachers in various subjects, including an Englishman to teach them the English language.

He also started organising co-operatives, schools and hospitals in the villages of his estates and tried to introduce improved farming methods. All these efforts for rural reconstruction went on while he pursued his creative writing. Tagore called this the period of his Sadhana-preparation, reflection, austerity and self-education for an active social life. He lived either at Seliadah or on his houseboat on the river Padma, visiting villages, talking to people and listening to their problems. Tagore's later educational experiments arose from this experience.

In 1901 he left Seliadah where he had undertaken these experiments and moved to Santiniketan where, with his father's consent, he started a boarding school. The Brahamacharyashram (or Ashram) School was inaugurated on 22 December 1901 with only a few pupils, his son being one of them, and with an equal number of teachers. It was to be run on the pattern of teachers and pupils living together amidst natural surroundings and willingly accepting an austere standard of living, often working with their own hands.

Of the five teachers, three were Christians-two of whom were Catholics and the third was his son's English teacher from Seliadah. The orthodox Hindus were offended by this situation and he did not get any assistance from them. No fees were accepted from students, all expenses being borne by Tagore himself. In the course of time, this Ashram School expanded as the poet's reputation grew.

Life at Santiniketan left its impression on the poet's literary work. He wrote about India's past and present, and stories of noble self-sacrifice. He published more realistic novels such as Choker Bali [Eyesore] (1901), Naukadubi [The wreck] (1903) and Gora (1910). He was trying to discover the eternal India that succeeds in achieving unity amidst a bewildering diversity of races, cultures and religions.

In 1912 Tagore left for the United Kingdom once again. Some of his poems and writings had already been translated into English and had attracted the attention of the well-known English painter Sir William Rothenstein and the poet W. B. Yeats. He made such an impression on the British writers and intellectuals that he was at once accepted as a great poet and intellectual. He was awarded the Nobel Prize for Literature in November 1913 and came back to India after visiting the United States of America, delivering there his 'Sadhana' lectures (The Realisation of Life, 1913). In 1916 Tagore went abroad again to Japan and then to the United States of America delivering lectures, published later in two volumes as Nationalism (1917b) and Personality (1917c).

This international experience gave him a new idea, that he must bring his country intocontact with the world at large. He felt that overemphasis on narrow nationalism led men and countries into paths of conflict. There should be an institution that emphasised the unity of the world's cultures and streams of knowledge. He considered Santiniketan to be that institution. He was thus already contemplating the foundation of Visva Bharati, an international centre of culture and humanistic studies.

The foundation stone of Visva Bharati was laid on 24 December 1918. A separate institution called Sri Niketan was established in 1921.

Education in India: Historical Background

By 1857, four years before Rabindranath was born, British

power in India had been consolidated and the general foundation of a colonial system of education had been laid. The stated aim of British policy was the promotion of English studies with English language as the medium of instruction and the creation of a class of Indians who had been brought up in an English way. As a result, the traditional system of village, Sanskrit and Islamic schools languished.

National universities had been established at Bombay, Madras and Calcutta, but secondary schools and universities were still the reserve of a small elite. The gulf between the fortunate upper classes and the vast masses of rural poor continued to widen. On the other hand, great socioeconomic changes were taking place in the country, and especially in Calcutta and in other towns as they grew in size. Railways were built; factories sprang up; municipal water supplies arrived. A new class of people came to adopt European dress, manners, attitudes and life styles. Old values and traditions came to be questioned. It was a period of social upheaval and reforms in India.

Towards the end of the nineteenth and in the early twentieth centuries the middle class, which had come into being following the establishment of universities in 1857, began to protest against the imposed system of education and its parallel language policy. It is true that in the middle of the nineteenth century, when the British system was being introduced, a powerful group of urban classes expressed their preference for such studies. But, seeing the consequences and with a growing awareness of the Indian cultural heritage and history, the middle classes had come to resent the education which was being offered. While Tagore preferred the traditional system to the new one, he did not want to bring it back without considerable changes.

This period also saw a rise in Indian nationalism. There was resentment against an imitation of British lifestyles and against British rule, coupled with increased awareness and appreciation of India's cultural traditions. Tagore's educational and other writings of the period reflect this nationalist trend. His concern with educational reform grew in intensity after 1901, and more so after 1905. Dissatisfaction with the existing system of education led to a general concern with reform.

A tragic series of family bereavements probably caused Tagore's withdrawal from the growing national struggle for independence in the country. He retired to his Ashram School to concentrate on its development and on the task of village reconstruction that he had initiated at Seliadah.

Tagore on Education

The difficulty in writing about Tagore's educational ideas lies in the fact that he did not set them down in a connected account. His views are found scattered in a large number of independent essays and journal articles, in speeches to various audiences and in letters to individuals over a number of years.Addresses to foreign audiences about his school at Santiniketan and on VisvaBharati are, of course, in English. Only recently have attempts been made to collect and publish these pieces in their original Bengali. There has been a tendency to group these diffuse writings into three broad divisions.

The First Phase: 1892-1901

Tagore considered lack of education to be the main obstacle in the way of India's progress and at the root of all its problems. The prevailing, colonial education system he found unsatisfactory since the only objective it appeared to serve was to produce clerks. to man government offices and British businesses in India. The basic objectives of any worthwhile national education system, such as promoting creativity, freedom, joy and an awareness of a country's cultural heritage, were completely ignored.

The education offered was not even modern, since it was unrelated to any developments going on the field of education outside India. Irrespective of the content, the medium of education was English-a foreign language-so that learning this language was an additional burden for young Indian students. Particularly, the educational process failed to develop scientific attitudes and the spirit of inquiry. On the other hand, it divided the Indian people into two classes: those who received this education and those who did not. The second group, comprising nearly everyone living in the countryside, remained almost completely cut off from the affluent, educated, Englishspeaking class living in cities and towns.

In the pre-colonial system, a common language promoted an unobstructed flow of culture, even if formal education was not available to all. However, there was no place even in informal educational activities for modern subjects, like history, science and geography, and it did not promote objectivity in thinking, nor facilitate desirable social change.

The Second Phase, 1901-18

Tagore's preoccupation during this second phase was with developing an appropriate system of national education for India. Each nation was different and this fact should be reflected, he thought, in its system of education. The Ashram School at Santiniketan was founded in 1901 on the basis of the ancient Indian forest schools.

In Tapovan [The Forest Schools of India] (1909) Tagore asserted that the forest school was typical of the Indian system of education with its emphasis on three basic elements of Indian culture, namely Advaita (non-duality) in the field of knowledge, friendship for all in the field of feeling, and fulfilment of one's duties without concern for the outcomes in the field of action. In his view, the forest school integrated education with Sadhana (disciplining one's senses and one's own life). But Tagore updated this form of school to include science and similar modern subjects.

The second significant essay of this period was Shikshar Vahana [The Vehicle of Education] (1915) emphasising the importance of the mother-tongue as the medium of education. The use of English in education hindered assimilation of what was taught, and kept education confined to urban centres and the upper classes. Thus, if the vast rural masses were to benefit, it was absolutely essential to switch over to the use of Bengali in the context of Bengal at all levels of education, including higher education.

The ideal school, according to Tagore, should be established away from the turmoil of human habitation under an open sky and surrounded by vistas of fields, trees and plants. Living in a forest was also associated with austere pursuits and renunciation. The vast background of nature represented a grand perspective against which all objects, all feelings assumed their due proportions. He also referred to the significance of educating feelings as distinct from educating the senses and the intellect. The word 'forest' used in this context, he explained, was not dense jungle, but Tapovana, the forest clearing.

A national system of education in India should try to discover the characteristic truths of its civilization. Those truths are not commercialism, imperialism or nationalism, but rather universalism. The aim was all-round development of the individual personality through harmonious interaction and union of the spirit with the environment.

About the place of religion in education, Rabindranath said: 'Nature and human spirit, wedded together, would constitute our temple and selfless good deeds our worship' (Dharma Sikhsha, 1912).

Tagore himself was a teacher at the Ashram School and also gave thought to educational methods. He taught English language, and in the evenings related stories from Indian history to the children. He wrote plays for the students to perform and entertaining verse for children, as well as simple textbooks in various subjects.

Tagore was against any conspicuous emphasis on materials, buildings, furniture or books that imitated Western educational institutions in India. He thought that this would make education too expensive for the common people. He was against bookish learning:

> Books have come between our mind and life. They deprive us of our natural faculty of getting knowledge directly from nature and life and have generated within us the habit of knowing everything through books. We touch the world not with our mind, but with our books. They dehumanize and make us unsocial.... Let the students gather knowledge and materials from different regions of the country, from direct sources and from their own independent efforts.

The Third Phase (1918-41)

Visva Bharati, Tagore's conception of a world university, was founded at the end of the First World War with a determination to go beyond aggressive nationalism and to build friendship with all nations.

After 1913, his travels abroad made him increasingly aware of what was going on in other countries. He came also to know a large number of intellectuals in the countries he visited. This in turn led him to emphasise co-operation between East and West, North and South (in today's jargon), in the field of humanistic studies and culture. From children's education and rural development, he increasingly shifted his attention to university education and developing the surrounding villages as one of the university's functions during this third phase. He wanted to devise an alternative form of education.

> In every nation, education is intimately associated with the life of the people. For us, modern education is relevant only to turning out clerks, lawyers, doctors, magistrates and policemen.... This education has not reached the farmer, the oil grinder, nor the potter. No other educated society has been struck with such disaster.... If ever a truly Indian university is established it must from the very beginning implement India's own knowledge of economics, agriculture, health, medicine and of all other everyday science from the surrounding villages. Then alone can the school or university become the centre of the country's way of living. This school must practise agriculture, dairying and weaving using the best modern methods.... I have proposed to call this school Visva Bharati.

Tagore was convinced that no form of education offered in India, be it at school or at university level, would be complete without knowledge of patterns of rural living and without an effort by the universities to rejuvenate rural life. He considered this to be an important aspect of Visva Bharati's total activity.

Writing about them in 1919 in his paper Ashantosher Karon [Cause of Dissatisfaction], he expressed his deep anguish at the contemporary attempts in India to establish new universities in exactly the same mould as existing ones due to a lack of will or a lack of courage to attempt new forms. This had become imperative in view of the fact that the civil service was saturated and, as the student members grew, the majority of graduates failed to get clerical or any other type of white-collar jobs and were good for nothing else. The time had thus come, Tagore urged, toattempt a change in the aims of university education.

How to make education real and our life force? In the addresses he gave and the essays he wrote from 1919 to 1936 he tried to answer this question. In his own words:

> We must try to understand how Indian genius expressed itself [...] Unless we try to put these together and discover the integrating factors behind these diverse streams of thought and make them a subject of study at our universities, we would only be borrowing knowledge from abroad. The natural habitat for knowledge is where it is produced. The main task of universities is to produce knowledge, its dissemination is its secondary function. We must invite those intellectuals and scholars to our universities who are engaged in research, invention or creative activity.14

While nations sought primarily to give their citizens a means of livelihood through education, Tagore believed that there was a more important aim-that of personal fulfilment and selfimprovement. It was important to borrow knowledge and experience from abroad, but not to use them as the foundation for Indian education.

Even so, if there was one European quality which Indian university students must acquire it was 'the desire to know, to find out about the laws of nature and to use them for the betterment of the conditions of human beings'.Science and its applications in the form of technology have led to the power and prosperity of Western countries. Unless India acquired knowledge of science and technology through its universities and schools, poverty and powerlessness would continue. To transform life and make it richer, healthier and more educated, it was imperative to resort to technology and science. But Tagore wanted science to be taught along with India's own philosophical and spiritual knowledge at Indian universities.

However, science without the constraint of self-knowledge, without appreciating that the quest for knowledge is the most important aim of human existence, leads to an endless desire for material goods and well-being, and the meaningless pursuit of the instruments of war and power, which are often the origin of conflict between nations and end, ultimately, in the suppression of the weaker by the stronger. That is why both spiritual and scientific knowledge are considered by Tagore as equally important.

In an address on the functions of the university,Tagore argued that a university is an attempt by a nation to aggregate knowledge at one place, to develop it and to disseminate it to the younger generation.

Long before universities in the West had been established, there existed in India universities, such as Nalanda and Vikramshila, where various branches of knowledge had been pursued by scholars for centuries during the Buddhist period of India's history. Students came to these universities from far and near in Asia to learn about the subjects taught, and to live with the teachers who were respected for their exemplary way of life. When universities came to be founded in Europe, the hold of religion was loosened. New methods of acquiring knowledge led to rapid growth in the fields of social, physical and life sciences.

Modern universities collect existing knowledge in various fields from within a country or abroad, preserve and develop it and make it available to the younger generations. But contemporary Indian universities had not been concerned about collecting and preserving the national heritage, and enriching it by fusing it with knowledge coming from abroad. Neither had they been concerned about improving life in the villages. 'Universities here are like a lighted railway compartment in a train passing through the countryside which is enveloped in darkness.'

Furthermore the use of the English language at universities presents a language barrier confining the flow of knowledge and information. Unless a beginning was made in using the mother-tongue as a medium of instruction in regional universities the flow of knowledge to the countryside would not be restored. Of course, English was needed to build bridges so as to benefit from the growing corpus of knowledge existing abroad in the fields of science, technology andother subjects, but its central importance in India's education process would cease.

In his Shikhar Suwangeekaran [Make education your own] (1936), he returned to his recurrent theme of the unnaturalness of the system of education in India, its lack of links with the nation and its management which was in the hands of a foreign government. The working of the government, its courts of law and its education system were conducted in a language completely unintelligible to the majority of Indians. He contrasted the situation in India with what he had seen in the USSR and in Japan, where the governments had been able to educate their people within a very short time. Educating India's entire population and restoring the flow of culture from the educated classes to the rural population would not come about unless the mother-tongue was adopted as the medium of teaching.

Second Experiment: Sri Niketan

Santiniketan developed continuously from 1901 to 1921. The school, called Patha Bhawan, eventually became affiliated to Calcutta University and students could thus take the matriculation examination. For a long time, the funding of the school was entirely assumed by Tagore. This was possible because teachers' salaries were very low. Most of Tagore's personal income, proceeds from the sale of his property, most of the Nobel Prize money and royalties from his books were the sources of school finance. Only after receiving the Nobel Prize and after being knighted by the British did the Indian Government begin to take an interest in him.

Tagore was convinced that some new form of schooling could be worked out for the village children in India based on life in the countryside. He had purchased an old building and some land at a village called Surul, not far from Santiniketan. Fortunately for Santiniketan, Tagore met Leonard Elmhirst in the United States in 1921. Elmhirst was at that time reading agricultural science at Cornell University and was keen on spending some time in India doing rural reconstruction work.

Tagore requested Elmhirst to join him. He told Elmhirst that Santiniketan was surrounded by a number of villages which, 'for some reason, appeared to be in a state of steady decline'.There was no sign of effort on the part of the villagers: there was no joy, no food, no health, no idea of the importance of their own initiative and no co-operation among them. Tagore wanted Elmhirst first to find out why and then suggest remedial action. The objective was to raise the villagers' income, but the higher aim according to Tagore was to make them happy.

Tagore was somewhat disappointed that Santiniketan had failed to achieve the ideal of bringing scientific knowledge to bear on life in the countryside. In order to improve the human condition in the villages of Eastern India, the population had to throw off their belief in fate and realise the importance of depending upon their own efforts. This is what Tagore had in mind when he launched the rural reconstruction work at Sri Niketan in a school called Shikshasastra. The objective of the new school was to provide an all-round education for village children, enabling them to earn a decent livelihood but also equipping them to improve rural life in all its aspects.

From the very beginning, the major thrust of the programme at Sri Niketan under Elmhirst came to be increasing the productivity of the land. But Tagore also wanted a total improvement covering agriculture, education, health and social life in the villages. Agricultural research and experiments would be undertaken at Sri Niketan and the fruits of this research were to be carried to the villages. At the same time, medical care and the eradication of malaria were considered equally important. At the centre, specialists in various fields worked together to overcome the difficulties of rural life. In addition, a scout movement was organised to mobilise the children as a starting point for drawing their parents into the village development programme.

A fundamental area of instruction at Sri Niketan was handicrafts; it was compulsory for all students to learn a trade. Another major activity was the launching of some 200 co-operative societies for agricultural credit, irrigation, granaries, etc. Experiments were made on new crops andon new varieties of existing crops that appeared to be suitable for local conditions. A dairy farm gave practical demonstrations of animal husbandry on scientific lines. The villagers were expected to adopt rural industries to supplement their income. The village welfare department initiated public works (repairing and excavating reservoirs), looked after village schools, maintained a mobile library for villages, organised social and cultural activities and ran the scout movement. There was a health section with a central dispensary; and a maternity and child-welfare section was added in 1940.

Sri Niketan aimed at combining work with joy. Picnics, excursions, games, music, theatrical performances and celebrating socio-religious festivals constituted regular features of the calendar. New Year's Day, the Rainy Season festival, the New Rice festival, the Spring festival were-and still are-all regular features. Tagore added Halkarshan (ploughing the land festival) and Van Mahotosava (tree planting). Apart from adding joy to dreary village life, some of these festivals brought students and villagers to work together.

For years Tagore tried to convince his countrymen through his speeches, stories, novels, poems and songs to work for rural revival. The call went unheeded until Gandhi came on the Indian political scene. Single handed, the poet had started his work: 'They call you mad. Wait for tomorrow and keep silent' (Poems, 1942).

> Of course, turning out songs is my proper vocation. But those who are unfortunate cannot afford to limit their choice to the works they do. They must also bear the burden of tasks they cannot do. The scale of our enterprise can never be a matter of pride to us, but let us hope that its truth will be. Ideas, if they have the vitality of truth in them, grow and spread in the course of time.

How correct Tagore was in this respect. The entire programme followed at Sri Niketan for rural development was adopted by India's five-year plans as the correct approach to rural community development.

Influences

Apart from the three remarkable Englishmen who were Tagore's collaborators, namely C. F. Andrews, William Pearson and Leonard Elmhirst, numerous other scholars came to Santiniketan at the poet's invitation to participate in the teaching programmes.

Tagore disowned being influenced by any of the well-known educationists. It was not any new theory of education but the memory of his schooldays that led him to establish his residential schools. 'I established my institution in a beautiful spot away from the town where the children had the greatest freedom possible under the shade of ancient trees.'

Through contact with nature, by making them aware of community relations and with the help of literature, festivals and religious teaching, he tried to develop the souls of his children. But this turned out to be not quite enough, so he introduced work education as 'a joyous exercise of our inventive and constructive energies that help to build up character.'

In many respects Tagore's ideas relating to the education of children resemble those of Rousseau, Fröbel, Dewey, Montessori and others. For instance, Rousseau considered nature as children's teacher, as does Tagore, but unlike Rousseau he retains a significant role for the teacher. Fröbel and Tagore both advocate harmony with all that exists to be achieved through education; they are both in favour of play and domestic activities as part of education during infancy and activity in the community as part of the educational process during childhood.

Fröbel stops here; but Tagore includes subsequent education under the purview of activity-oriented education. Both are for joy and festivities, and an awareness of the child's dignity as part of the educational environment. The resemblances between Fröbel and Tagore's ideas are indeed striking. The same istrue to some extent of his approach to children's education compared with some of his contemporaries, such as Dewey, Maria Montessori and Tolstoy.

As Sarkar (1961) points out, Tagore was familiar with many of these views, but all who knew the poet were aware that he was in no way indebted to them. His views were linked with the development of his own mind and spirit, and his profound understanding of India's traditional educational experience and philosophy.

His activity-oriented school for village children appears to have inspired Gandhi's ideas on basic education. Tagore's influence can also be seen in the report of the Kothari Commission on Education in India.

In Tagore's view, the higher aim of education was the same as that of a person's life, that is, to achieve fulfilment and completeness. There was a lesser aim, that of providing the individual with a satisfactory means of livelihood, without which a person would not be able to satisfy his/her basic requirements and thus fail to achieve either of these two aims. Tagore also imagined that the limitless development of man is possible only in an environment free from any kind of bondage. Apart from the scriptures, it would seem that he was influenced by the attitudes that arose in Europe during the Renaissance and the Age of Reason.

In his view, education was not intellectual development alone. It should also develop a student's aesthetic nature and creativity. The quest for knowledge and physical activity in an agreeable environment were integral parts of the process. Freedom and creativity are linked in Tagore's thought, one conditioning the other. The more people go beyond the limitations of their animal nature, the closer they come to humanism, freedom and unity and are then able to develop their creativity. This quest alone gives a meaning to life, and education is an effort to make life meaningful. Here the aims of the individual and those of the community have become almost one.

Tagore did not neglect the lesser aims of life and education. In the colonial system of education that existed at that time the whole focus of education was on employment, to the complete neglect of the higher aims of life. His intention was to correct this wrong emphasis, without ignoring science, technology and agricultural sciences, as well as training in village crafts. Without these, it was not possible to revive the derelict life of rural India. Both categories of aims should thus be considered the objective of education.

It was necessary, Tagore felt, to make the younger generation aware of their national cultural heritage and to grasp its significance for them. At the same time, education should bring children face to face with the cultures of other countries and persuade them to learn from them.

Tagore put great emphasis on the use of a national language as the vehicle of education at all stages of education. He wanted Indian universities to integrate themselves with society and make an effort to educate people living in the countryside. He did not want education to remain confined to the cities and to particular classes of society.

He was very much concerned with women's education. His educational institutions have almost always been co-educational and the number of female students is conspicuously large at Santiniketan. He wanted women and men to be offered similar theoretical courses with separate practical courses for women, since their roles in life differed from those of men.

Tagore considered teachers to be very important in any scheme of education. He wanted teachers to help young children to grow on their own as a gardener helps the young plants to grow. He wanted to use education as an instrument of change to make Indian young men and women more rational and less subject to meaningless social and individual rituals.

Tagore wanted his students to acquire a scientific temper; in other words, he wanted teachers to stimulate constructive doubt, the love of mental adventure, the courage and longing to conquer the world by enterprise and boldness in thought and in action. These were the virtues cultivation of which had made the West forge ahead.

Tagore was against any form of corporal punishment to impose discipline. He wanteddiscipline to come from within, from the pursuit of noble and high ambitions in life. Discipline would follow naturally when minor impulses and desires were willingly forgone to pursue grand creative desires.

He wanted his students to think in terms of the whole of mankind. He wanted them to become universal men and women like himself and to overcome feelings of narrow nationalism in order that the world could live and grow in peace and fellowship.

The poet passed away in 1941. The two institutions specific to Tagore's educational ideas and experiments still survive in the form of Patha Bhawan (the school section) at Santiniketan and in the form of Sikshasastra and Sri Niketan-of course, they have been modified a good deal over this long stretch of time. They form the core of the Santiniketan ideal. Visva Bharati survives too; it is now a central university and has changed considerably.

The emphasis that Tagore placed on the teaching of the fine arts and crafts, and on music, continues in the form of two separate autonomous institutions under the general supervision of Visva Bharati. These institutions are: the Kala Bhawan (the school of fine arts); and the Sangeet Bhawan (the school of music and dance).

Emphasis on the teaching of various Indian languages and on the teaching of Asian cultures, and the presence of an international faculty are not very evident. But there is a Cheena Bhawan (the school of Chinese language and culture), Hindi Bhawan, a School of Islamic Studies, and a good number of students from Far Eastern countries, particularly in the Kala Bhawan and the Sangeet Bhawan.

But one can see that Tagore's memory still dominates life on the university campus. The following poem from Gitanjali [Song offerings] brings together the ideals the poet kept before the nation, before mankind, and before his educational institutions.

Where the mind is without fear,
and the heart is held high,
Where the world is not broken up into fragments
by narrow domestic walls,
Where the words came out from
the depths of truth,
Where tireless striving stretches its arms
towards perfection;
Where the clear stream of reason has not lost its
way into the dreary desert sand of dead habits,
Where the mind is led forward by thee into
everwidening thought and action -
Into that heaven of freedom,
My father, let my country awake.

3

Tagore and Indian Society

If one individual is to be singled out for representing the values and traditions of India from the ancient times to the modern age, it cannot be any one other than Rabindranath Tagore (1861-1941).

He was the one person who incorporated the wisdom of the past, reflected in the spiritual and intellectual attainments of the Vedas and the Upanishads. Yet, he was never so immersed in India's seemingly other-worldly heritage, underlined in the philosophical concept of the world being an illusion (maya), as to negate rationalism. To use a cliché, he combined the best of both worlds.

Tagore scored in this respect over his other great contemporary, Mahatma Gandhi, for the Mahatma placed a far greater emphasis on the spirit of renunciation marking a rejection of the Western industrial civilization.

To a large extent, it is this attitude extolling the 'simple living, high thinking' outlook that is still favoured in India, even if it is not infrequently identified with hypocrisy.

Tagore set his face against such a rule of thumb approach to life if only because his horizon was much wider than Gandhi's. He had no time for Gandhi's rejection of European machines and preference for primitive Indian ones like the 'charkha', or the spinning wheel.

"If a man is stunted by big machines", Tagore wrote, "the danger of being stunted by small machines must not be lost sight of. The charkha in its proper place can do no harm ... but where ... it is in the wrong place, then the thread can only be spun at the cost of a great deal of the mind itself. The man is no less valuable than the cotton thread."

Poet, thinker, playwright, novelist, writer of short stories, dance dramas and songs, painter and educationist - Tagore's versatility was matched only by his genius. Truly, he was Gurudev, the epitome of the preceptor idealized in Indian myths and folklore.

Not surprisingly, Gandhi bestowed the title on Tagore - an honour that befits him even today - just as Tagore called Gandhi the Mahatma, recognizing the sterling qualities of a saint in the politician, who is embroiled in the heat and dust of quotidian battles.

It was left to Nehru to say that although Tagore and Gandhi were "entirely different from each other, and yet both of them (were) typical of India, both in the long line of India's great men".

If Tagore's legacy remains as relevant today as it was in his time, the reason is that he cherished certain ideals that have come to distinguish India in the present-day world. Hence, perhaps, the statues, busts and university chairs named after him which dot the world.

The first and foremost concept of Indian nationhood that he lauded was its inclusiveness. He recounts in one of his poems how the streams of Aryans, non-Aryans, Sakas, Huns, Pathans, Mughals et al have merged to give India its distinctive identity. It is not impossible that he developed this concept from a study of his own family, which he regarded as a product of the "confluence of three cultures, Hindu, Mohammedan and British".

It is this ideal of an integrated and vibrant multicultural society, a rainbow nation, which India holds up today as the only valid model which can ensure the survival and advancement of all. Otherwise, the so-called civilizational clashes between ethnic, religious and linguistic groups will tear the world apart. It is perhaps just as well that the great man died before India itself fell prey in 1947 to one such murderous conflict based on religion. And, then, the broken nation saw another divisive conflict in 1971 based on language and sub-nationalism, which led to the creation of Bangladesh.

Tagore would probably have been even more mortified by the second rupture because he came from that part of the subcontinent - East Bengal. In his time, he witnessed the colonial rulers partition Bengal in 1905, a traumatic upheaval for his Sonar Bangla. Fittingly, it is his song of love and reverence for the land where he was born (Amar Sonar Bangla) which is now the national anthem of Bangladesh.

Tagore recognized the seeds of the conflicts that tore apart India in Gandhi's use of religious symbols, both Hindu and Muslim as in the concept of Ram Rajya and the exhortation in favour of the Caliphate. He was as opposed to Gandhi's love for "small machines", with their numbing effect on the mind, as to his idealization of religious emblems, which can exert an equally stifling impact on the largely illiterate masses.

"I blamed Mahatmaji", Tagore wrote, "for exploiting (the) irrational force of credulity in our people." While Gandhi defended the Hindu idols, as the English clergyman and admirer of India C.F. Andrews recalled, "believing the masses (to be) incapable of raising themselves immediately to abstract ideals", Tagore could not "bear to see the people eternally treated as a child".

Many will see Tagore's depiction of the crafty politician mouthing nationalistic slogans to mobilize the credulous in his novel Gharey Bairey as a mirror image of the present political scene, just as his prescient vision that a revolution devours its own children, as in Char Adhyay, will be appreciated today although it was written in the context of the much-lionised anti-British revolutionaries and anarchists of his time.

Tagore wasn't without his critics at home and abroad. Even while accepting the Nobel Prize for Literature in 1913, he referred to the "calumnies and insults" he had received from his countrymen. The West, too, lost its interest soon enough. Graham Greene thought in 1937 "I cannot believe that anyone but Mr Yeats can still take his (Tagore's) poems very seriously". And Yeats himself had come to the conclusion by then that Tagore wrote "sentimental rubbish".

Notwithstanding these ups and downs, as in the life of all individuals, big and small, Tagore's thinking had a stamp of modernity which can act as guideposts for India and the world - just as his song, "Ekla Chalo Re" (walk alone), inspired Gandhi during the communal violence of 1946-47. And nowhere is Tagore's modern outlook more evident than in his paintings, with their remarkable stark originality, quite in contrast to the mellifluous nature of his verse. Perhaps more than any other aspect of his vast artistic output, it is in his paintings that apparently depict his real self - "I am by nature a savage" - that Tagore will live for generations.

Tagore and His India

Voice of Bengal

Rabindranath Tagore, who died in 1941 at the age of eighty, is a towering figure in the millennium-old literature of Bengal. Anyone who becomes familiar with this large and flourishing tradition will be impressed by the power of Tagore's presence in Bangladesh and in India. His poetry as well as his novels, short stories, and essays are very widely read, and the songs he composed reverberate around the eastern part of India and throughout Bangladesh.

In contrast, in the rest of the world, especially in Europe and America, the excitement that Tagore's writings created in the early years of the twentieth century has largely vanished. The enthusiasm with which his work was once greeted was quite remarkable. Gitanjali, a selection of his poetry for which he was awarded the Nobel Prize in Literature in 1913, was published in English translation in London in March of that year, and had been reprinted ten times by November, when the award was announced. But he is not much read now in the West, and already by 1937, Graham Greene was able to say: "As for Rabindranath Tagore, I cannot believe that anyone but Mr. Yeats can still take his poems very seriously."

The Mystic

The contrast between Tagore's commanding presence in Bengali literature and culture, and his near-total eclipse in the rest of the world, is perhaps less interesting than the distinction between the view of Tagore as a deeply relevant and many-sided contemporary thinker in Bangladesh and India, and his image in the West as a repetitive and remote spiritualist. Graham Greene had, in fact, gone on to explain that he associated Tagore "with what Chesterton calls 'the bright pebbly eyes' of the Theosophists." Certainly, an air of mysticism played some part in the "selling" of Rabindranath Tagore to the West by Yeats, Ezra Pound, and his other early champions. Even Anna Akhmatova, one of Tagore's few later admirers (who translated his poems into Russian in the mid-1960s), talks of "that mighty flow of poetry which takes its strength from Hinduism as from the Ganges, and is called Rabindranath Tagore."

Confluence of Cultures

Rabindranath did come from a Hindu family-one of the landed gentry who owned estates mostly in what is now Bangladesh. But whatever wisdom there might be in Akhmatova's invoking of Hinduism and the Ganges, it did not prevent the largely Muslim citizens of Bangladesh from having a deep sense of identity with Tagore and his ideas. Nor did it stop the newly independent Bangladesh from choosing one of Tagore's songs-the "Amar Sonar Bangla" which means "my golden Bengal"-as its national anthem. This must be very confusing to those who see the contemporary world as a "clash of civilizations"-with "the Muslim civilization," "the Hindu civilization," and "the Western civilization," each forcefully confronting the others. They would also be confused by Rabindranath Tagore's own description of his Bengali family as the product of "a confluence of three cultures: Hindu, Mohammedan, and British".1

Rabindranath's grandfather, Dwarkanath, was well known for his command of Arabic and Persian, and Rabindranath grew up in a family atmosphere in which a deep knowledge of Sanskrit and ancient Hindu texts was combined with an understanding of Islamic traditions as well as Persian literature. It is not so much that Rabindranath tried to produce-or had an interest in producing-a "synthesis" of the different religions (as the great Moghul emperor Akbar tried hard to achieve) as that his outlook was persistently non-sectarian, and his writings-some two hundred books-show the influence of different parts of the Indian cultural background as well as of the rest of the world.

Abode of Peace

Most of his work was written at Santiniketan (Abode of Peace), the small town that grew around the school he founded in Bengal in 1901, and he not only conceived there an imaginative and innovative system of education, but through his writings and his influence on students and teachers, he was able to use the school as a base from which he could take a major part in India's social, political, and cultural movements.

The profoundly original writer, whose elegant prose and magical poetry Bengali readers know well, is not the sermonizing spiritual guru admired-and then rejected-in London. Tagore was not only an immensely versatile poet; he was also a great short story writer, novelist, playwright, essayist, and composer of songs, as well as a talented painter whose pictures, with their mixture of representation and abstraction, are only now beginning to receive the acclaim that they have long deserved.

His essays, moreover, ranged over literature, politics, culture, social change, religious beliefs, philosophical analysis, international relations, and much else. The coincidence of the fiftieth anniversary of Indian independence with the publication of a selection of Tagore's letters by Cambridge University Press 3, brought Tagore's ideas and reflections to the fore, which makes it important to examine what kind of leadership in thought and understanding he provided in the Indian subcontinent in the first half of this century.

Gandhi and Tagore

Since Rabindranath Tagore and Mohandas Gandhi were two leading Indian thinkers in the twentieth century, many commentators have tried to compare their ideas. On learning of Rabindranath's death, Jawaharlal Nehru, then incarcerated in a British jail in India, wrote in his prison diary for August 7, 1941:

> "Gandhi and Tagore. Two types entirely different from each other, and yet both of them typical of India, both in the long line of India's great men ... It is not so much because of any single virtue but because of the tout ensemble, that I felt that among the world's great men today Gandhi and Tagore were supreme as human beings. What good fortune for me to have come into close contact with them."

Romain Rolland was fascinated by the contrast between them, and when he completed his book on Gandhi, he wrote to an Indian academic, in March 1923: "I have finished my Gandhi, in which I pay tribute to your two great river-like souls, overflowing with divine spirit, Tagore and Gandhi." The following month, he recorded in his diary an account of some of the differences between Gandhi and Tagore written by Reverend C.F. Andrews, the English clergyman and public activist who was a close friend of both men (and whose important role in Gandhi's life in South Africa as well as India is well portrayed in Richard Attenborough's film Gandhi [1982]). Andrews described to Rolland a discussion between Tagore and Gandhi, at which he was present, on subjects that divided them:

> "The first subject of discussion was idols; Gandhi defended them, believing the masses incapable of raising themselves immediately to abstract ideas. Tagore cannot bear to see the people eternally treated as a child. Gandhi quoted the great things achieved in Europe by the flag as an idol; Tagore found it easy to object, but Gandhi held his ground, contrasting European flags bearing eagles, etc., with his own, on which he has put a spinning wheel. The second point of discussion was nationalism, which Gandhi defended. He said that one must go through nationalism to reach internationalism, in the same way that one must go through war to reach peace."

Tagore greatly admired Gandhi but he had many disagreements with him on a variety of subjects, including nationalism, patriotism, the importance of cultural exchange, the role of rationality and of science, and the nature of economic and social development. These differences, I shall argue, have a clear and consistent pattern, with Tagore pressing for more room for reasoning, and for a less traditionalist view, a greater interest in the rest of the world, and more respect for science and for objectivity generally.

Rabindranath knew that he could not have given India the political leadership that Gandhi provided, and he was never stingy in his praise for what Gandhi did for the nation (it was, in fact, Tagore who popularized the term "Mahatma"-great soul-as a description of Gandhi). And yet each remained deeply critical of many things that the other stood for. That Mahatma Gandhi has received incomparably more attention outside India and also within much of India itself makes it important to understand "Tagore's side" of the Gandhi-Tagore debates.

In his prison diary, Nehru wrote: "Perhaps it is as well that [Tagore] died now and did not see the many horrors that are likely to descend in increasing measure on the world and on India. He had seen enough and he was infinitely sad and unhappy." Toward the end of his life, Tagore was indeed becoming discouraged about the state of India, especially as its normal burden of problems, such as hunger and poverty, was being supplemented by politically organized incitement to "communal" violence between Hindus and Muslims. This conflict would lead in 1947, six years after Tagore's death, to the widespread killing that took place during partition; but there was much gore already during his declining days.

In December 1939, he wrote to his friend Leonard Elmhirst, the English philanthropist and social reformer who had worked closely with him on rural reconstruction in India (and who had gone on to found the Dartington

Hall Trust in England and a progressive school at Dartington that explicitly invoked Rabindranath's educational ideals):

> "It does not need a defeatist to feel deeply anxious about the future of millions who, with all their innate culture and their peaceful traditions are being simultaneously subjected to hunger, disease, exploitations foreign and indigenous, and the seething discontents of communalism."

How would Tagore have viewed the India of today? Would he see progress there, or wasted opportunity, perhaps even a betrayal of its promise and conviction? And, on a wider subject, how would he react to the spread of cultural separatism in the contemporary world?

East and West

Given the vast range of his creative achievements, perhaps the most astonishing aspect of the image of Tagore in the West is its narrowness; he is recurrently viewed as "the great mystic from the East," an image with a putative message for the West, which some would welcome, others dislike, and still others find deeply boring. To a great extent this Tagore was the West's own creation, part of its tradition of message-seeking from the East, particularly from India, which-as Hegel put it-had "existed for millennia in the imagination of the Europeans."

Friedrich Schlegel, Schelling, Herder, and Schopenhauer were only a few of the thinkers who followed the same pattern. They theorized, at first, that India was the source of superior wisdom. Schopenhauer at one stage even argued that the New Testament "must somehow be of Indian origin: this is attested by its completely Indian ethics, which transforms morals into asceticism, its pessimism, and its avatar," in "the person of Christ." But then they rejected their own theories with great vehemence, sometimes blaming India for not living up to their unfounded expectations.

We can imagine that Rabindranath's physical appearance-handsome, bearded, dressed in non-Western clothes-may, to some extent, have encouraged his being seen as a carrier of exotic wisdom. Yasunari Kawabata, the first Japanese Nobel Laureate in Literature, treasured memories from his middle-school days of "this sage-like poet":

> His white hair flowed softly down both sides of his forehead; the tufts of hair under the temples also were long like two beards, and linking up with the hair on his cheeks, continued into his beard, so that he gave an impression, to the boy I was then, of some ancient Oriental wizard.

That appearance would have been well-suited to the selling of Tagore in the West as a quintessentially mystical poet, and it could have made it somewhat easier to pigeonhole him. Commenting on Rabindranath's appearance, Frances Cornford told William Rothenstein, "I can now imagine a powerful and gentle Christ, which I never could before." Beatrice Webb, who did not like Tagore and resented what she took to be his "quite obvious dislike of all that the Webbs stand for" (there is, in fact, little evidence that Tagore had given much thought to this subject), said that he was "beautiful to look at" and that "his speech has the perfect intonation and slow chant-like moderation of the dramatic saint."

Ezra Pound and W. B. Yeats, among others, first led the chorus of adoration in the Western appreciation of Tagore, and then soon moved to neglect and even shrill criticism. The contrast between Yeats's praise of his work in 1912 ("These lyrics...display in their thought a world I have dreamed of all my life long," "the work of a supreme culture") and his denunciation in 1935 ("Damn Tagore") arose partly from the inability of Tagore's many-sided writings to fit into the narrow box in which Yeats wanted to place-and keep-him.

Certainly, Tagore did write a huge amount, and published ceaselessly, even in English (sometimes in indifferent English translation), but Yeats was also bothered, it is clear, by the difficulty of fitting Tagore's later writings into the image Yeats had presented to the West. Tagore, he had said, was the product of "a whole people, a whole civilization, immeasurably strange to us," and yet "we have met our own image,...or heard, perhaps for the first time in literature, our voice as in a dream."

Yeats did not totally reject his early admiration (as Ezra Pound and several others did), and he included some of Tagore's early poems in The Oxford Book of Modern Verse, which he edited in 1936. Yeats also had some favorable things to say about Tagore's prose writings. His censure of Tagore's later poems was reinforced by his dislike of Tagore's own English translations of his work ("Tagore does not know English, no Indian knows English," Yeats explained), unlike the English version of Gitanjali which Yeats had himself helped to prepare.

Poetry is, of course, notoriously difficult to translate, and anyone who knows Tagore's poems in their original Bengali cannot feel satisfied with any of the translations (made with or without Yeats's help). Even the translations of his prose works suffer, to some extent, from distortion. E.M. Forster noted, in a review of a translation of one of Tagore's great Bengali novels, The Home and the World, in 1919: "The theme is so beautiful," but the charms have "vanished in translation," or perhaps "in an experiment that has not quite come off."

Tagore himself played a somewhat bemused part in the boom and bust of his English reputation. He accepted the extravagant praise with much surprise as well as pleasure, and then received denunciations with even greater surprise, and barely concealed pain. Tagore was sensitive to criticism, and was hurt by even the most far-fetched accusations, such as the charge that he was getting credit for the work of Yeats, who had "rewritten" Gitanjali. (This charge was made by a correspondent for The Times, Sir Valentine Chirol, whom E.M. Forster once described as "an old Anglo-Indian reactionary hack.") From time to time Tagore also protested the crudity of some of his overexcited advocates. He wrote to C.F. Andrews in 1920: "These people...are like drunkards who are afraid of their lucid intervals."

God and Others

Yeats was not wrong to see a large religious element in Tagore's writings. He certainly had interesting and arresting things to say about life and death. Susan Owen, the mother of Wilfred Owen, wrote to Rabindranath in 1920, describing her last conversations with her son before he left for the war which would take his life. Wilfred said goodbye with "those wonderful words of yours-beginning at 'When I go from hence, let this be my parting word.'" When Wilfred's pocket notebook was returned to his mother, she found "these words written in his dear writing-with your name beneath."

The idea of a direct, joyful, and totally fearless relationship with God can be found in many of Tagore's religious writings, including the poems of Gitanjali. From India's diverse religious traditions he drew many ideas, both from ancient texts and from popular poetry. But "the bright pebbly eyes of the Theosophists" do not stare out of his verses. Despite the archaic language of the original translation of Gitanjali, which did not, I believe, help to preserve the simplicity of the original, its elementary humanity comes through more clearly than any complex and intense spirituality:

> Leave this chanting and singing and telling of beads! Whom dost thou worship in this lonely dark corner of a temple with doors all shut?
>
> Open thine eyes and see thy God is not before thee!
>
> He is there where the tiller is tilling the hard ground and where the pathmaker is breaking stones.
>
> He is with them in sun and in shower, and his garment is covered with dust.

An ambiguity about religious experience is central to many of Tagore's devotional poems, and makes them appeal to readers irrespective of their beliefs; but excessively detailed interpretation can ruinously strip away that ambiguity.10 This applies particularly to his many poems which combine images of human love and those of pious devotion. Tagore writes:

> I have no sleep to-night. Ever and again I open my door and look out on the darkness, my friend!
>
> I can see nothing before me. I wonder where lies thy path!
>
> By what dim shore of the ink-black river, by what far edge of the frowning forest, through what mazy depth of gloom, art thou threading thy course to come to see me, my friend?

I suppose it could be helpful to be told, as Yeats hastens to explain, that "the servant or the bride awaiting the master's home-coming in the empty house" is "among the images of the heart turning to God." But in Yeats's considerate attempt to make sure that the reader does not miss the "main point," something of the enigmatic beauty of the Bengali poem is lost - even what had survived the antiquated language of the English translation. Tagore certainly had strongly held religious beliefs (of an unusually nondenominational kind), but he was interested in a great many other things as well and had many different things to say about them.

Some of the ideas he tried to present were directly political, and they figure rather prominently in his letters and lectures. He had practical, plainly expressed views about nationalism, war and peace, cross-cultural education, freedom of the mind, the importance of rational criticism, the need for openness, and so on. His admirers in the West, however, were tuned to the more otherworldly themes which had been emphasized by his first Western patrons. People came to his public lectures in Europe and America, expecting ruminations on grand, transcendental themes; when they heard instead his views on the way public leaders should behave, there was some resentment, particularly (as E.P. Thompson reports) when he delivered political criticism "at $700 a scold."

Reasoning in Freedom

For Tagore it was of the highest importance that people be able to live, and reason, in freedom. His attitudes toward politics and culture, nationalism and internationalism, tradition and modernity, can all be seen in the light of this belief. Nothing, perhaps, expresses his values as clearly as a poem in Gitanjali:

> Where the mind is without fear
> and the head is held high;
> Where knowledge is free;
> Where the world has not been
> broken up into fragments
> by narrow domestic walls; ...
> Where the clear stream of reason
> has not lost its way into the
> dreary desert sand of dead habit; ...
> Into that heaven of freedom,
> my Father, let my country awake.

Rabindranath's qualified support for nationalist movements-and his opposition to the unfreedom of alien rule-came from this commitment. So did his reservations about patriotism, which, he argued, can limit both the freedom to engage ideas from outside "narrow domestic walls" and the freedom also to support the causes of people in other countries. Rabindranath's passion for freedom underlies his firm opposition to unreasoned traditionalism, which makes one a prisoner of the past (lost, as he put it, in "the dreary desert sand of dead habit").

Tagore illustrates the tyranny of the past in his amusing yet deeply serious parable "Kartar Bhoot" ("The Ghost of the Leader"). As the respected leader of an imaginary land is about to die, his panic-stricken followers request him to stay on after his death to instruct them on what to do. He consents. But his followers find their lives are full of rituals and constraints on everyday behavior and are not responsive to the world around them. Ultimately, they request the ghost of the leader to relieve them of his domination, when he informs them that he exists only in their minds.

Tagore's deep aversion to any commitment to the past that could not be modified by contemporary reason extended even to the alleged virtue of invariably keeping past promises. On one occasion when Mahatma Gandhi visited Tagore's school at Santiniketan, a young woman got him to sign her autograph book. Gandhi wrote: "Never make a promise in haste. Having once made it fulfill it at the cost of your life." When he saw this entry, Tagore became agitated. He wrote in the same book a short poem in Bengali to the effect that no one can be made "a prisoner forever with a chain of clay." He went on to conclude in English, possibly so that Gandhi could read it too, "Fling away your promise if it is found to be wrong."

Tagore had the greatest admiration for Mahatma Gandhi as a person and as a political leader, but he was also highly skeptical of Gandhi's form of nationalism and his conservative instincts regarding the country's past traditions. He never criticized Gandhi personally. In the 1938 essay, "Gandhi the Man," he wrote:

> Great as he is as a politician, as an organizer, as a leader of men, as a moral reformer, he is greater than all these as a man, because none of these aspects and activities limits his humanity. They are rather inspired and sustained by it.

And yet there is a deep division between the two men. Tagore was explicit about his disagreement:

> We who often glorify our tendency to ignore reason, installing in its place blind faith, valuing it as spiritual, are ever paying for its cost with the obscuration of our mind and destiny. I blamed Mahatmaji for exploiting this irrational force of credulity in our people, which might have had a quick result [in creating] a superstructure, while sapping the foundation. Thus began my estimate of Mahatmaji, as the guide of our nation, and it is fortunate for me that it did not end there.

But while it "did not end there," that difference of vision was a powerful divider. Tagore, for example, remained unconvinced of the merit of Gandhi's forceful advocacy that everyone should spin at home with the "charka," the primitive spinning wheel. For Gandhi this practice was an important part of India's self-realization. "The spinning-wheel gradually became," as his biographer B.R. Nanda writes, "the center of rural uplift in the Gandhian scheme of Indian economics."

Tagore found the alleged economic rationale for this scheme quite unrealistic. As Romain Rolland noted, Rabindranath "never tires of criticizing the charka." In this economic judgment, Tagore was probably right. Except for the rather small specialized market for high-quality spun cloth, it is hard to make economic sense of hand-spinning, even with wheels less primitive than Gandhi's charka. Hand-spinning as a widespread activity can survive only with the help of heavy government subsidies. However, Gandhi's advocacy of the charka was not based only on economics. He wanted everyone to spin for "thirty minutes every day as a sacrifice," seeing this as a way for people who are better off to identify themselves with the less fortunate. He was impatient with Tagore's refusal to grasp this point:

> The poet lives for the morrow, and would have us do likewise.... "Why should I, who have no need to work for food, spin?" may be the question asked. Because I am eating what does not belong to me. I am living on the spoliation of my countrymen. Trace the source of every coin that finds its way into your pocket, and you will realise the truth of what I write. Every one must spin. Let Tagore spin like the others. Let him burn his foreign clothes; that is the duty today. God will take care of the morrow.

If Tagore had missed something in Gandhi's argument, so did Gandhi miss the point of Tagore's main criticism. It was not only that the charka made little economic sense, but also, Tagore thought, that it was not the way to make people reflect on anything: "The charka does not require anyone to think; one simply turns the wheel of the antiquated invention endlessly, using the minimum of judgment and stamina."

Celibacy and Personal Life

Tagore and Gandhi's attitudes toward personal life were also quite different. Gandhi was keen on the virtues of celibacy, theorized about it, and, after some years of conjugal life, made a private commitment-publicly announced-to refrain from sleeping with his wife. Rabindranath's own attitude on this subject was very different, but he was gentle about their disagreements:

> [Gandhiji] condemns sexual life as inconsistent with the moral progress of man, and has a horror of sex as great as that of the author of The Kreutzer Sonata, but, unlike Tolstoy, he betrays no abhorrence of the sex that tempts his kind. In fact, his tenderness for women is one of the noblest and most consistent traits of his character, and he counts among the women of his country some of his best and truest comrades in the great movement he is leading.

Tagore's persona' life was, in many ways, an unhappy one. He married in 1883, lost his wife in 1902, and never remarried. He sought close companionship, which he did not always get (perhaps even during his married life-he wrote to his wife, Mrinalini: "If you and I could be comrades in all our work and in all our thoughts it would be splendid, but we cannot attain all that we desire"). He maintained a warm friendship with, and a strong Platonic attachment to, the literature-loving wife, Kadambari, of his elder brother, Jyotirindranath. He dedicated some poems to her before his marriage, and several books afterward, some after her death (she committed suicide, for reasons that are not fully understood, at the age of twenty-five, four months after Rabindranath's wedding).

Much later in life, during his tour of Argentina in 1924-1925, Rabindranath came to know the talented and beautiful Victoria Ocampo, who later became the publisher of the literary magazine Sur. They became close friends, but it appears that Rabindranath deflected the possibility of a passionate relationship into a confined intellectual one.16 His friend Leonard Elmhirst, who accompanied Rabindranath on his Argentine tour, wrote:

> Besides having a keen intellectual understanding of his books, she was in love with him-but instead of being content to build a friendship on the basis of intellect, she was in a hurry to establish that kind of proprietary right over him which he absolutely would not brook.

Ocampo and Elmhirst, while remaining friendly, were both quite rude in what they wrote about each other. Ocampo's book on Tagore (of which a Bengali translation was made from the Spanish by the distinguished poet and critic Shankha Ghosh) is primarily concerned with Tagore's writings but also discusses the pleasures and difficulties of their relationship, giving quite a different account from Elmhirst's, and never suggesting any sort of proprietary intentions.

Victoria Ocampo, however, makes it clear that she very much wanted to get physically closer to Rabindranath: "Little by little he [Tagore] partially tamed the young animal, by turns wild and docile, who did not sleep, dog-like, on the floor outside his door, simply because it was not done."17 Rabindranath, too, was clearly very much attracted to her. He called her "Vijaya" (the Sanskrit equivalent of Victoria), dedicated a book of poems to her, Purabi-an "evening melody," and expressed great admiration for her mind ("like a star that was distant"). In a letter to her he wrote, as if to explain his own reticence:

> When we were together, we mostly played with words and tried to laugh away our best opportunities to see each other clearly ... Whenever there is the least sign of the nest becoming a jealous rival of the sky [,] my mind, like a migrant bird, tries to take ... flight to a distant shore.

Five years later, during Tagore's European tour in 1930, he sent her a cable: "Will you not come and see me." She did. But their relationship did not seem to go much beyond conversation, and their somewhat ambiguous correspondence continued over the years. Written in 1940, a year before his death at eighty, one of the poems in Sesh Lekha ("Last Writings"), seems to be about her: "How I wish I could once again find my way to that foreign land where waits for me the message of love!/... Her language I knew not, but what her eyes said will forever remain eloquent in its anguish." However indecisive, or confused, or awkward Rabindranath may have been, he certainly did not share Mahatma Gandhi's censorious views of sex. In fact, when it came to social policy, he advocated contraception and family planning while Gandhi preferred abstinence.

Science and the People

Gandhi and Tagore severely clashed over their totally

different attitudes toward science. In January 1934, Bihar was struck by a devastating earthquake, which killed thousands of people. Gandhi, who was then deeply involved in the fight against untouchability (the barbaric system inherited from India's divisive past, in which "lowly people" were kept at a physical distance), extracted a positive lesson from the tragic event. "A man like me," Gandhi argued, "cannot but believe this earthquake is a divine chastisement sent by God for our sins" - in particular the sins of untouchability. "For me there is a vital connection between the Bihar calamity and the untouchability campaign."

Tagore, who equally abhorred untouchability and had joined Gandhi in the movements against it, protested against this interpretation of an event that had caused suffering and death to so many innocent people, including children and babies. He also hated the epistemology implicit in seeing an earthquake as caused by ethical failure. "It is," he wrote, "all the more unfortunate because this kind of unscientific view of [natural] phenomena is too readily accepted by a large section of our countrymen."

The two remained deeply divided over their attitudes toward science. However, while Tagore believed that modern science was essential to the understanding of physical phenomena, his views on epistemology were interestingly heterodox. He did not take the simple "realist" position often associated with modern science. The report of his conversation with Einstein, published in The New York Times in 1930, shows how insistent Tagore was on interpreting truth through observation and reflective concepts.

To assert that something is true or untrue in the absence of anyone to observe or perceive its truth, or to form a conception of what it is, appeared to Tagore to be deeply questionable. When Einstein remarked, "If there were no human beings any more, the Apollo Belvedere no longer would be beautiful?" Tagore simply replied, "No." Going further-and into much more interesting territory-Einstein said, "I agree with regard to this conception of beauty, but not with regard to truth." Tagore's response was: "Why not? Truth is realized through men."

Tagore's epistemology, which he never pursued systematically, would seem to be searching for a line of reasoning that would later be elegantly developed by Hilary Putnam, who has argued: "Truth depends on conceptual schemes and it is nonetheless 'real truth.'" Tagore himself said little to explain his convictions, but it is important to take account of his heterodoxy, not only because his speculations were invariably interesting, but also because they illustrate how his support for any position, including his strong interest in science, was accompanied by critical scrutiny.

Nationalism and Colonialism

Tagore was predictably hostile to communal sectarianism (such as a Hindu orthodoxy that was antagonistic to Islamic, Christian, or Sikh perspectives). But even nationalism seemed to him to be suspect. Isaiah Berlin summarizes well Tagore's complex position on Indian nationalism:

> Tagore stood fast on the narrow causeway, and did not betray his vision of the difficult truth. He condemned romantic overattachment to the past, what he called the tying of India to the past "like a sacrificial goat tethered to a post," and he accused men who displayed it - they seemed to him reactionary - of not knowing what true political freedom was, pointing out that it is from English thinkers and English books that the very notion of political liberty was derived. But against cosmopolitanism he maintained that the English stood on their own feet, and

> so must Indians. In 1917 he once more denounced the danger of 'leaving everything to the unalterable will of the Master,' be he brahmin or Englishman.

The duality Berlin points to is well reflected also in Tagore's attitude toward cultural diversity. He wanted Indians to learn what is going on elsewhere, how others lived, what they valued, and so on, while remaining interested and involved in their own culture and heritage. Indeed, in his educational writings the need for synthesis is strongly stressed. It can also be found in his advice to Indian students abroad. In 1907 he wrote to his son-in-law Nagendranath Gangulee, who had gone to America to study agriculture:

> To get on familiar terms with the local people is a part of your education. To know only agriculture is not enough; you must know America too. Of course if, in the process of knowing America, one begins to lose one's identity and falls into the trap of becoming an Americanised person contemptuous of everything Indian, it is preferable to stay in a locked room.

Tagore was strongly involved in protest against the Raj on a number of occasions, most notably in the movement to resist the 1905 British proposal to split in two the province of Bengal, a plan that was eventually withdrawn following popular resistance. He was forthright in denouncing the brutality of British rule in India, never more so than after the Amritsar massacre of April 13, 1919, when 379 unarmed people at a peaceful meeting were gunned down by the army, and two thousand more were wounded.

Between April 23 and 26, Rabindranath wrote five agitated letters to C.F. Andrews, who himself was extremely disturbed, especially after he was told by a British civil servant in India that thanks to this show of strength, the "moral prestige" of the Raj had "never been higher."

A month after the massacre, Tagore wrote to the Viceroy of India, asking to be relieved of the knighthood he had accepted four years earlier:

> The disproportionate severity of the punishments inflicted upon the unfortunate people and the methods of carrying them out, we are convinced, are without parallel in the history of civilized governments, barring some conspicuous exceptions, recent and remote. Considering that such treatment has been meted out to a population, disarmed and resourceless, by a power which has the most terribly efficient organisation for destruction of human lives, we must strongly assert that it can claim no political expediency, far less moral justification.... The universal agony of indignation roused in the hearts of our people has been ignored by our rulers - possibly congratulating themselves for imparting what they imagine as salutary lessons.... I for my part want to stand, shorn of all special distinctions, by the side of those of my countrymen who for their so-called insignificance are liable to suffer a degradation not fit for human beings.

Both Gandhi and Nehru expressed their appreciation of the important part Tagore took in the national struggle. It is fitting that after independence, India chose a song of Tagore ("Jana Gana Mana Adhinayaka," which can be roughly translated as "the leader of people's minds") as its national anthem. Since Bangladesh would later choose another song of Tagore ("Amar Sonar Bangla") as its national anthem, he may be the only one ever to have authored the national anthems of two different countries.

Tagore's criticism of the British administration of India was consistently strong and grew more intense over the years. This point is often missed, since he made a special effort to dissociate his criticism of the Raj from any denigration of British-or Western-people and culture. Mahatma Gandhi's well-known quip in reply to a question, asked in England, on what he thought of Western civilization ("It would be a good idea") could not have come from Tagore's lips. He would understand the provocations to which Gandhi was responding -

involving cultural conceit as well as imperial tyranny. D.H. Lawrence supplied a fine example of the former: "I become more and more surprised to see how far higher, in reality, our European civilization stands than the East, Indian and Persian, ever dreamed of.... This fraud of looking up to them-this wretched worship-of-Tagore attitude is disgusting." But, unlike Gandhi, Tagore could not, even in jest, be dismissive of Western civilization.

Even in his powerful indictment of British rule in India in 1941, in a lecture which he gave on his last birthday, and which was later published as a pamphlet under the title Crisis in Civilization, he strains hard to maintain the distinction between opposing Western imperialism and rejecting Western civilization. While he saw India as having been "smothered under the dead weight of British administration" (adding "another great and ancient civilization for whose recent tragic history the British cannot disclaim responsibility is China"), Tagore recalls what India has gained from "discussions centred upon Shakespeare's drama and Byron's poetry and above all...the large-hearted liberalism of nineteenth-century English politics."

The tragedy, as Tagore saw it, came from the fact that what "was truly best in their own civilization, the upholding of dignity of human relationships, has no place in the British administration of this country." "If in its place they have established, baton in hand, a reign of 'law and order,' or in other words a policeman's rule, such a mockery of civilization can claim no respect from us."

Critique of Patriotism

Rabindranath rebelled against the strongly nationalist form that the independence movement often took, and this made him refrain from taking a particularly active part in contemporary politics. He wanted to assert India's right to be independent without denying the importance of what India could learn-freely and profitably-from abroad.

He was afraid that a rejection of the West in favor of an indigenous Indian tradition was not only limiting in itself; it could easily turn into hostility to other influences from abroad, including Christianity, which came to parts of India by the fourth century; Judaism, which came through Jewish immigration shortly after the fall of Jerusalem, as did Zoroastrianism through Parsi immigration later on (mainly in the eighth century), and, of course-and most importantly-Islam, which has had a very strong presence in India since the tenth century.

Tagore's criticism of patriotism is a persistent theme in his writings. As early as 1908, he put his position succinctly in a letter replying to the criticism of Abala Bose, the wife of a great Indian scientist, Jagadish Chandra Bose: "Patriotism cannot be our final spiritual shelter; my refuge is humanity. I will not buy glass for the price of diamonds, and I will never allow patriotism to triumph over humanity as long as I live." His novel Ghare Baire (The Home and the World) has much to say about this theme.

In the novel, Nikhil, who is keen on social reform, including women's liberation, but cool toward nationalism, gradually loses the esteem of his spirited wife, Bimala, because of his failure to be enthusiastic about anti-British agitations, which she sees as a lack of patriotic commitment. Bimala becomes fascinated with Nikhil's nationalist friend Sandip, who speaks brilliantly and acts with patriotic militancy, and she falls in love with him. Nikhil refuses to change his views: "I am willing to serve my country; but my worship I reserve for Right which is far greater than my country. To worship my country as a god is to bring a curse upon it."

As the story unfolds, Sandip becomes angry with some of his countrymen for their failure to join the struggle as readily as he thinks they should ("Some Mohamedan traders are still obdurate"). He arranges to deal with the recalcitrants by burning their meager trading stocks and physically attacking them. Bimala has to acknowledge the connection between Sandip's rousing nationalistic sentiments and his sectarian - and ultimately violent-actions. The dramatic events that follow (Nikhil attempts to help the victims, risking his life) include the end of Bimala's political romance.

This is a difficult subject, and Satyajit Ray's beautiful film of The Home and the World brilliantly brings out the novel's tensions, along with the human affections and disaffections of the story. Not surprisingly, the story has had many detractors, not just among dedicated nationalists in India. Georg Lukács found Tagore's novel to be "a petit bourgeois yarn of the shoddiest kind," "at the intellectual service of the British police," and "a contemptible caricature of Gandhi." It would, of course, be absurd to think of Sandip as Gandhi, but the novel gives a "strong and gentle" warning, as Bertolt Brecht noted in his diary, of the corruptibility of nationalism, since it is not even-handed. Hatred of one group can lead to hatred of others, no matter how far such feeling may be from the minds of large-hearted nationalist leaders like Mahatma Gandhi.

Admiration and Criticism of Japan

Tagore's reaction to nationalism in Japan is particularly telling. As in the case of India, he saw the need to build the self-confidence of a defeated and humiliated people, of people left behind by developments elsewhere, as was the case in Japan before its emergence during the nineteenth century. At the beginning of one of his lectures in Japan in 1916 ("Nationalism in Japan"), he observed that "the worst form of bondage is the bondage of dejection, which keeps men hopelessly chained in loss of faith in themselves."

Tagore shared the admiration for Japan widespread in Asia for demonstrating the ability of an Asian nation to rival the West in industrial development and economic progress. He noted with great satisfaction that Japan had "in giant strides left centuries of inaction behind, overtaking the present time in its foremost achievement." For other nations outside the West, he said, Japan "has broken the spell under which we lay in torpor for ages, taking it to be the normal condition of certain races living in certain geographical limits."

But then Tagore went on to criticize the rise of a strong nationalism in Japan, and its emergence as an imperialist nation. Tagore's outspoken criticisms did not please Japanese audiences and, as E.P. Thompson wrote, "the welcome given to him on his first arrival soon cooled." Twenty-two years later, in 1937, during the Japanese war on China, Tagore received a letter from Rash Behari Bose, an anti-British Indian revolutionary then living in Japan, who sought Tagore's approval for his efforts there on behalf of Indian independence, in which he had the support of the Japanese government. Tagore replied:

> Your cable has caused me many restless hours, for it hurts me very much to have to ignore your appeal. I wish you had asked for my cooperation in a cause against which my spirit did not protest. I know, in making this appeal, you counted on my great regard for the Japanese for I, along with the rest of Asia, did once admire and look up to Japan and did once fondly hope that in Japan Asia had at last discovered its challenge to the West, that Japan's new strength would be consecrated in safeguarding the culture of the East against alien interests. But Japan has not taken long to betray that rising hope and repudiate all that

> seemed significant in her wonderful, and, to us symbolic, awakening, and has now become itself a worse menace to the defenceless peoples of the East.

How to view Japan's position in the Second World War was a divisive issue in India. After the war, when Japanese political leaders were tried for war crimes, the sole dissenting voice among the judges came from the Indian judge, Radhabinod Pal, a distinguished jurist. Pal dissented on various grounds, among them that no fair trial was possible in view of the asymmetry of power between the victor and the defeated. Ambivalent feelings in India toward the Japanese military aggression, given the unacceptable nature of British imperialism, possibly had a part in predisposing Pal to consider a perspective different from that of the other judges.

More tellingly, Subhas Chandra Bose (no relation of Rash Behari Bose), a leading nationalist, made his way to Japan during the war via Italy and Germany after escaping from a British prison; he helped the Japanese to form units of Indian soldiers, who had earlier surrendered to the advancing Japanese army, to fight on the Japanese side as the "Indian National Army." Rabindranath had formerly entertained great admiration for Subhas Bose as a dedicated nonsectarian fighter for Indian independence.24 But their ways would have parted when Bose's political activities took this turn, although Tagore was dead by the time Bose reached Japan.

Tagore saw Japanese militarism as illustrating the way nationalism can mislead even a nation of great achievement and promise. In 1938 Yone Noguchi, the distinguished poet and friend of Tagore (as well as of Yeats and Pound), wrote to Tagore, pleading with him to change his mind about Japan. Rabindranath's reply, written on September 12, 1938, was altogether uncompromising:

> It seems to me that it is futile for either of us to try to convince the other, since your faith in the infallible right of Japan to bully other Asiatic nations into line with your Government's policy is not shared by me.... Believe me, it is sorrow and shame, not anger, that prompt me to write to you. I suffer intensely not only because the reports of Chinese suffering batter against my heart, but because I can no longer point out with pride the example of a great Japan.

He would have been much happier with the postwar emergence of Japan as a peaceful power. Then, too, since he was not free of egotism, he would also have been pleased by the attention paid to his ideas by the novelist Yasunari Kawabata and others.

International Concerns

Tagore was not invariably well-informed about international politics. He allowed himself to be entertained by Mussolini in a short visit to Italy in May-June 1926, a visit arranged by Carlo Formichi, professor of Sanskrit at the University of Rome. When he asked to meet Benedetto Croce, Formichi said, "Impossible! Impossible!" Mussolini told him that Croce was "not in Rome." When Tagore said he would go "wherever he is," Mussolini assured him that Croce's whereabouts were unknown.

Such incidents, as well as warnings from Romain Rolland and other friends, should have ended Tagore's flirtation with Mussolini more quickly than it did. But only after he received graphic accounts of the brutality of Italian fascism from two exiles, Gaetano Salvemini and Gaetano Salvadori, and learned more of what was happening in Italy, did he publicly denounce the regime, publishing a letter to the Manchester Guardian in August. The next month, Popolo d'Italia, the magazine edited by Benito Mussolini's brother, replied: "Who cares? Italy laughs at Tagore and those who brought this unctuous and insupportable fellow in our midst."

With his high expectations of Britain, Tagore continued to be surprised by what he took to be a lack of official sympathy for international victims of aggression. He returned to this theme in the lecture he gave on his last birthday, in 1941:

> While Japan was quietly devouring North China, her act of wanton aggression was ignored as a minor incident by the veterans of British diplomacy. We have also witnessed from this distance how actively the British statesmen acquiesced in the destruction of the Spanish Republic.

But distinguishing between the British government and the British people, Rabindranath went on to note "with admiration how a band of valiant Englishmen laid down their lives for Spain."

Tagore's view of the Soviet Union has been a subject of much discussion. He was widely read in Russia. In 1917 several Russian translations of Gitanjali (one edited by Ivan Bunin, later the first Russian Nobel Laureate in Literature) were available, and by the late 1920s many of the English versions of his work had been rendered into Russian by several distinguished translators. Russian versions of his work continued to appear: Boris Pasternak translated him in the 1950s and 1960s.

When Tagore visited Russia in 1930, he was much impressed by its development efforts and by what he saw as a real commitment to eliminate poverty and economic inequality. But what impressed him most was the expansion of basic education across the old Russian empire. In Letters from Russia, written in Bengali and published in 1931, he unfavorably compares the acceptance of widespread illiteracy in India by the British administration with Russian efforts to expand education:

> In stepping on the soil of Russia, the first thing that caught my eye was that in education, at any rate, the peasant and the working classes have made such enormous progress in these few years that nothing comparable has happened

> even to our highest classes in the course of the last hundred and fifty years... The people here are not at all afraid of giving complete education even to Turcomans of distant Asia; on the contrary, they are utterly in earnest about it. 26

When parts of the book were translated into English in 1934, the under-secretary for India stated in Parliament that it was "calculated by distortion of the facts to bring the British Administration in India into contempt and disrepute," and the book was then promptly banned. The English version would not be published until after independence.

Education and Freedom

The British Indian administrators were not, however, alone in trying to suppress Tagore's reflections on Russia. They were joined by Soviet officials. In an interview with Izvestia in 1930, Tagore sharply criticized the lack of freedom that he observed in Russia:

> I must ask you: Are you doing your ideal a service by arousing in the minds of those under your training anger, class-hatred, and revengefulness against those whom you consider to be your enemies?... Freedom of mind is needed for the reception of truth; terror hopelessly kills it.... For the sake of humanity I hope you may never create a vicious force of violence, which will go on weaving an interminable chain of violence and cruelty.... You have tried to destroy many of the other evils of [the czarist] period. Why not try to destroy this one also?

The interview was not published in Izvestia until 1988-nearly sixty years later.27 Tagore's reaction to the Russia of 1930 arose from two of his strongest commitments: his uncompromising belief in the importance of "freedom of mind" (the source of his criticism of the Soviet Union), and his conviction that the expansion of basic education is central to social progress (the source of his praise, particularly in contrast to British-run India). He identified the lack of basic education as the fundamental cause of many of India's social and economic afflictions:

> In my view the imposing tower of misery which today rests on the heart of India has its sole foundation in the absence of education. Caste divisions, religious conflicts, aversion to work, precarious economic conditions - all centre on this single factor.

It was on education (and on the reflection, dialogue, and communication that are associated with it), rather than on, say, spinning "as a sacrifice" ("the charka does not require anyone to think"), that the future of India would depend.

Tagore was concerned not only that there be wider opportunities for education across the country (especially in rural areas where schools were few), but also that the schools themselves be more lively and enjoyable. He himself had dropped out of school early, largely out of boredom, and had never bothered to earn a diploma. He wrote extensively on how schools should be made more attractive to boys and girls and thus more productive. His own co-educational school at Santiniketan had many progressive features. The emphasis here was on self-motivation rather than on discipline, and on fostering intellectual curiosity rather than competitive excellence.

Much of Rabindranath's life was spent in developing the school at Santiniketan. The school never had much money, since the fees were very low. His lecture honoraria, "$700 a scold," went to support it, as well as most of his Nobel Prize money. The school received no support from the government, but did get help from private citizens-even Mahatma Gandhi raised money for it.

The dispute with Mahatma Gandhi on the Bihar earthquake touched on a subject that was very important to Tagore: the need for education in science as well as in literature and the humanities. At Santiniketan, there were strong "local" elements in its emphasis on Indian traditions, including the classics, and in the use of Bengali rather than English as the language of instruction. At the same time there were courses on a great variety of cultures, and study programs devoted to China, Japan, and the Middle East. Many foreigners came to Santiniketan to study or teach, and the fusion of studies seemed to work.

I am partial to seeing Tagore as an educator, having myself been educated at Santiniketan. The school was unusual in many different ways, such as the oddity that classes, excepting those requiring a laboratory, were held outdoors (whenever the weather permitted). No matter what we thought of Rabindranath's belief that one gains from being in a natural setting while learning (some of us argued about this theory), we typically found the experience of outdoor schooling extremely attractive and pleasant.

Academically, our school was not particularly exacting (often we did not have any examinations at all), and it could not, by the usual academic standards, compete with some of the better schools in Calcutta. But there was something remarkable about the ease with which class discussions could move from Indian traditional literature to contemporary as well as classical Western thought, and then to the culture of China or Japan or elsewhere. The school's celebration of variety was also in sharp contrast with the cultural conservatism and separatism that has tended to grip India from time to time.

The cultural give and take of Tagore's vision of the contemporary world has close parallels with the vision of Satyajit Ray, also an alumnus of Santiniketan who made several films based on Tagore's stories.28 Ray's words about Santiniketan in 1991 would have greatly pleased Rabindranath:

> I consider the three years I spent in Santiniketan as the most fruitful of my life.... Santiniketan opened my eyes for the first time to the splendours of Indian and Far Eastern art. Until then I was completely under the sway of Western art, music and literature. Santiniketan made me the combined product of East and West that I am.

India Today

At the fiftieth anniversary of Indian independence, the reckoning of what India had or had not achieved in this half century was a subject of considerable interest: "What has been the story of those first fifty years?" (as Shashi Tharoor asked in his balanced, informative, and highly readable account of India: From Midnight to the Millennium). If Tagore were to see the India of today, more than half a century after independence, nothing perhaps would shock him so much as the continued illiteracy of the masses. He would see this as a total betrayal of what the nationalist leaders had promised during the struggle for independence-a promise that had figured even in Nehru's rousing speech on the eve of independence in August 1947 (on India's "tryst with destiny").

In view of his interest in childhood education, Tagore would not be consoled by the extraordinary expansion of university education, in which India sends to its universities six times as many people per unit of population as does China. Rather, he would be stunned that, in contrast to East and Southeast Asia, including China, half the adult population and two thirds of Indian women remain unable to read or write. Statistically reliable surveys indicate that even in the late 1980s, nearly half of the rural girls between the ages of twelve and fourteen did not attend any school for a single day of their lives.

This state of affairs is the result of the continuation of British imperial neglect of mass education, which has been reinforced by India's traditional elitism, as well as upper-class-dominated contemporary politics (except in parts of India such as Kerala, where anti-upper-caste movements have tended to concentrate on education as a great leveller).

Tagore would see illiteracy and the neglect of education not only as the main source of India's continued social backwardness, but also as a great constraint that restricts the possibility and reach of economic development in India (as his writings on rural development forcefully make clear). Tagore would also have strongly felt the need for a greater commitment-and a greater sense of urgency-in removing endemic poverty.

At the same time, Tagore would undoubtedly find some satisfaction in the survival of democracy in India, in its relatively free press, and in general from the "freedom of mind" that post-independence Indian politics has, on the whole, managed to maintain. He would also be pleased by the fact noted by the historian E.P. Thompson (whose father Edward Thompson had written one of the first major biographies of Tagore:32

> All the convergent influences of the world run through this society: Hindu, Moslem, Christian, secular; Stalinist, liberal, Maoist, democratic socialist, Gandhian. There is not a thought that is being thought in the West or East that is not active in some Indian mind.

Tagore would have been happy also to see that the one governmental attempt to dispense generally with basic liberties and political and civil rights in India, in the 1970s, when Prime Minister Indira Gandhi (ironically, herself a former student at Santiniketan) declared an "emergency," was overwhelmingly rejected by the Indian voters, leading to the precipitate fall of her government.

Rabindranath would also see that the changes in policy that have eliminated famine since independence had much to do with the freedom to be heard in a democratic India. In Tagore's play Raja O Rani ("The King and the Queen"), the sympathetic Queen eventually rebels against the callousness of state policy toward the hungry. She begins by inquiring about the ugly sounds outside the palace, only to be told that the noise is coming from "the coarse, clamorous crowd who howl unashamedly for food and disturb the sweet peace of the palace."

The Viceregal office in India could have taken a similarly callous view of Indian famines, right up to the easily preventable Bengal famine of 1943, just before independence, which killed between two and three million people. But a government in a multi-party democracy, with elections and free newspapers, cannot any longer dismiss the noise from "the coarse, clamorous crowd."

Unlike Gandhi, Rabindranath would not resent the development of modern industries in India, or the acceleration of technical progress, since he did not want India to be shackled to the turning of "the wheel of an antiquated invention." Tagore was concerned that people not be dominated by machines, but he was not opposed to making good use of modern technology.

"The mastery over the machine," he wrote in Crisis in Civilization, "by which the British have consolidated their sovereignty over their vast empire, has been kept a sealed book, to which due access has been denied to this helpless country." Rabindranath had a deep interest in the environment - he was particularly concerned about deforestation and initiated a "festival of tree-planting" (vriksha-ropana) as early as 1928. He would want increased private and government commitments to environmentalism; but he would not derive from this position a general case against modern industry and technology.

On Cultural Separation

Rabindranath would be shocked by the growth of cultural separatism in India, as elsewhere. The "openness" that he valued so much is certainly under great strain right now - in many countries. Religious fundamentalism still has a relatively small following in India; but various factions seem to be doing their best to increase their numbers. Certainly religious sectarianism has had much success in some parts of India (particularly in the west and the north). Tagore would see the expansion of religious sectarianism as being closely associated with an artificially separatist view of culture.

He would have strongly resisted defining India in specifically Hindu terms, rather than as a "confluence" of many cultures. Even after the partition of 1947, India is still the third- largest Muslim country in the world, with more Muslims than in Bangladesh, and nearly as many as in Pakistan. Only Indonesia has substantially more followers of Islam. Indeed, by pointing to the immense heterogeneousness of India's cultural background and its richly diverse history, Tagore had argued that the "idea of India" itself militated against a culturally separatist view- "against the intense consciousness of the separateness of one's own people from others."

Tagore would also oppose the cultural nationalism that has recently been gaining some ground in India, along with an exaggerated fear of the influence of the West. He was uncompromising in his belief that human beings could absorb quite different cultures in constructive ways:

> Whatever we understand and enjoy in human products instantly becomes ours, wherever they might have their origin. I am proud of my humanity when I can acknowledge the poets and artists of other countries as my own. Let me feel with unalloyed gladness that all the great

> glories of man are mine. Therefore it hurts me deeply when the cry of rejection rings loud against the West in my country with the clamour that Western education can only injure us.

In this context, it is important to emphasize that Rabindranath was not short of pride in India's own heritage, and often spoke about it. He lectured at Oxford, with evident satisfaction, on the importance of India's religious ideas-quoting both from ancient texts and from popular poetry (such as the verses of the sixteenth-century Muslim poet Kabir).

In 1940, when he was given an honorary doctorate by Oxford University, in a ceremony arranged at his own educational establishment in Santiniketan ("In Gangem Defluit Isis," Oxford helpfully explained), to the predictable "volley of Latin" Tagore responded "by a volley of Sanskrit," as Marjorie Sykes, a Quaker friend of Rabindranath, reports. Her cheerful summary of the match, "India held its own," was not out of line with Tagore's pride in Indian culture. His welcoming attitude to Western civilization was reinforced by this confidence: he did not see India's culture as fragile and in need of "protection" from Western influence.

In India, he wrote, "circumstances almost compel us to learn English, and this lucky accident has given us the opportunity of access into the richest of all poetical literatures of the world." There seems to me much force in Rabindranath's argument for clearly distinguishing between the injustice of a serious asymmetry of power (colonialism being a prime example of this) and the importance nevertheless of appraising Western culture in an open-minded way, in colonial and postcolonial territories, in order to see what uses could be made of it.

Rabindranath insisted on open debate on every issue, and distrusted conclusions based on a mechanical formula, no matter how attractive that formula might seem in isolation (such as "This was forced on us by our colonial masters - we must reject it," "This is our tradition-we must follow it," "We have promised to do this-we must fulfill that promise," and so on). The question he persistently asks is whether we have reason enough to want what is being proposed, taking everything into account. Important as history is, reasoning has to go beyond the past. It is in the sovereignty of reasoning-fearless reasoning in freedom-that we can find Rabindranath Tagore's lasting voice.

4

Philosophy of Rabindranath Tagore

The tendency towards a newer and fresher reconstruction of Indian Philosophic thought has been noticeable during the past two decades. In India the impetus was given by the fresh thought infused by Christian Civilization. At times such an infusion has the effect of annihilating the original thought of the country wherever such thought is weak and irrational. At other times and places, it has the opposite effect of provoking fresh thought conflict. Every conflict has also the effect of making one probe deeper into one's own thought, and when this conflict is intellectual, without being dogmatic, it stimulates assimilation. This has been the case wherever the thought which was provoked by this Christian conflict was strong and profound-as in India.

Thus stimulated and thrown on the defensives the Indian philosopher diving deep into his own culture and thought, brought to the surface several tendencies, quite old but now re-lived in his own being Thought that soared without a material foundation now tried to find its bed-rock in human life and being. It is characteristic of Rabindranath's philosophy to call it the 'Religion of Man'.

In his Religion of Man, Rabindranath sketches beautifully and arrestingly the way of expression of the Universal Spirit-within the conditions of space and time. He shows that the Spirit had at first taken the quantitative direction and found at last a quantitative mass-infinity undoubtedly an infinity but as far from real infinity of Spirit. Mere mass without integral organisation leads of to disruption and results in the giving -up of beauty and simplicity for the sake of gorgeousness and unnecessary, unwieldy and uncouth decoration. This could be seen in forms of the pre-historic mosters. Their very size prevented them form protecting themselves against attacks from less massive and more lithe and better organized creatures.

Spirit bloated and grew vast as it were misinterpreting its own fundamental nature of intensive infinity. But checked and prevented from growing vaster by the very fact of the survival of the fittest and made to recognise that size by no means makes for efficiency in deference, there originated an orientation towards real evolution of spirit which is conscious interiority and intelligent adjustment. Man's evolution as a spiritual being was assured thereafter and coherent organisation became the chief character of evolutionary history. Real power consists not in size but in organisation and intelligent direction. As this development progressed, we may say that the unfolding of the main purpose now pronouncedly became human instead of remaining natural.

The natural passes over in its conscious character into the human. Therefore does man start with the artificial by reconstructing conditions far from those of the animal (for that has been civilization) only shows that the spiritual end has been the transformation of the unconscious organization into the conscious. It is not true to say that human destiny is at cross-purposes with that of Nature. Natural process and human organisation are but one continuous enfoldment of the self-same purpose of Spiritual Life. The natural process and human organisation tend to the expression of the Divine- God.

The highest truth of man is the full creative expression of himself in the light of eternal Life of Man, the man himself universalised. From the repetitive and the imitative instinctive-life, through all the sorrows and defeats, the spirit in nature tries to follow this trend up towards the complete exemplification of this purpose of Spirit is Man (purushottama) who is the goal of individual human beings. (Upeya).

If we are confronted with the question whether or not we should take present human beings as representative, in however little measure of the universal, we must admit that man is yet unborn, but thought unborn he is yet with us in our inmost purposes, and wherever man has caught the purpose of universal life, he has to that extent become the true man-a universal being. Not in his primitive desires which are as yet animal because unconscious expressions of an urge towards his true nature, (every urge within the human breast and animal life but the expression of the spirit within, struggling to release its meaning and life), but in his rationalised consciousness which recognises the greater and the All - 'surplus'. This is the purpose and goal of individual life.

Reason is universal and truly spiritual, and reason in man is the sure code guide towards universal Life. This Reason, however, is not the intellect which tries to thwart the main ends of universality but confines itself to particular ends, but it is intuition which is the appreciator of the harmony of life and its meaning and which guides the conduct of man accordingly. We find, thus, that Rabindranath holds the humanistic thesis that the goal of the world or cosmos is human and that its realisation is a possibility only when the individuals act consciously towards the fullest exemplification of the Universal Man. This inner realisation or consciousness of Man is essentially the recognition of oneself.

Some people hold that evolutionary history is a fantasy and an illusion. It has no reality. It is mere appearance. In fact, they even go to the extent of saying that the individual human being himself is an illusion, caught up in an illusion, trying to reach an illusion. Rabindranath holds that the individual souls are not illusion, that the world of which we know is certainly not an illusion, though it is an appearance-quite a different thing. It is an intimation of the more real thought by itself and in itself if it is as yet un under standable. To deprive truth of its appearance is to deprive it of its best part. "When you deprive truth of its appearance, it loses the best part of its reality. For appearance is a personal relationship, it is for me ... "This appreciation which seems to be the surface but which carries the message of the inner spirit" is something that cannot be denied reality because it is the only manner we can know the real at all.

To create an opposition between reality and appearance is to misjudge the nature of reality. It is due to the perversity of intellectual obscurantists and abstractionists turned mystical, that such a change has been maintained and human values sacrificed. Rabindranath, though an intuitionist, does not sacrifice, as pseudo-mistics have done, the world of values. To him the human values are absolute truth. He does not join the intuitionists who maintain that in some sense the reality which is experiences or the appearance is a distorted or segmented reality.

The charge which Bergson levels against intellect as the fundamental instrument of mind which has an innate separate and utilitarian bent and which therefore distorts reality to further the ends of practical life is only partially true. Bergson has greater influence on modern thought. His intuition resembles superficially the integrative consciousness of Hindu thought, and facile writers on

Indian Philosophy have adapted his description without looking deeper into it.

Intellect has the primary and inevitable tendency to abstract experience and to contemplate on those abstracted experiences, which also abstracted, lose life and movement, their peculiar individuality and completeness. When it is ecercised to its fullest, it becomes a satisfying instrument neither valuable nor practicable. But when it is used within limits for the purpose of understanding, it becomes defining and analysing activity. But such a definition and analysis can be valuable only when one has complete knowledge of the object.

The real then has to be understood as a whole and not in segments. Knowledge of it can be complete only when its unique character is realised. To enter into the object and understand it as a whole is the way of intuition. The whole is a definite uniqueness, not a vague undefined experience, though to describe it by words may not be possible. When Bergson calls Intuition 'intellectual sympathy', he means intellect as limited in its tendency and as having for its main purpose wholeness and completeness, and as characterised by emotion or instinctive dynamism.

Bergson intellect can be abused as much as intuition can be. Everything is sanctified or defiled by the goal to which it tends. Instincts are proclaimed holy when they aim at the liberation of true values within the individual life. Reason, then must apply to experience and evaluable it, draw out its significance and express its inmost aspiration. It is only then that it becomes truly spiritual. To hold that intellect and intuition are opposities, emergents out of life which contradict and thwart the purpose of each other, is to hold a view which is damaging to philosophy and to life alike. Nor are action and thought contradictories.

Pragmatism is perfectly right when it affirms this criterion of workability. Only it fails to see the real springs of practical action. Ultimate knowledge is really a synthesis, a synthesis of thought and action. This knowledge will lead not to the abstract impersonality of knowledge and reality but to the concrete personality of reality. Reality is a synthesis, a whole that ought to be apprehended as a Whole - not merely as nature, nor merely as spirit but as a unity comprising both the subjective and the objective. In man as a psycho-physical being, it finds its first resolution of this dualism of the subjective and the objective.

The objective - view of the scientist is a partial representation of the whole. The Scientist is too preoccupied with the constancies in nature, its laws of causality and regular occurrence. He tries to discover those impersonal principles of nature that order it. He certainly does not know the future but he can deduce or calculate the chances. But the fact of chance always makes him uncertain as to the individual events happening one way or the other. The past is capable of exact determination but the future is pregnant with the impossibilities of today and of the past. The nature of the world seems therefore incapable of any purely mechanical explanation.

The subjective world-view on the other hand depends only upon one's personal whims and fancies. Having constructed a world of imagination the individual seeks to live in his own creation. The individual thus concentered in his own person, living an isolated life, unrelated to other lives ends in a life of glorified fantasy of egoistc existence.

The world, according to the subjective thinker is individual creation, having no objective or trans-subjective reference. But even he finds that there is such a thing as objective commonness in existence, which is referred to as identical by all beings, even if such an identity is only for the sake of practical life. This objectivity is affirmed of the world with respect to the individual selves who experience it, because it is obvious that the individual knowledge is too little and narrow to enable him to create a universe more than himself.

Even subjective Idealists like Berkeley also maintain that there must be a Spiritual Being greater then the individual whose creative fancy this world is. This they call God. Therefore, we find that the subjectivist tends more and more to the recongnisation of a greater and an All who alone fashions and creates this world, and has as his fundamental nature creative activity. Before His manifestation we are nothing, and our understanding of Him fails to grasp the plan of the unfoldment of His Nature.

The objective world also strives to gain significance through subjective life that so fashions it as to express the sure purpose of Spirit. There is an inner pulsation within it that seems to vibrate in unison with the purpose of human Life: else it would not be possible to organise it. Within it Spirit is struggling to express itself. Its very orderliness (which some idealists think is imposed by man's schematising mind) suggests the organised nature of its being.

The world, therefore, is spiritual not because its substance is spirit (spirit is no substance here but purposive governing activity), but because its order and unfoldment are coterminous with the world of the subject and his ideals. The world is ideal because its ground is in something which is forcing expression in and though its texture. This ethical trend within its being is what makes even the most hardened realists affirm the ideal character of reality. Idealism is true only when we understand it in terms of ethical life, not in terms of the philosophers of Absolutistic schools of thought who somehow call themselves idealists.

This possible organisation of the objective world by the subject is a conscious process - a process which is planned by the individuals who have recognised this ideal as the goal of Man. In personality, then, the resolution of subjective individualism and objective impersonalism take place. The Personality of Man attains its fullest scope and measure when its infinity is realised within the finite, when the absolute values of Spirit are adequately represented and assured within the relative.

For, "Man has found out the great paradox that what is limited is not imprisoned within its limits; it is ever moving and therefore shedding its finitude every moment. In fact, imperfection is not a negation of perfection ; finitude is not contradictory to infinity ; they are but completeness manifested in parts, infinity revealed within limits."

Rabindranath holds the view that the Ideal Man is constantly immanently sustaining the process of the revelation of His Being in terms of the relative and the finite. Such sustaining may be compared to the teleological immanence of Spirit of Aristotle' theory. We are conscious of this Ideal in our most lucid moments, in our appreciation of art and nature, in Beauty, in other words, in the sacrificial moment when we offer ourselves entirely for the person we love, in the expression of our truth which is direct and unequivocal, and in the justest acts of equity. We cannot deny that which we feel so surely.

Even the most extreme of the amoralists and immoralists cannot deny that life is governed by such principles as beauty, truth and equity, because we know in the depths of our being that we are thoroughly governed by such Ideals. We even affirm that the Ideal is immanent within us sustaining our very life. The more consciously we express and the more consciously we are guided by this ideal power, the more we become men, or as Tagore would express it, Man. The arguments of Tagore therefore, for the existence of God are cosmo-teleological as well as ontological But to be able to express our faith in God we have to be conscious of our real Self.

"We have our personal self. It has desires which struggle to create a world where they could have their unrestricted activity and satisfaction. While it goes on, we discover that our self-realisation reaches its perfection in the abnegaion of self. This fact has made us aware that the individual finds his meaning in a fundamental reality comprehending all individuals - the reality which is the moral and spiritual basis of human values. This belongs to our religion. As science is the liberation of our knowledge in universal reason, which cannot be other than human reason, religion is the liberation of our individual personality in the universal person who is human all the same."

Thus the ideal of reason which science lays down, is the liberation of itself from finite and relativity ; the ideal of love is the liberation of the individual love from the finitude of its individual relations or selfishness. Sometimes one feels that this must be a progressive process-this release of the individual love from the bond of individual relationship, even as the body of scientific laws goes on liberating itself from the relativity to which it is restricted by the very nature of experience. It must, however, be remembered that in Science there is an objective impersonality which integrates itself with other laws of science, equally impersonal. But the movement of love is, on the other hand, personal ; and its enlargement does not lead to impersonal contemplation but to concrete expression towards all. There is an ascent to perfection - a gradual liberation by the submission of our wills to the sovereignty of the Universal will, which is unversal Love. There is a gradual submission of our desires to the happiness of the family; the family is sacrificed for the happiness of the nation, the race, and finally, Man.

All sacrifice is inevitably attended with pain. But even pain becomes a valuable asset, it becomes the measure of our Love. All suffering is due to the inability to sacrifice oneself -or rather to adjust oneself to the perfect Ideal which constantly seeks expression through us. This pain is the intrinsic quality of sacrifice, is indeed, the joy of love and giving for the sake of Man. Humanity must realise this Universal will and submit to its greatest expression which cannot be expressed in terms of human experience.

The voice of Conscience might be considered to be the chord which catches the rhythmic vibrations of the Universal Mind. The voice of beauty, the call of Truth, is the same for all, in the sense that it manifests the universality of its nature. So, it is absolutely certain that there is a universal Mind which works through the relative finite centres or selves. No less imperative is the call of Love. "Want of love is a degree of callousness: for love is the perfection of consciousness. We do not love because we do not comprehend, or rather we do not comprehend because we do not love".

The private individual has to shed his privateness and assume universal significance which is that of the Universal Person. The Upanishad says "Know thou the one soul. It is the bridge leading to the Immortal Being. This is the ultimate end of man, to find the One which is in him; which is his truth, which is his Soul ; the key with which he opens the gate of spiritual life, the heavenly Kingdom."

The freedom which characterises moral life is really the freedom of the Spirit which has assumed several modes of expressing the infinite in terms of the finite. To ask why there is so much suffering if there is a God or a universal Being is to ask a question of inconsequence. The freedom of the individual is a condition necessary for the creative life of spirit. Craving for uniformity, men create a state of uniformity,but it has not attraction of distinction nor the richness of beauty, nor the rhythm of music. All true love is characterised by joy, and that is because all love is soul-offering.

. All true co-operation is based on the free acceptance of love which cannot be brought into being by force. If there is freedom which sometimes ends in severance of relationsindependence-it is because there is another element which forces the individual into loving and union. But the element of severance is, according to Tagore, only an appearance, and the element of union is the ultimate truth. Anarchy that regions in the moral life of the individual is a condition precedent to real co-operative life, the life of love. Just as we have to pass though 'the valley of the shadow of death' to attain to Happiness, we have to pass through the stage of saverance ere we attain to Love.

The more we adjust our ends to the universal goal as revealed by our conscience (which is not to be mistaken with the norms and standards of life but which in some measure expresses the fundamental universality of the values of truth, love and beauty) the more we become truly free.

Then the Godhead becomes one with the individual, the infinite is revealed in the finite mind. This could be possible only if the universal Being is really human and not the phantom of intellectual philosophy. God is a person of universal significance, whose nature is Love and Beauty. His relation to men is integral, or organic. "It is only the Vaishnava religion that has boldly declared that God has bound himself to man, and in that consists the greatest glory of human existence. In the spell of the wonderful rhythm of the finite he fetters himself at every step and thus gives his love out in music in his most perfect lyrics of beauty.'

It is because the personality of God is human, there is possible the rapport with the Infinite All. It only means that God's Personality is superior to the impersonality of the logical Absolute. The impersonality of God is his Truth-aspect. God interpreted through Logic appears to be an abstraction, a concept. But God understood in terms of value, of moral life and religion is personality.

"Some modern philosophers of Europe who are directly or indirectly indebted to the Upanishads, far from realising their debt, a negation of all that is in the world. In a word, that the infinite being is to be found nowhere else except in metaphysics. It may be that such a doctrine is to be is found and still is prevalent with a section of our countrymen. But that is certainly not in accord with a pervading spirit of the Indian Mind".

The metaphysical Absolute is a result of pure scholasticism. It is a tenet held by none except the intellectualist thinkers. All religious thinkers accept no such description of God. Nor is the destination of man the abstraction of the Absolute. There is not the slightest evidence to support the view that increasing understanding, sympathy and cooperation tend to make real personalities disappear. It is only those who have developed the fundamental persistence of immortal existence. "It is precisely the stability and originality of people of character that keeps the world from stagnation," say Rabindranath. The truth of our private selves does not lie in our idiosyncracies but in the moral nature of the freedom that we possess and exercise.

Rabindranath believes in the Joy of existence. He accepts the Unity of all things, Advita the Absolute Divine All. In God according to Rabindranath the super-personal God en rapport with individual God manifests himself in the parts. But no part can absorb the whole. The part cannot defeat the ends of the whole by the accentuation of itself. It must subordinate its individuality to the whole; if it does not, it perishes. Civilization is the continual discovery of the transcendental Humanity or God. All men, therefore should try to live for Man, for it is His Joy that the world reveals.

Therefore is the significance of the parts and the snatches of finite experience realised only when we go beyond the purely partial, and investigate the purpose for which the parts stands, not merely in order to plan out the whole as the metaphysician or the geographer does. It is only the artist who sees the All and the One, and understands the goal of human existence. Without the vision of the All, we are certain to sink down in the morass of internecine quarrels, and Civilization would become nothing other then selfish enterprise.

The Artist is the real Seer,' he has sees beyond the temporal and the fragmentary and the temporal. The Poets and the Artists alone can save the world, for theirs is the Vision of Beauty, Truth and Bliss. They alone can plan the future with sympathy and true Love. They alone, having intuition, perceive the Man sub specie eternitatis, whilst the individual beings look at it in fragments.

Rabindranath has taken uponhimself the task of planning such an education and his International University at Bolpur aspires to bring into being a culture which shall reflect the Man and not any particular individual or nation or race. Not the renunciation of life but the fulfillment of Life is immortal Joy and unending beauty. That should be the main aim of Knowledge. The world is the Creative Excellence of the Man, the Lila, play of Divine Perfection.

In evaluating Rabindranath's Philosophy, at the very outset, it must be said that it makes no pretence at offering a complete exposition of the moot-points of intellectual philosophers. In spite of its poetic character, there are certain features that demand attention and appreciation even, from the intellectualists.

There is a spiritual purpose, says Rabindranath, that runs through the ages. This Purpose is Man. Rabindranath's theory does not, however, clearly explain how the Divine Mind finds projection in the individual. Rebindranatn assumes that this perfection of Man will find its fullest expression in an altogether utopian order of existence where the intellectual and the intuitive cooperation of all the several peoples of the world shall reign supreme and the peoples shall give to one another their particular riches of spiritual experience. Thus the completest Deity comes into being. Man, then is the whole Universe of existence come to complete expression in human terms. Two interpretations are possible here. We may conceive of the whole universe as the One Purushottama appeating diversified but yet holding the unity which is the very nature of His Spiritual existence.

The several individuals, then, are parts somehow, reaching beyond themselves, even as our individual organs strive for the maintenance of the unity of the body,-- to express the infinite purpose of the Deity, whose instruments they become. A more conscious realisation of the interdependence of the parts and the whole makes for complete Oneness. It is necessary in the case of human beings that the unconsciousness that is a characteristic of functioning of the organs of the body must give place of the conscious and deliberate offering of the several parts of the life of the whole which is Man.

The other alternative is the Divine expresses Himself fully each of His perfections Plato affirms that the world only mirrors the eternal Ideas and this mirroring is animperfect andunreal manifestation. Rabindranath is a realist and does not accept that the world is illusory. Plato holds that the individually, and in each individual he is complete and full.

The Goal of the Process is then Society. Rabindranath inclinesto the former view. The Goal is Man. Here again we have two alternatives. (1) Should the surrender of the parts to the whole be made once and forever? This course has a parallel in the Social contract theory of Hobbesor (2) should the surrender be a conscious endeavour at every moment of individual existence? The former surrender becomes nugatory after a time for there is no love and real affection but mere habit, the latter love and real affection but mere habit, the latter becomes the real revealing affection to the unity of the whole. The description of evolution by Rabindranath has novel reatures. It is quite distinct from anything that we know of in India or western thought, and effectively reconciles several western theories.

Evolution of Spirit into Matter and a return to itself through its texture is the real Though of the East. The summit of this return is Man. The immanent urge within matter is Spirit. How this urge expresses itself through extension at first and then by a return to its intensive character has been explained. Rabindranath Pure Idea God,the Highest Essence can be known only by discovering the essences in existence and subsuming then under the most universal Being.

Rabindranath affirms the realisation of the pure Being in the values of the universe, of space and time. it is not through intellectual generalisation that will lead to the Concrete Universal Being, Man, but the loving that surrender to the All. The Universal is other than the general This concept is the most intriguing in Rabindranath. Whatever he means this to be identical with the Leviathan of Hobbes or with the Utopia of the Anarchists; whether the Absolute of Bosanquet orthe World of souls who have attained co-operative freedom is not quite clear.

Concurs with the view of those thinkers who have been deeply influenced by Aristotle, viz Bergson, Lloyd Morgan, and General Smuts. That Spirit as vital energy fashions and creates now forms or patterns of life for the pupose of expressing itself adequately and that the progress of evolution is guided by the principle of adequate expression of Spirit is the main thesis of these thinkers. Lioyed Morgan and Bergson agree in so far asthey posit new forms of spirit as reflex, instinct, intellect, and intuition. We cannot derive any one of these forms from the rest, though they are equally manifestation of the identical Elan.

Tagore does not however, visualise the emergance of these forms clearly. He seems to follow Bergson in so far as the impeding of one form of Spirit by another is concerned, though not with respect to all forms of Spirit. The quantitative movement of Spirit impedes the qualitative. He follows more closely Yadava Prakasa's cleavage theory of evolution. Originally spirit began to function in the direction of quantitative infinity- and matter was the result. When it began its movement towards intensity and qualitative infinity, it created Life and man. Its f inal expression through Man is the transcendent -over humanity-God.

The original matrix of existence is the Absolute Undifferentiated Spirit. In the theory of Yadava,the cosmic process is immediate, and sudden. In Rabindranath it is closely linked with time. In both theories,the identity of the One Spirit becomes the unity of the three in relative existence, and by becoming such it reveals an intenser harmony and humanity. More so in Rabindranath's Philosophy.

The theory of Raabindranath does not account for the nature of the many-ness of the individuals as fully and satisfactorily as maybe desired. But his theory of sacrifice of less perfect individuals for the purpose of the most perfect being, Man, deserves consideration. General Smut explains that in evolution less perfect wholes are subsumed under larger and more perfect wholes.

The completer whole reveal some peculiar characteristic over and above the qualities of lesser wholes, that compose it if not altering them. There is visible a newer function emerging from such an interrelation of wholes. Functionally, its activity is not the mere sum of the functions of the units which from it. At first, in evolution, small cells (unicellular organisms) are independent units. Later they group themselves to form more complex bodies with diversified functions. these groupings brings into being functional characteristics like instinct, intellect, consciousness, and intuiion. These functional characteristics are therefore the quality of the wholes, the more complex and diversified, the more dominant and delicate are these forms of spiritual activity.

The highest is the organisation on the physical basis of wholeness is the human body. These units now progress towards the still more complex spiritual units, the family,. Society, community, State, and finally, Deity. The last is the completest personally, the most real and perfect whole. Its nature is transcendent to anything contained in the several units. in an ideal sense the Deity as the spirit moving towards the whole is immanent at every stage of the process.

In Rabindranath's theory, however, the Ideal is more powerfully present. His idealistic tendency is greater, and resembles strongly the Hegelian. If we can compara this Ideal Deity with Man, Narayana, we have not only the explanation. Of Evolution but also the realisation of the Most perfect whole,.the Supreme Personality, God who is organic with the world. It is not clear in Rabindranath's philosophy whether hemeans the ideal implication of the parts in the whole, or the natural biological implication of the units in the whole as in Smuts' theory.

Ranbindranath, speaks about the sacrifice of the individual units for the gradual realisation of the unity of the family, community, nation, state, universe, each in turn being sacrificed for the sake of MAN. Rabindranath does not mean to annual the individuals or communities, but he intends to make them whole, so as to bring into being the Ideal expression of MAN.

As a Seer, Rabindranath sees this ideal purpose of Man, as a poet he sings about Him, for this perfect being is not a mere emergent possibility but an actual fact when we Love deeply, truly and spontaneously. Evil andchance are not the truth of existence. Despair is not the last word; tragedy is not the highest summit of spirituality. Delight through sacrifice is the highest truth of existence. All this world is the Lila, the creative Delight of Man-to Him who Sees this within Himself.

5

Educational Ideas of Rabindranath Tagore

Rabindranath Tagore's role in the innovation of educational ideas has been eclipsed by his fame as a poet. He was a pioneer in the field of education. For the last forty years of his life he was content to be a schoolmaster in humble rural surroundings, even when he had achieved fame such as no Indian had known before. He was one of the first, in India, to think out for himself and put in practice principles of education which have now become commonplace of educational theory, if not yet of practice.

Today we all know that what the child imbibes at home and in school is far more important than what he studies at college, that the teaching is more easily and naturally communicated through the child's mother-tongue than through an alien medium, that learning through activity is more real than through the written word, that wholesome education consists in training of all the senses along with the mind instead of cramming the brain with memorized knowledge, that culture is something much more than academic knowledge.

But few of Rabindranath's countrymen took notice of him when he made his first experiments in education in 1901 with less than half a dozen pupils. A poet's whim, thought most of them. Even today few of his countrymen understand the significance of these principles in their national life. The schoolmaster is still the most neglected member of our community, despite the fact that Rabindranath attached more merit to what he taught to children in his school than to the Hibbert lectures he delivered before the distinguished audience at Oxfoard.

Mahatma Gandhi adopted the scheme of teaching through crafts many years after Rabindranath had worked it out at Santiniketan. In fact the Mahatma imported his first teachers for his basic School from Santiniketan.

If Rabindranath had done nothing else, what he did at Santiniketan and Sriniketan would be sufficient to rank him as one of the India's greatest nation-builders.

With the years, Rabindranath had won the world and the world in turn had won him. He sought his home everywhere in the world and would bring the world to his home. And so the little school for children at Santiniketan became a world university, Visva-Bharati, a centre for Indian Culture, a seminary for Eastern Studies and a meeting-place of the East and West. The poet selected for its motto an ancient Sanskrit verse, Yatra visvam bhavatieka nidam, which means, "Where the whole world meets in a single nest."

"Visva-Bharati", he declared, " represents India where she has her wealth of mind which is for all. Visva-Bharati acknowledges India's obligation to offer to others the hospitality of her best culture and India's right to accept from others their best."

In 1940 a year before he died, he put a letter in Gandhi's hand,

"Visva-Bharati is like a vessel which is carrying the cargo of my life's best treasure , and I hope it may claim special care from my countrymen for its preservation."

Growth of Viswa-Bharati

A study of the evolution of Visva-Bharati during the lifetime of its founder, Rabindranath Tagore, offers an insight into what this institution was intended to achieve. Rabindranath founded a school for children at Santiniketan and it was around this nucleus that the structure of an unconventional university developed through careful planning.

In 1863, on a seven-acre plot at the site of the present institution, Debendranath Tagore, the poet's father, had built a small retreat for meditation, and in 1888 he dedicated, the land and buildings, towards establishment of a Brahmavidyalaya and a library. Rabindranath's school Brahmacharyasrama which started functioning formally from December 22, 1901 with no more than five students on the roll, was, in part, a fulfilment of the wishes of his father who was a considerable figure of his time in the field of educational reforms. From 1925 this school came to be known as Patha-Bhavana.

The school was a conscious repudiation of the system introduced in India by the British rulers and Rabindranath initially sought to realize the intrinsic values of the ancient education in India. The school and its curriculum, therefore, signified a departure from the way the rest of the country viewed education and teaching. Simplicity was a cardinal principle. Classes were held in open air in the shade of trees where man and nature entered into an immediate harmonious relationship.

Teachers and students shared the single integral socio-cultural life. The curriculum had music, painting, dramatic performances and other performative practices. Beyond the accepted limits of intellectual and academic pursuits, opportunities were created for invigorating and sustaining the manifold faculties of the human personality.

After Rabindranath was awarded the Noble Prize in 1913, he was invited to numerous visits all over the world and he came closely to know a large part of the world and its people. By 1917 the range of his experience and the restlessness of his exploration led to his own self-clarification regarding the idea of a centre of Indian culture at Santiniketan.The centre as conceived by him was to provide "for the coordinated study of the different cultures".

As "music and the fine arts are among the highest means of national self expression... in the proposed centre of our culture, music and art must have prominent seats of honour". This centre should not only be a centre of the intellectual life of India but the centre of the economic life as well. Participating thus in all the major spheres of Indian life, the institution would attain a representative character and enter into an encounter with the rest of the world.

The institution chose for its motto the Vedic text "Yatra visvam bhavtyekanidam" (where the world makes a home in a single nest). On 23 December 1921 Visva-Bharati became a registered public body which adopted a constitution of its own. The aims and object as set forth on the occasion have since then remained the objectives of Visva-Bharati.

Vidya-Bhavana or the Institution of Higher Studies and Research was the manifestation of the ideal of the proposed centre of comprehensive studies in the cultures of the East and the West. The centre was viewed principally as a community of scholars, Indian as well as foreign, who would be engaged in creation & dissemination of systematised and philanthropic reasoning. The concern was epistemological.Those who followed included Mortiz Winternitz, V.Lesny of Prague, Carlo Formici and Giuseppe Tucci of Rome, Sten Know of Oslo. They added a new dimension to the work that was being carried on by a remarkable group of Indian scholars and creative artists of rare dedication, the services of some of whom Rabindranath had secured even from the days of the Brahmacharyasrama.

In 1937 Cheena-Bhavana, the department of Sino-Indian studies was established, and even today it remains, by any standard, a remarkable symbol of cultural collaboration. In 1939, the Hindi-Bhavana with certain distinct projects of studies was founded. Kala-Bhavana which was originally the institute for both Fine Arts and Music came into existence in 1921 but in 1934 it branched off into two independent institutions, Kala-Bhavana and Sangit-Bhavana each with its own distinct discipline. In generating more informed and cultured interest and more ample educational components, these two institutions played pioneering role in our country.

Santiniketan

To study the mind of man in its realisation of different aspects of truth from diverse points of view.

To bring into more intimate relation with one another, through patient study and research, the different cultures of the East on the basis of their underlying unity.

To approach the West from the standpoint of such a unity of the life and thought of Asia.

To seek to realize in a common fellowship of study the meeting of the East and the West, and thus ultimately to strengthen the fundamental conditions of world peace through the establishment of free communication of ideas between the two hemispheres.

And, with such ideals in view, to provide at Santiniketan, a centre of culture where research into and study of the religion, literature, history, science and art of Hindu, Buddhist, Jain, Islamic, Sikh, Christian and other civilisations may be pursued along with the culture of the West, with that simplicity in externals which is necessary for true spiritual realisation, in amity, good fellowship and co-operation between the thinkers and scholars of both Eastern and Western countries.

Sriniketan

To win the friendship and affection of villagers and cultivators by taking a real interest in all that concerns their life and welfare, and by making an effort to assist them in solving their most pressing problems.

To initiate a dialogue between academic study and research of rural economy / culture and on-field experience.

The Institute of Rural Reconstruction was founded in 1922 at Surul at a distance of about three kilometres from Santiniketan. It was formally inaugurated on February 6, 1922 with Leonard Elmhirst as its first Director. Thus the second but contiguous campus of Visva-Bharati came to be located in 1923 at a site which assumed the name of Sriniketan. The chief object was to help villagers and people to solve their own problems instead of a solution being imposed on them from outside.

In consonance with the ideas about reconstruction of village life, a new type of school meant mainly for the children of neighbouring villages who would eventually bring the offering of their acquired knowledge for the welfare of the village community was also conceived. This school, Siksha-Satra, was started in Santiniketan in 1924 but was shifted to Sriniketan in 1927. The Lok-Siksha Samsad, an organization for the propagation of non-formal education amongst those who had no access to usual educational opportunities, was started in 1936.

Siksha-Charcha for training village school teachers followed next year.

A Central University

In May 1951, Visva-Bharati was declared to be a Central University and "An Institution of National Importance" by an Act of Parliament. It was granted the status of a unitary, teaching and residential university. The status and function of all the major institutions have been redefined in successive Amendment Acts and the University has continued to grow by giving accreditation to new institutions in response to needs newly felt.

The school has reshaped itself into a full fledged modern University with diverse concern and interests The defining maxim of excellence remains intact.

A Way of Life

From the very beginning Rabindranath tried to foster a self-sufficient social life along with new values of creative as well as participatory culture. The most joyful expressions of the community are the festivals which at different times of the year celebrate the cycle of the seasons and the diverse manifestations of nature. Dances and songs presented on such occasions draw as much upon Rabindranath as other cultural resources of all parts of India. The community comes together in these festivals and for the young students in particular, it is an unobtrusive process of cultural enrichment.

Certain cultural events and festivals had come down as a legacy from the inception of the institution. The open-air devotional service that is held on 7 Poush (on or about 22 December) every year under the Chatim tree where Debendranath once meditated is an occasion of particular significance for the institution since it is the foundation day of the asrama. In accordance with the trust deed, a mela (festive fair) popularly known as the Poushmela is held to mark the occasion. Another three day village fair, called Maghmela is held early in February every year at Sriniketan.

There is prayer-hall, referred to as Mandir, where every Wednesday a non-denominational community prayer service is held. This prayer-hall is the place of congregation for all important occasions of commemoration for the community. It was the founder's belief that the moral influence radiating from here would afford a silent but constant guidance to the members of the community. All in all Santiniketan is the name for an attitude, a value, a way of life which suffuses an educational process, contains it, sustains it, yet transcends it.

Location

Visva-Bharati is ensconced in a rural setting in the district of Birbhum, about 160 km by road from Kolkata. The nearest railway station is Bolpur (Santiniketan) on the Eastern Railway and the air-terminal is Kolkata Airport. The University campus at Santiniketan, about 3 km from the railway station can be reached in a little over two hours from Kolkata by train. By train it is about 146 km. The University has two campuses, one at Santiniketan and the other at Sriniketan, which is about 3 km from Santiniketan. The institutional buildings and departments are distributed among them.

6

Tagore's View on Pluralism and Cultural Conflict

The issue of pluralism and cultural conflict occupied Rabindranath Tagore throughout his life. Several factors have to be kept in mind in trying to follow his view on this issue. I shall mention only two of the most vital. In the first place, he was a multi-faceted personality: not merely a thinker or philosopher, but also a creative artist, a man of action, and a man engaged in a diversity of pursuits.

In each of them he reached new heights and opened new possibilities. Unlike professional philosophers he did not seek to construct a system. Instead, he brought to bear upon each issue a multiplicity of insights. It would be a grievous error to seek to present him as a one-dimensional intellectual to try to simplify and systematize what refuses to be simplified and systematized. In trying to understand his view on any issue, one has to take into account his different insights as expressed in his various works and activities.

Secondly, Tagore not only had a long life, but to the very end he also kept renewing himself through daring new experiments and explorations. This is most dramatically evident in his drawings and paintings which belong to the last phase of his life and which present a dark and disturbing Dionysian personality in sharp contrast to the Apollonian figure of sweetness and light with which people had been familiar for several decades. But the transformations, albeit somewhat less dramatic, may also be seen in his other activities and expressions.

One has, for example, only to compare the poetry of Manasi (1890) and Chitra (1896) with that of Gitanjali (1910), then Balaka (1916), then Mohua (1929) and Sesh Lekha (1941) to realise how the world within him changed, time and again, without losing any of its richness of texture and significance. Again, the reverential attitude and idealized view which Tagore had towards Hindu India's traditional Brahmanical culture and social organization when he founded the brahmacharyasram at Santiniketan in 1901 changed almost radically by the time the foundation stone of Visvabharati was laid in 1918.

The experiment in Sriniketan showed further shifts in his outlook and priorities. I refrain from citing examples from other areas, but the main point to keep in mind is that Tagore's views kept changing and developing, that his mind was open to new experience and ideas and did not confine itself to a narrow set of conclusions, and that, although he was basically an idealist, he was also very much alive to the actualities of life and responded to them with a liveliness that did not weaken with age.

Having said this, I must immediately admit that for all his multiplicity and transformation there would appear to have formed quite early in his life some central core which gave all a substantial measure of togetherness and a certain conscious direction. This central core is best indicated by the expression, 'Unity in Diversity', which he often used in his essays and addresses. Throughout his life he consistently opposed uniformity and contrasted it to the ideal of unity. But true unity, Tagore believed, gave full recognition to diversity and sought harmony which, instead of reducing diversity, enriched each one of the discrete units. A deeply religious person, he had an unshakable faith in the existence of a supreme being who was both immanent and transcendent, but he did not subscribe to the notion propounded by Sankara that the world is maya or illusion, that the Absolute is the only reality, that atman, in the last analysis, is identical with brahman.

I have already cautioned that to look for a coherent system in his works would be worse than useless. There were shifts and variations, ambiguities and contradictions, but I incline to think that basically he believed that God, Nature and Man needed one another, that the endless variety of forms in nature was essential to the Supreme Being's self-realization, that between the Supreme Being and each individual self there existed an intimate relationship of playfulness which was inexhaustible and which gave meaning to both. God, Nature and Man formed a cosmic unity in which each retained its distinct identity.

I am quite aware that this is a very bald way of presenting a profound intuition which Tagore expressed in a thousand beautiful metaphors and analogies in his poems, songs, plays and expository prose. I am not a religious person and, therefore, I recognize myself as an outsider when I refer to Tagore's God. However, I feel at the same time certain that Tagore's core idea of unity in diversity has great relevance to the issue under discussion. Even to a non-religious humanist like myself that idea seems to be quite sound and has strong intellectual, aesthetic and moral appeal.

The intrinsic worth of that idea may be considered, even if it is taken out of its religious or metaphysical context. I shall briefly indicate the relevance of this idea at two clearly secular levels and then close with a pointer to the tragic sense which a secular humanist shares with a religious humanist like Tagore.

The first of these secular levels concerns the relation of the individual to any reified collectivity. To Tagore every individual is unique and irreplaceable, and freedom is essential to every individual's survival and development. Creativity, inquiry, conscience all are rooted in the individual's freedom. The individual grows not by submerging individuality, but by relating freely to other individuals, to history and nature while retaining its distinct identity.

Tagore was thus basically a libertarian. He was opposed to every form of authoritarianism or tyranny domestic, institutional, social, cultural, political and economic. No walls are to be raised to circumscribe the self, whether by others or by itself. It is through harmony with one's milieus ? social, cultural and physical that the individual frees itself from its initial narrowness and discovers the macrocosmic universe within its microcosmic self.

The purpose of education is to cultivate this harmony by responding to the plenitude of forms in nature and their rhythm, by voluntarily engaging in a variety of cooperative activities with other individuals through love, creativity and knowledge. Humanity will continue to grow and discover its inner wealth not by putting everyone into a common mould which seeks efficiency at the cost of freedom and creativity, but by appreciating the variousness of individuals and the universe and by pursuing the ideal of harmony.

This ideal of harmony, of achieving unity in diversity, was, for Tagore, no abstract notion, but was rooted in his personal experience and intuition. Nevertheless, he could not but recognize the existing gulf between the ideal and the actual. This is less evident in his songs, poems or expository prose than in his stories, novels or plays. It is not always noted by Tagore's interpreters that in the majority of his works which deal with persons and events, those individuals who are enlightened or who possess strong consciences or fine sensibilities sooner or later find themselves in conflict situations which defeat their pursuit of harmony. Any number of examples can be cited, but a few should suffice.

In Sacrifice, the King, moved by compassion, decides to abolish animal sacrifice to the dark goddess, and finds his wife, brother, the priest and the people turning against him. Joy Sinha, the young man of conscience, chooses to sacrifice his own life to achieve what seems to be but a fragile and temporary peace. The idealist Nikhilesh in The Home and the World is alienated both from his home and his people by his intellectual and moral integrity.

Mrinal in "Strir Patra" had to choose voluntary exile from her family and community because she could no longer bear their mean, insensitive, custom-bound, oppressive way of life. I am not sure that Tagore knew any more than I do how to resolve such a conflict situation and achieve genuine unity or reconciliation. So, while pursuit of harmony remained the ideal (with Tagore, the ideal was grounded in the cosmic order), in actual life it was discord which often proved to be stronger and prevailed. Exploration of the psychological and institutional sources of discord was central to his major works of fiction.

At the second secular level, it is not the relation between a plurality of individuals or between the individual and institutions, but between various cultures and collectivities which Tagore sought to understand, and to the regulation of which he offered guidelines. On the one hand, he perceived and appreciated the distinctive achievements of various cultures; on the other, he stressed the common nature and pursuit of the human species, the inalienable humanity of humankind.

Time and again he warned against cultural chauvinism which pitted one culture against another, and he wrote and spoke in favor of a universal culture to which the cultures of various peoples would contribute their finest achievements and from which they in their turn would draw nourishment. He was passionately opposed to nationalism, chauvinism, xenophobia, cultural aggressiveness and every form of imperialism or dominance of one people by another. The culture of a people is formed by history, geography, ethnic factors, language, religious beliefs and forms of social organization. It is not static, but capable of growth.

We have now reached a period of history where it is possible to evolve a universal culture without destroying or weakening the various indigenous cultures of the world. However, as in the case of individuals, here, too, the gulf between the ideal and actual proves to be very great. At one time Tagore had believed that India might provide the model where a diversity of peoples and cultures would be reconciled, and that they would evolve a unity where plurality would not be a source of conflict. But he lived to see the growing division in India between the Hindus and the Muslims, and among the Hindus between the traditional upper castes and the lower castes. He had at one time greatly admired the aesthetic refinement and the tradition of chivalry in Japan. And then Japan completely disillusioned him by launching a war of aggression against defenseless China.

The removal of illiteracy in the Soviet Union had elated him, but its bombing of Finland exposed to him its aggressive and ruthless nature. He had publicly opposed

Gandhi's non-cooperation, because he wanted reconciliation between the East and the West and believed that Europe, with it modern knowledge and democratic institutions, had much to offer. But in the end he saw the West bent on destroying itself and with it the fabric of modern civilization.

The contrast between the spirit of hope in his lectures on The Religion of Man (1931) and the sense of dark despair in Crisis in Civilization (1941) is a revelation of the great tragedy of our time. "I had at one time believed," he wrote two months before his death, "that the springs of civilization would issue out of the heart of Europe. Today, when I am about to quit the world, that faith has gone bankrupt."

Nonetheless, being more than an idealist or an artist, Tagore did try during the last twenty years of his life to create an institution which would embody some of his basic ideas. Visvabharati was to be a place where, in a rural setting, many cultures will meet, enrich each other, and help in the evolution of a universal culture appropriate to our age. He invited scholars, artists, scientists, philosophers from different parts of India and abroad to meet young minds who also came from distant places with a genuine keenness to learn.

At the same time, he wanted the university to relate intimately to the rural community, and established Sriniketan as complement to Santiniketan. He sought to remove the old walls of distrust, ignorance and pride which separate the people of one nation from another, community from community, caste from outcast, city from village. Visvabharati was a unique educational experiment befitting a man of Tagore's genius and supernumerary energy, vision, and creativity.

However, Tagore's brave efforts to create an institutional model which would approximate his ideal and inspire others to make similar experiments met with serious problems and obstacles even while he was still there to guide his associates and followers. The interwar decades in India saw the high tide of nationalism, and his vision of universalism and cultural unity between East and West provoked strong and widespread opposition from his own countrymen.

In fact, the last twenty years of his life were also the loneliest; and his anguish and sense of alienation cried out from many of his paintings and a good part of his prose and poetry of this final period. The 30s were a dark decade when the world was moving inexorably 'towards the most devastating war in history'. It was hardly a time when people were in a mood to listen to the voice of reason or any message of reconciliation and peace.

Moreover, Tagore did not succeed in achieving harmony between Visvabharati and Sriniketan. The deeply rooted hierarchical and elitistic tradition of India's brahmanical culture stood in the way of the university people appreciating the vital importance of education for rural development. Despite Tagore's strenuous efforts, Santiniketan never accepted Sriniketan on equal terms. Besides, scholars who came from abroad, attracted by Tagore's ideas and personality, found it difficult to win friendly acceptance from their local colleagues, and most of them left after a little while.

Weakened by age and illness, harried by lack of adequate financial resources for running the institutions, unable to find colleagues and followers who genuinely shared his ideals and visions, struggling against powerful currents of contemporary history, both Indian and international, Tagore witnessed the beginnings of decay set in at Visvabharati before his death in 1941. In the last more than half century, the situation has gone from bad to worse. His ideals today are hardly more than a memory. The institutions remain, but with neither vision nor dynamism of spirit.

And here lies the heart of the great tragedy which is as much Tagore's as it is ours. Pluralism is a fact of life, and so is cultural conflict. It is also certain that the road to survival and growth stretches along tolerance of differences, reconciliation, harmonization of different cultures and pursuit of unity in diversity. But there are dark forces and urges in the human psyche which are destructive in nature the Instinct of Thanatos or Death. Unless effective ways are found to regulate and subordinate them to the instinct of Eros or Life, the ideals of humanism, whether religious or secular, have hardly a chance to materialize.

The problem is both psychological and institutional, or situational. What Freud called "deafness of mind" has to be cured, and the aggressive tendencies in man have to be successfully controlled by cultivation of the spirit of reason. On the other hand, our civilization has to be radically reconstructed so that it incorporates everyone in its benefits, and its fruits are not unjustly distributed.

This involves a two-fold revolution ? one within the human psyche, the other in the structure of societies and civilizations. It seems to me that while humanists have rightly focussed their attention on the ideals which humanity must adopt and pursue to survive and grow, neither Tagore nor any other humanist could formulate and substantiate effective methods which would bring about this twofold revolution.

On the one hand, the lust for power and possession and the aggressive tendency inherent in that lust and, on the other, the iniquitous structure of our civilization, which deprives the majority of the people and ensures the control and enjoyment of the benefits of power and possession by a few, are the principal sources of conflict.

Our tragedy is that despite the lifelong efforts of extraordinary persons like Tagore, these sources continue to dominate the contemporary human condition. I see it as a supreme irony of history that what is called "globalization" today, made feasible by modern technology, is only leading towards imposition of one dominant culture, namely the American, on the rest of the world by a process of cultural cannibalism, instead of promoting the principle of unity in diversity.

7

Tagore, History and Cultural Studies

There was a time when in Europe, shattered by the torment of the First World War, the name Rabindranath Tagore (1861-1941) could evoke an enthusiasm bordering on idolatry. This is no longer the case. Today many people have perhaps heard the name but few will associate it with a famous Bengali poet on whom the Nobel prize for literature was conferred in 1913.

The basis for foreign recognition has been fragile as the non-Bengali-reading public only knew Tagore's work either from the few clipped paraphrases in English made by himself, or from some later, fairly weak, translations done by others in the forties and the fifties. It seems that until recently the personality cult of Tagore prevented a more sober and critical assessment of his Bengali works, while the available English texts do not do him full justice. After all, the original Bengali works run into thousands of pages and cover almost every literary genre. However, to date they are known only to the Bengali-reading public both in India and Bangladesh.

A new impulse to produce better translations of and to encourage a less mawkish involvement with Tagore arose in the mid-eighties. The first fruits of this new preoccupation can be seen in the recent works published by such people as William Radice (1987; 1991), Martin Kämpchen (1989; 1990), and Kẹtaki Kushari Dyson (1991). As Tagore was and still is known mainly as a poet, these translations are for the most part (on the whole rather well executed) renderings of poetry.

But Tagore wrote more than poems and songs, more than short stories, novels, travelogues, plays and letters. As a perceptive intellectual of his times he also commented on politics, social questions and religious and cultural matters in numerous essays and lectures. This body of religious, cultural and political writings has been little studied so far, in spite of the fact that it made an important contribution to the canon of Bengali nationalist literature of the late nineteenth and the early twentieth century, a truth to which Tapan Raychaudhuri in his book *Europe Reconsidered, Perceptions of the West in Nineteenth Century Bengal,* (1988) frankly testifies.

Subaltern Studies

Also in the two recent books by Partha Chatterjee (1993 2nd ed.; 1993) on Bengali and Indian nationalism in the colonial nineteenth century we find only scant reference to Tagore. Chatterjee, belonging to the prestigious historiographical school of the *Subaltern Studies* and now one of the editors of the volumes bearing the same name, prefers to analyse the conceptualizations of Indian nationalism by the earlier great Bengali writer Bankimchandra (1838-1894). In this Chatterjee follows the current postmodern, text-based trend of writing cultural history within the Subaltern Studies.

The latter's founder, Ranajit Guha, frequently refers to Bankimchandra, while Sudipta Kaviraj, also belonging to the Subaltern Studies group, has devoted a fresh study to this writer. The above-mentioned niche of Subaltern Studies seems to be meandering along slowly to join the field of Cultural Studies proper. The latter is a multidisciplinary attempt at writing and interpreting human culture. After it sprang up formally in Birmingham at the Centre for Contemporary Cultural Studies and gained importance in the seventies, it is now rising to prominence in the North American, and Australian human sciences.

Largely an outcome of the postmodern experience, it seems to hold out credible but heavily contested promises to build novel and creative passages towards a more refined, if fragmented, understanding of how cultural production comes about and what forces make it 'work' in human societies.

Its early theoretical 'canon' of Cultural Studies embraces among other schools Marxism, the Frankfurter Schule, English literary theory and a bit of classical Anarchist thought, as well as authors like Clifford Geertz, Bourdieu, and Stuart Hall. This canon is now expanding in various directions and incorporates many new fields of sociological and historical study such as women's and minority studies.

The most recent unfolding of Cultural Studies can be grasped from a number of anthologies, among which the ones edited by Lawrence Grossberg, Cary Nelson, Paula Treichler (1992); Simon During (1993); and Valda Blundell, John Shepherd, Ian Taylor (1993), are the more prominent. The monographs by Norman K. Denzin (1992) and Fred Inglis (1993) offer vigorously critical and historical surveys of the entire field.

Leiden Tagore Projects

The Leiden projects on Tagore, which are conducted by myself, draw critically upon the theoretical frameworks and possibilities offered by both the Subaltern Studies and Cultural Studies. Thus the present Tagore projects will be drawn into the orbits of these fields. This will widen the horizons of the study of Bengali culture as well as those of Cultural Studies as a whole. Fragments of Tagore's poetry, nationalist and religious thought will be presented in this light as instances of Bengali cultural studies.

The first result, to appear in the course of 1995, is a translation from Bengali into Dutch of the *Gitali* (1914), a volume of Tagore's poetry which has hitherto been translated into English only once, and that somewhat poorly. The Gitali is the last of three consecutive volumes of which the first, *Gitanjali* (1910), partly paraphrased into English by Tagore himself in 1912, brought his fame to the attention of the Western world. My translation of the Gitali will appear in the series 'Kern Institute Miscellenea'.

This literary presentation will soon be followed by two studies in English. The first one (with translations from various Bengali sources) will deal with the constructions of nineteenth century Indian nationalism, understood by its protagonists as being of a predominantly Hindu-cultural character, and its diverse ideological and political perspectives within the context of the British Raj. This volume will bring to light certain aspects of the (cultural) nationalism of this period, which neither Tapan Raychaudhuri, Partha Chatterjee, nor Sudipta Kaviraj have treated in detail in their respective explorations.

Around the turn of the century Tagore wrote with penetrating insight about European nationalism and its relevance to the Indian reality. Tagore wrote in a period in which what Benedict Anderson (1993) calls 'print capitalism' was already well established in India. The printed word had become a major vehicle for spreading ideology among the educated middle class, using not only English, but also the vernaculars. By means of the printed word Tagore tried to disseminate a distinctive brand of nationalism in which cultural theories, (mainly liberal Hindu) religious inspiration, historical imagination as well as invention and humanist ethos blended almost inseparably.

This blend with its shifting accents forms the subject of the second publication. It will contain a full English translation from Bengali with annotations of *Dharma*, a volume of Tagore's early religious essays, published in book form in 1908. In these essays Tagore construes a national religious ideology with different strands, ranging from utterly individualistic religious experience to broad concepts of a unitary Indian nation whose predominant flavour is humanist religious and spiritual.

The exercise of translation and annotation (a rather traditional performance) is refined by commentatorial readings of the texts themselves. These readings will highlight some disturbing problems of the original texts and pose some disagreeable questions about the texts. It will be underscored that these problems and questions have not lost much of their historical and social pertinence.

Among the more agonizing problems is the present rise of religious political discourse, commonly labelled fundamentalism and communalism. But also nationalism with its seeming pretensions to secular religiosity shakes the (post)modern worldview down to its very roots. Within the context of modern Indian political and cultural history, I will extract the genealogy of these phenomena right back to the period in which Tagore was active.

This will to some extent enable us to gain a better understanding of the way in which Indian cultural productions exerted their influence in colonial society and in whose interest, and how various politically motivated readings of the same cultural product evokes different responses and different re-readings.

8

Benefits of Aesthetic Education

Aesthetic education seems to be most easily defined by what it is not. It is not the teaching of logical form or matters of fact, and it is not satisfied to remain at the level of surface text. Generally aesthetics seems to be the defining characteristic of the Arts,with which it is usually identified.

Monroe Beardsley saw the central task of aesthetic education as the improvement of taste, claiming that this required the development of two dispositions (1) the capacity to obtain aesthetic gratification from increasingly subtle and complex objects that are characterised by various forms of unity, and (2) an increasing dependence on beautiful objects as sources of aesthetic satisfaction.

Beautiful objects for him were inherently beautiful, They were perfect. They adhered to the rules of good composition. They allowed people to feel pleasure when they contemplated the objects disinterestedly. They caused pleasure due to intrinsic properties such as color, line, shape, proportion, harmony, symmetry, etc.; They revealed a spiritual force in the universe; They were whatever pleases people of good taste and they had properties to which people respond with love.

Somewhat circularly, he claimed that a person was having an aesthetic experience during a particular stretch of time "if and only if the greater part of his mental activity during that time is united and made pleasurable by being tied to the form and qualities of a sensuously presented or imaginatively intended object on which his primary attention is concentrated".

This classically traditional definition makes explicit its assumptions of intentionality, holistic sensuous qualities, imagination, and form but it does not address the question of how or why we would want to teach it in schools, a topic which has only been considered in the last thirty years. Transferred to the Arts, it requires that production of or performance in the arts is intentional rather than divinely inspired or genetically imposed.

The question of taste alone is highly contentious and one would wonder whether beauty is the ideal to which students are directed these days. There seems to be an assumption that through intentionally creating artworks which "come together appropriately" (as opposed to craft), students will come to develop a disposition to experience the aesthetic moment. But in many schools this aesthetic moment is ignored. The emphasis is given to the product qua product and to documentation of the student's learning process through production portfolios or visual diaries. The rational reflection and self-consciousness of discipline-based art education marginalise the aesthetic experience.

It is often assumed that the aesthetic experience is equally marginalised in schools by prevailing cultural pressures of accountability and pragmatism and the dominant functionalism of education. Arts are justified in the curriculum only because they pass on the cultural heritage of our society, or because they train students in skills that might lead to a worthwhile occupation as a carpenter, musician or painter in adult life, or even because they might decrease social malaise and alienation by making leisure time more enjoyable.

Such functionalism assumes that progress is only possible if there are measurable or demonstrable outcomes. The arts become more accountable as progress is measured in the number of products or performances. They are therefore presented in a theoretical language of criticism within which they can intentionally produce works of art. Such theoretical structures provide the frame and standards through which students can be graded and against which they can evaluate other works of art or art performances, However whether such a theory is testable, worthwhile or even possible has rarely been considered. On formalist assumptions of aesthetics, it is sufficient for it to be internally coherent.

Where theories are not grounded on evidence, they proliferate, and the arts world slides into a cultural relativism of movements, Curriculum reformers bypass such contextualism by requiring a more solid foundation for evaluation. Rarely is this an educational one. As Danto said, when art becomes confused about aesthetic standards or discards the guiding standards of representation or artistic skill, the guiding value will become commercial, making the arts into a commodity in which the price or audience an artwork commands becomes the criterion of its success. So education in the arts becomes accountable in terms of the employment status of its graduates, the salary they can command, even their visibility in large museums theatres and the press.

Most aestheticians react to this as if a fundamental category mistake has been made. One cannot reduce the aesthetic to a number, or even to its pragmatic function. Success in the arts is so contextually dependent that one could never measure it by objective standards. It would be like trying to measure love or happiness, which are felt states rather than measurable products. Artists make earn money making artworks or performing, but that is not why they do it and that is not why we teach it in schools.

To formalists like Beardsley and Dickie, if Arts education was to be aesthetic, it had to be "disinterested". "Art for Art's sake" has become something of a cliché, especially at a period where political hegemonies seem to drive all. If the Arts were to be a "discipline" in a Hirstian forms of knowledge sense, they would derive their identity from their formal structures, their ability to represent transcendental values of Beauty. Many drama and visual arts teachers tacitly assume the notion that besides aesthetics, arts are defined by their representational value at least in imitating Ideal form through mimesis. Music teachers particularly refer to the aesthetic formalism of Clive Bell, based almost on Pythagorean notions of divine harmony.

An attempt to bring formalist transcendentalism closer to a physical reality was made by psychologists like Arnheim, and Gombrich, by naturalising form in the brain through genetic structures. In his theory of multiple intelligences, Howard Gardner has raised the status of aesthetics in music by identifying it as a biologically inherited trait. These presumptions operate still within a modernist frame, making aesthetic experiences essentialist rather than politically and culturally contingent.

The formalist position runs the risk of retreating into a sublime essentialism that has nothing to do with the sordid or ugly, the political or mundane. The discovery that aesthetic standards presented as timeless and universal are in practice neither timeless nor universal - that they largely reflect beliefs and values typical of European patriarchy - has led to a more critical, historically grounded analysis of artistic concepts, institutions and practices generally. Dickie and Danto particularly remind us of the institutional presence in art, that its values are defined within a changing social context and that in the twentieth century at least, formalism is either trite or empty. The grounding of aesthetics must take a different form in a postmodern era.

The disappearance of the grand narrative has resulted in a broader and deeper understanding of the many social and cultural variables that contribute to prevailing notions of taste, aesthetic value and artistic genius. As such arts teachers are now involved in helping children to enter aesthetic awarenesses not only of their own cultures but those of others from the past and present. To what extent this crossing of and comparison between cultural paradigms is possible has not been much debated in teacher training institutions.

Other barriers have been rendered invisible in educational programmes, especially in the seamless construction of a learning area called the Arts differentiated from Languages, Science, Social Science, and Maths. What is thus differentiated can vary quite dramatically, with uncritical selections made variously from the Performing Arts, Design, Music, Literature, Visual Arts, Film, Painting, Sculpture, Drama, Dance, Poetry, Architecture, Jewellery-making. Different theoretical assumptions drive the selection according to the weight placed on self-expression (especially by psychologists), technical skills, beauty, aesthetic performance, cultural conformity or originality. Could the integrating quality be a notion of aesthetic response?

Beardsley, Osborne, Weitz, Kaelin and others would say yes, and a brief history of the development of the Arts area indicates the asthetic assumption that works of art are still believed to have the capacity to induce higher levels of worthwhile experience which justifies their inclusion in the curriculum. Learning in the arts is "fundamentally experiential, creative, and developmental and must involve students in perceiving, transforming, expressing and appreciating", as if these aspects somehow contained and defined the aesthetic.

No use for drama teachers to complain that creativity on stage was a different thing entirely from creativity with a violin or clay. Such decontextualision of imagination and creativity, and even self-expression in this manner is a mark of Beardsley's transcendentalism. Theoretical work in contemporary aesthetics by such influential academics as Goodman, Cavell, Danto, Davidson, Gadamer, has not much filtered down into schools but it raises the questions about the possibility of an aesthetic quality separate from its expressions in art-worlds.

Most of these writers recognise the aesthetic as a human convention, even where it is tied to a nominalist realism. The Arts becomes identified as a humanity, designed to make us aware of and sensitive to the varieties of human differences as expressed through the arts. Could "aesthetics" as a categorical term be replaced by the humanities? Aesthetics has recently benefited from 'an ethical turn' a revival of long-standing debates about the moral function of narrative and the social impact of the arts, drawing aestheticians into the cultural value of arts education but it is not clear how mutually inclusive this categorisation could or should be.

Environmental issues could be said to be founded in a aesthetic notion of the essential beauty and sublimity of nature. The sciences too are recognised as human artefacts based on realism. What is it that is makes an aesthetic experience in the arts differ from one in logic or science? Some educators looking to the arts because they offer opportunities to move beyond consolidated texts and change human values through revitalising symbol and artistic ritual. Art is the lie that becomes the truth. Aesthetic education helps us to understand others as humans. What it is about this form of aesthetic experience that is unique to the arts remains to be examined continuously.

9

Tagore on Self-reliance Thinking and Action Research

Rabindranath Tagore (Nobel laureate in literature, 1913) is perhaps more well known in the world as a poet, lyric composer and artist than as a social development philosopher and social action researcher. Little of his voluminous contributions to the discourse on the meaning of independence of India from the point of view of its economic and social development, are known to the wider world. These writings present a remarkably unified and consistent philosophy of Man, society, nation and economic and social development that sharply challenged contemporary Indian thinking. They also provide a deep articulation of participation and self-reliance thinking in which a school has been developing since around the seventies or so, about three decades after his death (1941).

Human creativity, self-reliance and collective economic and social action that are the central concepts in what is known as "Participatory Action Research" (PAR) today were the cornerstones of Tagore's own philosophy of nationhood and development. Humanist Tagore went on relentlessly invoking these concepts as his anxious and passionate contribution to India's independence struggle, in his voluminous writings and speeches from the early twentieth century through the late twenties. He was a very lone traveller in this still to be born 'paradigm' of development and social action in his days, and even clashed uncompromisingly with Gandhi on the mission of Man notwithstanding very deep mutual respect these two great philosophers held for each other.

Tagore not only gave original and profound articulation of the above concepts; he also applied his thinking in practical experimentation with village development as a zamindar (landlord) in his estate in East Bengal and also as an educator as a part of the programme of the Biswabharati University founded by him in Shantiniketan.

Thoughts of Tagore on Self-reliance

Nature of Humans

Tagore viewed human beings fundamentally as a species that seeks fulfilment in creative acts, doing what has not been done and daring to do the impossible. He saw thus "feeding the mind" as more important to the human than feeding and clothing the body that are regarded as the "basic needs" of the human in modern development discourse.

"In his experiments with creating life the Creator suddenly becomes quite daring when he comes to creating human beings. He does not confine the freedom of its soul. Outwardly the species is thrown naked, armourless and weak in all respects while its soul is freed to fly. Elated by the joy of this freedom it cries out: *'I shall do the impossible!'*, meaning I shall not accept that what has been happening all the time will continue to happen – what does not happen will also happen" .... He is not attached only to what is near at hand, he is bringing under his hand what is not near at hand....In his labour he seeks not only success, but labour itself is pleasure to him; he seeks constantly to reach deeper than the surface, from the seen to the unseen, from the easy to the difficult, from dependence to self-reliance, from following the instinct to pursuing reason.

This is how he has been victorious. If some say that 'this is what our forefathers did, and, therefore, if we seek to do something else we shall lose our indigenous identity", then ... they may preserve what they call their indigenous identity, but they lose their greatest identity – their humanhood. [such people] are slaves to the surroundings, have no sense of independence in their mind....they do not at all know that a human has to accomplish the impossible by one's own strength; he will not be confined to what has happened - he will advance toward what has not happened... (Tagore 1921, 321-322)

"All great civilizations of the world are creations of daring. Daring of human strength, intellect, desires. Humans have moved on crossing oceans and mountains as their strength refused to acknowledge any obstacle; their intellect transcended the apparent truth and moved on proudly by tearing the spells of blind prejudice, from the great to greater truth, from the atoms to sub-atoms, from far to farther, from the near to the nearest; the aspirations of humans have not regarded any ailments, poverty and wants as invincible and have not sat idle giving up efforts to overcome them, and have gone on trying repeatedly.... "In this daring there is great inconsideration.

This inconsideration is working today in those who are crushing on the ground from airplanes and dying. Those thousands who one day vowed to cross the sea and drowned, were driven by this inconsideration. It is that fierce excitement of this inconsideration which even today is driving humans to conquer now the north pole and now the south pole beating the ice-demons...(Tagore 1914a, 257-258)

Primacy of mind over body

"If we want to eradicate the external poverty we have to rouse the inner strength that lies in intellect, knowledge, and comradeship that promotes cooperation. "One may say, external work also stirs the mind. It does so, if the work itself insinuates processes of thinking in the mind. This does not happen in clerical work as all clerks in the country know.

In narrow habitual work only external skills grow, and the imprisoned Mind keeps encircling around the habitual path like the blinded bullock. This is why, people in all lands have looked down upon work that is mainly a repeated recitation of some particular physical activity. Carlyle has preached the dignity of labour in very loud voice; but through ages people of the world have testified to the indignity of labour.

Those who work as labourers make themselves machines in dire compulsion...to feed the stomach sacrificing the mind, as they are on the point of dying of hunger. But to console him/her as having dignity by sacrificing one's more important half, is nothing but ridiculing him...Mind is the wealth of the human, [and] no external respect can save one from the intense inglory of mindless labour. (Tagore, 1925a).

Atmoshakti and Nationhood

Atmoshakti (atmo = self; shakti = strength) - by way of one's own creativity, knowledge, intellect, labour, love and service - was a foundational concept in Tagore's development thinking. He wanted to see fulfilment of people's atmoshakti in the realisation of their material, cultural and spiritual aspirations, and was fervently against waiting upon and demanding deliverance of any need from external agencies such as the government, whether it be people's own or foreign. He stood firmly on the concept of atmoshakti in discussing both the meaning and tasks of nation as well as the tasks of (village) community.

In his view people do not get their nation just by gaining independence, but have to create their nation by applying their atmoshakti in working for its development. The concept of "nation" to Tagore was a mental concept, to be gained by a people applying their atmoshakti together to fulfil common needs, and uniting in such process into a sense of nationhood, shunning favours both from the state as well as from foreign powers.

"Starting with Buddha all those Sadhus and Saints of India of the middle ages, whoever has come bringing some great message, have all opposed unmindful mechanical external rituals. They had defied all obstacles to talk to the soul of humans. They did not say, like the miserly, like the calclative wise men, that first the external, then the soul; first food and clothing, then fulfilment of atmoshakti. They gave tribute to the human by demanding big from her/him; and it was in response to that big tribute that their hidden inner wealth expressed itself in diverse ways in literature, music, manifold arts, and thereby enriched society. They had given light to men and women, given them awakening, i.e. gave them realisation of their own soul - in such giving all is given". (Tagore 1925a, 404)

"The claim that it is my nation because I have been born here - this is the word of those who are involved with the external features of the world. But because the true character of humans is his/her inner character of atmoshakti, that is why the nation that one creates by one's knowledge, intellect, love and labour is truly one's nation. In 1905 I had called the Bengalis and told them this, that 'create your nation from within by your atmoshakti because it is through creation that a sense becomes a 'truth'. The creator finds himself/herself in his/her own creation.

To get a nation means to realise (discover) one's very own soul in all its dimensions within the nation. We find our soul truly within the nation only when we are engaged in building the nation ourselves by our thoughts, labour and service. Our nation is a product of our very soul, this is why our soul is spread out over the nation, expressing itself.(Tagore, 1921, 323-324) " Animals are born in particular lands, but the land does not become theirs just because they are born there. Humans create their own land themselves.

In that act of creation and care for maintenance of that creation the ties between them become deep, and they are able to love that land of their creation more than their lives. People of our land are only being born on the land, but are not creating it; this is why they have no occasion of uniting with each other, they do not have any sense of harm if the land is harmed. We have to inspire them to gain their nation by creating it.

This act of creation is diverse, and requires diverse energies of the people. We feel ourselves as a part of the nation by applying our diverse energies in diverse paths with a single goal. ..(Tagore, 1925b, 421) "...We have to win over the nation not from the hands of others, but from our own lack of engagement, from our own indifference. When we bring ourselves to the door of the British for any task of development of our nation we have by that act only deepened our own lack of engagement.

This is because what the British government does is not our doing, so that despite how much we gain by such doings of the British from the outside we lose our nation to the same extent, i.e. we achieve success at the cost of our soul. When we know that the nation is my very soul, and that is why the nation is so dear to me, then we can never bear looking up to others to build our nation...."(Tagore, 1921, 323-4)

"nation is a living entity, a mental concept": It is a sense of union derived from "memory of glories of the past and vision of future with similar glory - to suffer together, enjoy together, hope together - these are the main thing...to suffer together has been mentioned because the bond of pain is stronger than the bond of joy"(Tagore, 1902b, 518).

"How can union between people be achieved? This can be achieved only by working together - there is no other way of achieving true union." (Tagore 1905a, 612) foreign favours a song on national atmoshakti by Tagore mother, will you send your son to the alien's door? they slight us, throw stones at us seeing our beggar's bowl. we have humbled ourselves chasing him, hoping he will give me something in slight. shall we go on chasing him, leaving what our own mother has bestowed on us? we have no strength of our own? this is a mighty lie, our strength has not yet died - we shall pour our own strength and our devotion at your feet, O mother!

"Receiving favours from others is the true sign of a pessimist, of hopeless poverty. I shall never agree that we have no way out except to beg from others - I believe in my own land, I respect atmoshakti... I know for sure that...if the foundation of the fulfilment for which we are eager today rests on others' fleeting pleasures, if it is not specially India's own, then it will keep failing again and again. (Tagore 1903a, 535)" "Independence of communities is independence of India in its true sense. (Tagore 1903b, 553)

"The village whose people have united in all ways to provide education, health care, earnings and joy to each other - that village has truly lit the lamp on the path of independence of India." (Tagore, 1925b, 422) "the flow of the human heart is no less important than the flow of river. This flow had always kept the villages of Bengal healthy and joyful [but] now the flow of the Bengalees' heart has become dissociated from the village. That is why its temples are emaciated - there is none to repair them; its ponds are polluted - there is none to clean the mud; the mansions of the elite are abandoned - one does not hear the joy of festivities there. Today My Lord the State is the Master to give us water; My Lord the Sate is the Master to provide health care; one has to go and kneel before the state for provision of education as well. The tree that used to blossom its own flowers is spreading all its shriveled branches in petitions for a shower of flowers from the sky.

"In ancient India the state was in the form of the kings. Those who were in the position of the society's guardians took charge of giving education and religious education to the whole country without remuneration. It is not that the king did not have the responsibility of supporting and rewarding them - but this was partial support; actually this resonsibility bestowed upon every household.

Education and religious education in the society would not be totally jeopardized if the king stopped his support or if the nation suddenly became kingless. It is not that the king did not get ponds excavated - but he contributed in this the same way that any well-to-do person in the society did. The jar of water of the nation did not get empty if the king got unmindful. ...the king might be morally responsible whether he would go to war, go hunting, would do his kingship duties or spend his time in enjoyment - but the people would not vitally wait upon him for their welfare - the tasks of the society got distributed upon every person in society in diverse and splendid ways.

"In such a system what we understand by moral obligation circulated throughout the whole of society. Each one had to sacrifice one's personal interests and practice abstinence. Each one had a moral obligation to society. It should be evident from this, that the life force of different societies is situated in different places. The heart of a nation lies wherever the responsibility for the welfare of the ordinary people is concentrated.

The whole nation gets vitally hurt if that centre is hit. In Europe the whole nation faces destruction if the King's power is devastated. This is why in Europe politics is such a serious matter. In our nation serious crisis truly arises only if the society (community) becomes disabled. This is why so far we have not staked our lives for independence of the nation but have tried in all ways to save independence of the society....

"...In recent times we have learnt by studying in the British schools that the greatest duty of the people is to pester the government to gain its attention irrespective of the nature of our needs. We have not understood that we do not treat the ailments of our own bodies by constantly [poking] in others' bodies.

"...The very heart of our existence is lying uncovered and unguarded today...This, and not shortage of water, is what our crisis is today.... Today we need either charity from the state, or need to press our demands to it...

"Without further hesitation we must take over in our own hands the self-administration of our village. We have to rouse our own panchayet (association for village selfadmiistration) before the fist of the state-created panchayet presses in the throat of our village. We ourselves shall protect the peasant; we ourselves shall educate their children; we ourselves shall accomplish village development, arrange for health care, and we ourselves shall save our zamindars and prajas (subjects) from the destructive hand of litigation. We should never think of taking the help of the king in these matters - because to take help in these matters means to invite and institute the powerful in the midst of the independent rights of the weak." (Tagore, 1905a. 616)

"The way for us to live is to rouse our own strength in all respects. Our glory does not lie in sitting idle and consuming the wealth of our forefathers; when we shall feel throughout the society that we are spreading this wealth, only then we shall truly respect ourselves and come out of the spell." (Tagore, 1903b,555-556)

"[Let] our descendants be able to say with pride that these are all ours, it is we who have built these all. It is us who have made our land fertile, purified our water reservoirs and our air; extended our learnings and enbraved our hearts. Let them be able to say that this very beautiful land - this motherland giving us its fruits and water and the cool breeze -thus established with morals and labour, standing on its valour, it is our creation -anywhere we look everything is filled with our thoughts efforts and soul, resounding with our joy-songs and vibrating with the tireless footsteps of travellers on paths of ever-new hopes" (Chakravarty, 57).

"Let no one understand that I do not want to have any relation with the government at all...I am saying the contrary. I am saying that we should seek to establish a [gentlemanly] relation with the government. Gentlemanly relation implies freedom. A relation that does not wait for my own desire or otherwise is a relation of slavery, it is bound to keep decaying and get severed one day. But a relation of free give-and-take gets progressively more intimate.

"Many of us imagine and say also that if the government gives us everything that we are demanding then our joy and love for it will be boundless. Such thinking is totally baseless. One party will go on wanting, and the other party will go on giving - where will the end of such process be? ...the more we receive through such a donor-recipient relation the more does the demand from generosity rises, and the amount of dissatisfaction keeps skyrocketing. It is as bad for us as it is uncomfortable for the donor in a relation where what I get does not rest on our own strength.

"On the other hand a relation of exchange, of give and take, is good for both - here the quantum of demand naturally tends to be fair, and diferences assumes the possibility of being resolved through negotiation. The only way to attain such a state of decency in the country is to establish the nation's independent strength in the service of the society. A relation between two strengths is what is decent and lasting, the source of joy and respect...

"This is why I was saying, that our nation can get upto the last bit of what is possible to get, if we can give to the nation the last bit of what we can give. The more we shall give the more will a relation of receiving be strengthened.

"Our right to self-rule is lying on our doorstep - none has snatched it and none can snatch it. We can provide education in our villages, health, road development, everything, ourselves, if we desire it, if we unite for this. For this there is no need to wear the belt of the government. But we do not desire it, we do not unite...

"We are getting upset at the failure of each of our demands because we have made our demands our principal assets. We are identifying this excitedness with our patriotism. We are not only seeking consolation in our weakness but also taking pride in it! (Tagore 1904, 572-575)

"Whether we beg with folded arms or with red eyes, it is not so easy to earn glory thereby- whatever we can do ourselves by our own strength for the country benefits us in two ways - one is gaining the fruit of this, secondly to work ourselves is a gain by itself which is even greater than gaining the fruit...The inglory of begging is that even if we gain the fruit we are deprived of the fulfilment of doing the work ourselves. (Tagore 1905b, 581-2)

Destiny has given the strength in the voice of Mahatmaji to give this call, because he has truth in him. Hence this was indeed our great opportunity. But he gave the call only in a very narrow area. He called everyone to spin the charka (spinning wheel), to weave the cloth.... Is this the call for the great creativity of the new epoch? When nature called the bees to live the narrow life of making bee-hives, hundreds of thousands of bees responded to that call only to make themselves impotent; in this self-sacrifice by which they belittled themselves they moved away from the path of liberation [which is nothing but revelation, as Tagore said in another place in the same essay (p 329)].

A nation the majority of whose people do not hesitate to make themselves impotent responding to some enticement or rule are imprisoned in their own hearts. To spin the wheel is in one sense extremely easy, and that is why it is difficult for all humans. The call of the easy is not for humans, this is a call for the bees.

Humans can reveal the wealth within themselves only when their supreme strength is invoked... Isn't Europe making humans impotent in its army establishments and in its factories; cutting the humanity of humans to the size of dwarfs to satisfy greed and such other designs... Humans can be dwarfed both by large as well as small machinery, by engines as well as by the charka. Where the charka is natural it does not do any harm, rather it does good - but because of the richness of the human mind the charka damages the mind more than it damages the cord where it is not natural. And the mind is not less valuable than the cord.(Tagore,1921; 328-334)

"If we reduce our demand from the Mind then the Mind becomes lazy and listless. To glorify the charka in welfare thinking for the nation is the way to make the humiliated Mind idle... Those in the world who have made great sacrifices for their land, for humanity, have visualised the welfare of humanity by their mind's eyes. If we want the sacrifices of people we need to assist in this visualisation.

Great quantities of cord and khaddar [a coarse variety of cloth spun by the charka) are not big images of glory of the nation. This is the picture of the calculative person who cannot rouse that great uncalculative force which is not only prepared to embrace pain and death in the joy of thinking of the great, but is also unmindful of rejection by others and even of failure." (Tagore,1925b,419)

"Some may say that spinning the thread is also an act of creation. This is not so. The reason is, in working with the charka people become a part of the charka; i.e. they do what could have been done by a machine. He makes it spin. The machine has no mind and hence it is alone - it has nothing outside it. Likewise the person who is spinning the thread is also alone; the thread of his charka does not link him with anyone else. He has no need to know that he has a neighbour...He is a machine, lonely, isolated....But even if the person who is working to drive away a disease from the village has unfortunately to work fully alone, yet the beginning and the end of his work are intimately linked with thinking for the whole village.

Through this very work he feels an intimacy with the whole village. He feels conscious joy in creating the village. Indeed, in his work is the beginning of self-rule of the village. Then if people of the whole village put their hands together we understand that the village is advancing toward truly finding itself by creating itself. This finding is what is truly gaining self-rule...(Tagore, 1925b,421-22) "We have to give evidence before we get self-rule, that we shall be able to self-rule after we get it in our hands. There is wide space for giving this evidence.

Expressions of love for our nation through service to the nation does not wait for any external change of situation, it rests only on earnestness. If we see today that that expression is idle and indifferent, then I do not believe that this lethargy will disappear if we only get formal indpendence as a favour of others. I do not believe in such self-deception that first our external impediment will be removed and then our love for the land will overcome resistances from the mind and will manifest itself in service of the land. The person who says "first the fountain pen and then I shall write the epic", we have to understand that his fascination is for the fountain pen and not for the epic....(Tagore, 1929,443-444)

Action Research to promote self-reliant village developmentIn 1890, at the age of thirty, Tagore was assigned by his father responsibility for running the family estates (zamindari) in the district of Pabna, basing himself in Shilaidaha. Humanist Tagore established deep contact with the villagers and village life, and soon started developing ideas and making experiments with self-reliant village development in accordance with his philosophy of atmoshakti and service to society. He advocated, in writing and through his speeches, the formation of one or more village communities (pallishamaj) in every village to take charge of co-operative-based self-reliant village development, which would among other tasks take charge of literacy for all, development of local industries, community health care and recreation, safe drinking water, model farming, collective paddy stores, domestic industry-based work for women, campaigns against drinking of liquor, developing fellow-feeling and solidarity among the villagers, and collection of demographic, economic and social statistics on every village. He initiated experimentation on self-reliant village development In three places -

Shelaidaha, Kaligram and Sriniketan -that were forerunners of such experiments anywhere in the sub-continent. He was manifestly unsuccessful in this effort in Shelaidaha where he himself was the chief "animator", with a typical response by the villagers: "are we so stupid? we shall give our hard labour to make the well and Mr. Zamindar will get the credit for this?"

This failure in animating village self-reliance by Tagore himself has never been analysed in depth, and the present author suspects that here the "animator's" overwhelming personal status and enrobed presence and styles (unlike Gandhi, Tagore is not known to have ever taken off his shirt in public to integrate with the peasants!) were the negatives that caused the failure of this effort. More successful was the effort in Kaligram Pargana (subdistrict) where the chief "animator" was an outstanding worker and teacher, Atul Sen.

Under Atul Sen's leadership villagers of this Pargana established the Kaligram Welfare Society which initiated a lot of community activities in the villages. These included the establishment within a very short time of three health care centres, more than two hundred primary schools inlcuding night schools, three middle English schools and one high school, and the building of quite a number of roads, water tank repairs, clearing of forests, etc., followed by the setting up of an agricultural bank and a community paddy store.

Financing of these activities was done jointly by the Kaligram Welfare Society and the estate of the Tagore family. The subjects of the estate paid 3 paisa per Taka of estate rent to the fund of the Welfare society, and the estate paid an equal amount to the fund. In special cases for construction of school rooms etc. Tagore used to make additional contribution. Disputes among the subjects used to be settled by shalish (people's dispute resolute forums) organised by the Welfare Society. As a result for many years not a single case of dispute went to the court, a phenomenon that was mentioned in government reports of the time.

Tagore introduced the system of loans to poor peasants who were traditionally burdened with heavy debt to the village money lenders. In perhaps the first known such loan programme for poor peasants in the subcontinent, he introduced a system of lending to them from the estate in Kaligram at low interest rates against mortgage of their harvests: the harvest was to be deposited to the estate from which the loan was to be repaid and the peasants would take the surplus harvest home. There was provision for writing off the interest if the harvest was poor for any debtor.

By village development Tagore did not mean only economic development but sought to promote joyful unions of villagers and cultivation of culture and beauty by them as well as environment care. He sought to promote tree plantation festivities by school children on special days; festive spirits in community road construction projects; and flower gardening in the peasant households, preaching that "cultivation of beauty is an imperative for the nation."

Unfortunately, this pioneering "action research" by Tagore in Kaligram got into trouble when underground "revolutionary" terrorism gained ground and many social activists all over Bengal came under suspicion from the authority. Police arrested and jailed Atul Sen and many of his co-workers suspecting them as terrorists. From hindsight today the great drawback of Tagore's village development effort was a lack of attention to the development of internal leadership from among the villagers who could replace external leadership in the effort.

The effort in Kaligram gradually faded out as the external leaders were jailed. But at that time Tagore's basic idea of community self-rule and selfinitiatives for village development were miles ahead of development thinking of the time oriented toward delivery of development by the authorities. Tagore, the creative social philosopher and experimentor committed to people's collective self-rule, never stopped experimenting.

In 1922 he founded the Biswabharati university and, as a part of this university, Sriniketan as an action research institution, putting it under the charge of an idealist British young man, Lenard Elmhurst as its first Director. Another idealist worker, Kalimohan Roy was Elmhurst's principal associate in village work. Tagore himself did not personally involve himself in the work of the centre but was of course the "Guru" behind this effort.

The motto of Sriniketan was put in a bulletin issued by the centre, containing words like the following:

"we shall do our own work ourselves, we shall not wait upon others to do things for ourselves, self-reliance and cooperative work are the two mantras for our life. we belong to the village and the village belongs to us, our good is in the good of the village. We shall develop our village; this is not the task of any one alone, this is a task for all of us. We are taking charge ourselves of advancement of our agriculture, our industries, our business, our health, our educatioin, our joy, everything."

Sriniketan inspired and assisted community initiatives for village development in numerous villages. The work included adult and child education, clearing of jungles and turning them into farming plots and vegetable gardens, road construction, experimentation with cooperative farming, collective paddy stores, livestock production, promotion of cottage industry, malaria eradication by cleaning villages and improving drainage systems, setting up people's health care centres providing cheap medical service and medicines funded by villagers' contributions, welfare work for indigenous people, village socio-economic surveys, tree plantation, research on village economy, and many other such initiatives.

The project moved in typical action research style, involving villagers in exploring what they could do together for their economic and social advancement without any predesigned development agenda. The workers of Sriniketan integrated closely with the villagers, 'animated' them in taking self-development initiatives as well as worked themselves in these initiatives, gave or arranged for training the villagers in different activities, and helped them in dire difficulties.

Tagore emphasised solidarity (in his words, "unity of the hearts"), among the villagers and between the villagers and workers of the project, as a central value in tis effort. His greatest emphasis was on literacy for all, with the philosophy he expounded in his writings presented earlier, to repeat, that what one learns is secondary; what is primary is that literacy is a road for travel of the minds of the people to each others' minds for interaction with each other, and thereby find the greater humanity within oneself and oneself within greater humanity.

The work spread in quite a number of villages. Adult education centres - a number of them night schools - grew up in a number of them, where not only literacy but Baul and Kirtan singing, story telling from the mythical classics, and lectures and discussions on health care and other essential subjects were also a regular feature. In several villages quite a number of health cooperatives as well as general village development societies were formed.

Bulletins on social education were printed and distributed as a regular feature. Under the initiative of Sriniketan a number of "service-brigades" of youth were also fomed to orient shcool-going youth in village service as part of their overall development. Along with sports and pysical exercises these brigades participated in initiatives to clean bushes and drains, repair roads, distribute quinine, nurse the sick and such other social services.

Tagore's emphasis on the need for cooperative work in the context of the state of economic development in Bengal at that time is exemplified in his address at a provincial conference in Pabna in 1908: " In Europe and America labour-saving machinery of many types have been invented which we cannot use because of our poverty - it is not possible to use them on small pieces of land and meagre resources.

Modern machinery can be used to reduce expenses considerably and facilitate farming if if all in a village got together and put their land together for cultivation. If they collected all the sugarcane of a village for threshing in one machine then they will gain and not lose buying an expensive threshing machine; by combining all jute plots they can themselves press them in a machine; if all milkmen joined hands they can produce milk butter and ghee etc. at a lower cost and better; if weavers get together to bring the weaving machine in their village and work with them then they will all gain from the higher cloth production;...hence if the villagers themselves get together to use relevant machinery and raise their employment status staying where they are, they can gain in all respects. In addition, this is one way to indoctrinate people in the principle of unity."

Tagore's thinking on the introduction of machinery in the village economy of India can be subjected to critical scrunity from the point of view of labour displacement in a country with growing population pressure, which would have perhaps warranted a more carefully selective introuction of machinery.

Sriniketan experimented also with agricultural credit cooperatives but the field record of repayment fom these coperatives was not very satisfactory, and over time most of these credit coperatives were closed down. But Tagore was the first known development thinker to talk of the co-operative principle for village development that early in the history of development thinking in India, as an economic rationale in its own right and also as a way of uniting people for collective self-development combining economics and culture, and to promote fellow feeling among villagers.This was the meaning to him of independence (swaraj).

As he had said once earlier, "Swaraj can become a truth upon the firm foundation created through the exercise of collective self-rule, through its manifestation, through the spread of pride in this among the people.When this foundatin is lacking in the villages, in the heart [of people] and outside, and when this lacking becomes the cause of lack of food for the people, lack of education, lack of health care, lack of joy, then the idea that some external ritual can establish swaraj in this country is totally disrespectful."

10

Tagore's Concept of Social Integration

Civil society was one of Tagore's chief concerns. He repeatedly wrote and spoke of it, and in his own way tried to foster it by experimenting with institutions which would serve as the foundation of civil society. E.P. Thompson, in his introduction to Tagore's Nationalism observes, "For Tagore, more than any other thinker of his time, had a clear conception of civil society, as something distinct from, and of stronger and more personal texture than, political and economic structures." The Visva-Bharati he proposed (a far cry from the central university of today) was the growing concrete shape of the foundation imagined for the superstructure of civil society. We have to give the Visva-Bharati he proposed a close look; a few other things also deserve our consideration.

Tagore, says E.P. Thompson, 'was a founder of anti-politics'. This means that even during the phase of the most widespread political activities in India's struggle for independence Tagore continued to maintain that village reconstruction was a more fruitful activity for the purpose of the real deliverance of the Indian people. Not only Indians, but India survived in India's villages. The uninterrupted continuity of Indianness in the Indian villages was possible not because they could offer any effective resistance to the successive hordes of invaders and colonizers, but because these invaders and colonizers thought they could afford not to take their existence into serious account.

Down the ages and stages of foreign rules, the Indian (but not exclusively Hindu) civil society survived the political upheavals and economic transitions without an impact of fundamental character. The trickle of benefits that accrued to the village society as a result of changing economic forces did not inspire the crossing of any technological border which could have exercised a decisive influence. Macaulay's ideas about westernization of Indians were true only about a fringe of Indian urban society. Outside the urban fraction, the plural civil society went on in Indian villages much in the manner of a hundred years ago.

The British Indian army and the British Indian lower bureaucracy performed for British Imperialism whatever British imperialism desired to squeeze out of this sub-continent. Distance and discontinuity amongst villages were not annihilated, and the civil society in rural India remained more or less beyond the pale of impregnation of Western social, political and economic ideas and the consequent changes in structures which could have been induced by radically new ideas,

Tagore recognized this and was, in fact, pleased with this. But he did not idealize all aspects of living in this society. He was put out by the feudalistic limitedness — economic, social and moral — and repeatedly pointed out the need for reforms, and, in his own way, carried out some reforms on his own means in estates he managed on behalf of his father. He found in this plural civil society the seat of Indian creativity, the fountainhead of multifarious cultural manifestations which together constituted the unity of Indian culture. To respect the vitality and legitimacy of civil society is at one and the same time to discountenance the totalization, monopolization, mechanization, abstraction which are features of aggressive, neo-colonial societies. Neo-colonialism is the new economic mask of the belligerent nationalism of the recent past.

Tagore wanted to posit the civil society he experienced in Indian societies against the covert neo-colonial aggression making its appearances in his own day. He proposed another antidote in the form of a new university that he conceived, his Visva-Bharati. The motto with which the university was founded included:

> This is Visva-Bharati where the world
> makes a home in a single nest . . .
> We are of the faith that Truth is one and
> undivided, though diverse may be the ways
> which lead us to it. Through separate
> paths pilgrims from different lands arrive
> at the same shrine of truth. . . .
>
> . . .
>
> So unto this Visva-Bharati we render our
> homage by weaving garlands with flowers
> of learning gathered from all quarters
> of the earth. To all devotees of Truth, both
> from the West and from the East, we extend our hand with love,

Compared with the objectives of any institution of higher learning at any time anywhere, the motto of Visva-Bharati must be considered unique. Pursuit of learning is not acknowledged as an end in itself. It is set against the perspective of the achievable unity and solidarity of all civil societies, along with their distinct heritages of value and the perpetually active cultural and spiritual exercises. Tagore conceived of his institution as 'The Center of

Indian Culture', but we need to know of the proposed activities in slightly greater detail than will be revealed by the mere name of the Center.

In Tagore's own words, "On each race is the duty laid, to keep alight its own lamp of mind, as its part in the illumination of the world. To break the lamps of any people, is to deprive it of its rightful place in the world festival." The noblest experience is that of the ever brightening world festival of light, every ray of which is the effulgence of one national mind or another. The effulgence starts at the moment of origin of any particular society, and every contribution of undeniable value will be progressively added through the perpetually evolving life process of that society — of every society.

The attraction of the world festival of light is spontaneous and unquenchable in every human heart unless this be irredeemably brutalized. The love of this light is the urge for answers for all the problems of existence which agonize every human heart. The social mind, in a combined single and collective effort, thinks, feels and gropes. Education energizes this groping and helps find slices of truth. Society makes this slice of truth its own wherever it may have originated. What is of crucial importance is the perception of truth and not the source from which it arrives. Yet, the significance of the sources of the arrival of truth cannot be detached from the truths themselves, and hence education is a concourse of truth and the sources and processes of its arrival.

In more concrete terms he says:

> My suggestion is that we should generate somewhere a centripetal force which will attract and group together from different parts of our land and different ages all our materials of learning and thus create a complete and moving orb of Indian culture.

At one and the same time he cautions:

We have come to understand in modern times that any special truth, or special culture which is wholly dissociated from the universal, is not true at all.

Indeed his understanding of the Indian past was that:

Our forefathers did spread a single pure white carpet, whereon all the world was cordially invited to take its seat in amity and good fellowship.

The basic impulse for Tagore's conceptions of 'The Center of Indian Culture' as a seat where all the distinct cultures of the world should meet and creatively negotiate at the level of equality and complete acceptance of one another was supplied by his vision of India's history. In ancient India, as perhaps in all ancient societies, social, personal life was lived at a safe distance from the political and revolved around features of civil society. Thoughts were directed mainly to the evolution of diverse aspects of the civil society, Hence, successive periods of the Indian history proved receptive to various groups of settlers or even invaders and assimilated all the novel and noble features of these peoples. Indian culture remained a developing synthesis, seeking harmonization with alien but welcome, distinct but absorbable elements.

In his interpretation of India's history, he undertakes to show how the history of India constitutes a process of assimilation through different epochs of history, through periods of trials and struggles with aggressive antagonistic forces. The specific historical situations which served as the objective basis for the two primary epics of India, the Ramayana and the Mahabharata, give us an insight into the emergence of a new age, with a new outlook upon the life of societies, races and ideas which were initially hostile to each other, This remains the abiding spirit of the history of India.

At that stage the achievement consisted in the reconciliation of two opposite principles, that of self-preservation, represented by the Brahmin, and that of self-expression, represented by the Kshatriya. When the first overtures towards social union were being made, it became necessary for the Aryans to come to an understanding with the non-Aryan strata of the population. At a succeeding phase, the Sakas and the Huns poured into India in repeated hordes, and this threatened that the very racial and cultural identity of Indians being would be swept away.

But an act of self-preserving resistance and sheer cultural vitality enabled India to assimilate the invaders. The retention of racial identity to the extent it is a reflex of a distinct cultural identity is a sine qua non for the synthesizing attitude and act. The urge for protection of cultural identity manifested itself through new compilations and collections of the extant cultural materials which served to define and preserve the synthesizing cultural identity.

Visualizing the whole as complete made for a new, inspiring self-awareness. The surviving, as well as renewing self-awareness, is a condition of an ever-enriching culture which generates its own principle of creative continuity and its vigor for enfranchising others. Race-mingling and value-absorbing became a unified and unhindered process. Harmony of component differences came to be organically effected through a long history which confronted India with complex problems of meaningful adjustment. In a climatic passage in his A Vision of India's History Tagore observes:

> . . . The India of to-day has roused herself once more to search out her truth, her harmony, her oneness, not only among her own constituent elements, but with the great world. The current of her life, which had been dammed up in stagnation has found some breach in the wall and can

> feel the pulse of the tidal waves of humanity outside. We shall learn that we can reach the great world of man, not through the effacement, but through the expansion of our own individuality. We shall know for certain that, just as it is futile mendicancy to covet the wealth of others in place of our own, so also to keep ourselves segregated and starved by refusing the gift which is the common heritage of man because it is brought to us by a foreign messenger, only makes for utter destitution.

Thus, vision of Indian history, as it has progressed through centuries of conflict and resolution in integration in a higher synthesis, is the broad perspective that has lent meaning and intelligibility to Tagore's conception of an international university which expresses the spiritual craving of an ancient civilization. This spirit seeks fulfillment in a complete freedom of creativity which alone assures individual as well as collective self-realization.

11

Political Ideas of Rabindranath Tagore

Modern European nation-states came into existence when the old feudal and imperial socio-political systems of the classical and medieval periods proved obsolete and inadequate with the advent of the Renaissance and the Reformation. The Industrial Revolution, which gave rise to a new form of machine economy and mercantile capitalism, was especially influential in their formation. In time, these nation-states created their own empires, which began to disintegrate with the burgeoning of nationalist awareness in the colonized Third World societies.

Nationalism has proven difficult to define. Foucault calls it a "discursive formation", while Benedict Anderson characterises it as "imagined community". According to Mariategui, "The nation...is an abstraction, an allegory, a myth that does not correspond to a reality that can be scientifically defined". On the contrary, Lawson suggests "Nationalism is a reaction of peoples who feel culturally at a disadvantage". In spite of its "fictive" nature and the difficulty of defining it with any degree of precision, nationalism has become, as Anderson argues, "the most universally legitimate value in the political life of our time".

Dipesh Chakrabarty goes a step further to claim that European imperialism and Third World nationalism have together achieved the "universalisation of the nation-state as the most desirable form of political community". Empire is comparatively easy to define; it refers to the policy of territorial expansion or acquisition of foreign lands for purposes of material, cultural and political gain for the dominant or imperial nation. In the case of the more recent "classical imperialism," it refers to European expansionist policies, or systematic Europeanisation of the globe, which began with "informal imperialism," or the "imperialism of free trade" in the eighteenth and nineteenth centuries.

In this chapter, to interrogate Tagore's ideas on the intersecting discourses of empire and nation in his travel writings, and argue that many of the pitfalls of the two institutions put forth by this inveterate champion of human subjectivity and global unity have been duly emphasised by other socio-cultural critics and thinkers before and after him. Tagore is well known for his diatribes on both empire and nation, which he saw as "hideously profane cult[s]" or "cult[s] of Devil-worship", responsible for a "whirlwind of race antipathy" and for turning the world into "a tower of skulls".

However, when we think of Tagore's views of empire and nation, generally we turn to his more canonical writings, such as his essays on Nationalism, or his novels The Home and the World and Four Chapters, or the poem "The Sunset of the Century," which are all primarily dedicated to these two themes. He was equally preoccupied with the thematic of empire and nation in much of his travel writings, especially in many of the letters he wrote to family and friends during his trips within the subcontinent as well as to Europe, America, China, Indonesia, Russia and Persia, and the occasional speeches or interviews he gave during these visits.

As in his canonical works, in these letters, interviews and speeches, he characteristically dismisses both nation and empire as the twin axis of egoism and evil, and urges humanity to reach out for a cultural confederation between races/nations, attainable through a global dialogue, or a creative interlocution between the East and the West. Tagore believed that inclusivism and synergic interaction between cultures would propel the world towards harmony and global fellowship, through the appropriation of Santam, Sivam, and Advaitam, principles he borrowed from the Upanishads. Elucidating this three-fold ideology, in a letter to Charles Andrews, sent from Kashmir, Tagore observes:

> The first stage towards freedom is the Santam, the true peace, which can be attained by subduing self; the next stage is the Sivam, the true goodness, which is the activity of the soul when self is subdued; and then the Advaitam, the love, the oneness with all and with God. Of course this division is merely logical; these stages, like rays of light, may be simultaneous or divided according to the circumstances, and their order may be altered, such as the Sivam leading to Santam. But all we must know is that the Santam, Sivam, Advaitam, is the only goal for which we live and struggle. (Letters 50)

This comment immediately establishes the poetic and spiritual basis of Tagore's political ideas. He exhorts humanity to bring about inner unity of the self, by overcoming worldly distractions, so as to attain oneness with the world. It involves a two-way process, since it requires the individual to deny his mind and senses to accomplish selfhood, and withdraw into his soul to become one with the world. Only by sacrificing the duality of the self and the world or I and you, can the human individual (and by extension a nation) become part and parcel of the whole. In the Brihadaranyaka Upanishad, Yagnavalkya explains this principle to Maitreyi:

> As long as there is duality, one sees the other, one hears the other, one smells the other, one speaks to the other, one thinks of the other, one knows of the other; but when for the illumined soul the all is dissolved in the Self, who is there to be seen by whom, who is there to be smelt by whom, who is there to be heard by whom, who is there to be spoken to by whom, who is there to be thought of by whom, who is there to be known by whom?

Thus, the only process for getting rid of the duality of self and other is eradication of the self (ego), which immediately connects the individual with the larger world. In a letter from New York, advocating this principle of non-duality as a way of emancipation from the political and moral contortions modern man has spun around himself, and for bringing about a peaceful and united world, Tagore advises: "Let us be rid of all false pride and rejoice at any lamp being lit in any corner of the world, knowing that it is a part of the common illumination of our house". This selfless rejoicing of things big or small, with an express feeling that they are all equal, requires the individual and nation to rise above the taints of pride and passion, or of worldly Maya, and appreciate that, to quote from Chandogya Upanishad, "What is in the macrocosm is in the microcosm", and vice versa.

Empire and Nation

Tagore was born at a critical juncture in Indian history, in 1861—four years after the great indigenous uprising against the East India Company was successfully crushed, and three years after "the British Parliament passed the Government of India Act, transferring 'all rights' that the company had hitherto enjoyed on Indian soil directly to the crown". This transfer of power consolidated the British imperial hold on the subcontinent, creating an environment in which the Indians were enslaved by an alien power in their homeland. They became the beasts of burden for another society, toiling away so that the English could be fed, clothed, nourished and, as Tagore tauntingly suggests in a letter from Russia, "become great and do great things for mankind".

Being a humanitarian at heart, he could not understand or accept the rationale behind this British exploitation and injustice in India. He wondered why the Indians were used as a lamp stand to irradiate English life, while the Indians themselves remained smeared in trickles of oil. Why should the British systematically pilfer the Indian coffer and inflict the indignity of poverty and pandering on the local people? Why couldn't the two sides seize the moment of encounter between the East and the West in a creative, constructive spirit, for establishing mutuality and equality between the races, instead of the blind and irrational contempt and corresponding hatred and vengefulness that prevailed between the groups?

Tagore's rejection of the Empire and imperialism was deep seated in his consciousness, and he categorically expresses his outrage against this hierarchical political system in his travel writings. His basic stricture against this oppressive practice was that it was based on the binary of self and other—one race imposing its political and cultural will viciously and violently on another, giving rise to a culture of ruthless exploitation, manipulation, and prejudice. Tagore articulates his universal rejection of this repressive political structure in a letter from London, responding to a woman who had accused him of being unduly critical of the British people in one of his lectures:

> I deeply feel for the races who are being insulted and injured by the ruthless exploitation of the powerful nations belonging to the West and the East. I feel as much for the negroes, brutally lynched in America, often for economic reasons, and for the Koreans, who are the latest

> victims of Japanese imperialism, as for any wrongs done to the helpless multitude in my own country. (Letters 127-28)

Tagore felt morally outraged by the fact that one nation should rule over another by brute force, and thrive on the life-blood of the victim nation. This was an insult to human dignity on both sides, as it flagrantly violated the law of autonomy of the self. Moreover, as an ideal or action, it was unscrupulous, even scandalously criminal. It created a mold of victimizer-victim, ruler-ruled, master-slave and deterred the races from growing out of this symbiotic relationship and fulfilling their true human potential. This scramble for new land was motivated by what Hobsbawm would call greed, or what Said later described as a wish for cultural dominance.

Tagore saw it as a corollary of "homicidal pride of sect and lust for gain" (Parasya Jatri 148). To him, this hegemonism was as morally detrimental to the English as it was to Indians. In a letter to Romain Rolland, dated 19 October 1919, he cautions:

Parasitism, whether based upon power or upon weakness, must breed degeneracy... And the time seems fast approaching when the soul will be sucked dry from the civilization of Europe also by the growing lust for gain in her commerce and politics, unless she has the wisdom and power to change her mind and not merely her system.

Tagore was particularly disturbed by the inherent violence in the relationship between the colonizer and colonized nations, which he captured in a poignant metaphor, used in a letter to Charles Andrews, elaborating the long-standing struggle between England and Ireland: "It is a python which refuses to disgorge this living creature which struggles to live its separate life". This tendency of one nation to consume another by animal force, in order to meet its own greed, unleashes a cycle of endless violence, taking its toll on innocent people.

In a letter from Persia he recollects his experience of the reckless bombing of Iraqis by the occupying British soldiers, who were gleefully killing innocent children and women to establish their might and economic right over the land. Depicting an incident that is eerily and ironically similar to Iraq's current experience in the hands of the Americans, (which goes to validate Tagore's argument that the monolithic modern civilization has brought considerable material prosperity, but humanity still remains trapped in a vicious cycle of greed, lust and war for lack of a guiding moral principle), Tagore comments in utter disbelief:

> A British air force is stationed at Baghdad. Its Christian chaplain informs me that they are engaged in bombing operations on some Sheikh villages. The men, women and children done to death there meet their fate by a decree from the stratosphere of British imperialism—which finds it easy to shower death because of its distance from its individual victims. So dim and insignificant do those unskilled in the modern arts of killing appear to those who glory in such skill! Christ acknowledged all mankind to be the children of his Father; but for the modern Christian both father and children have receded into shadows, unrecognisable from the elevation of his bombing plane—for which reason these blows are dealt at the very heart of Christ himself. (Dutta, Anthology 127)

Tagore's reference to Christ reaffirms his allegiance to the principle of Ahimsa or non-violence as, like Christ, he was a proponent of human fellowship, love, and sympathetic neighbourliness, and opposed to barbaric ferocity between individuals or nations. The poet's love for non-violence was central to his imagination, and in many ways he was a precursor of Gandhi in introducing and popularising the ideal of non-violence on the Indian political stage. His novel The Home and the World, which came out in 1915, had championed the doctrine of non-violence in his protagonist Nikhil, well before Gandhi embarked on his Satyagraha movement, with non-violent non-cooperation as the main strategy to withstand the imperial might.

Besides, in the wake of the Amritsar massacre on 13 April 1919, it was Tagore who made the first public protest against the heinous incident. He repudiated his Knighthood (conferred on him in 1915), in an open letter to the viceroy, published in the Indian press on 2 June, when no other Indian politician was willing to risk his career confronted by the Rowlatt legislation. Moreover, he did this well before Gandhi returned his awards to the viceroy on 1 August 1920.

Tagore's message on the unholy alliance between imperialism and violence was potent but simple, cogently summed up in his Izvestia interview in Russia, "Violence begets violence and blind stupidity. Freedom of mind is needed for the reception of truth; terror hopelessly kills it. The brute cannot subdue the brute. It is only the man who can do it".

Tagore was opposed to imperial arrogance and its capacity for misery and injustice in the world, but he was equally critical of the parochialism and chauvinism fomented by nationalism. In a letter from Vienna, Austria, he affirmed: "I have said over and over again that the aggressive spirit of nationalism and imperialism, religiously cultivated by most of the nations of the West, is a menace to the whole world".

He recurrently saw an ongoing nexus between the two forces as, like Hobson, he judged imperialism as an expression of national egoism, and both as potent sites of power discourse. He argued that the Europeans had come to India and other parts of the world driven by their love and pride for their own nation. They plundered other countries only to further the prosperity of their own land, and to establish its power and authority in the world. Their patriotism blinded them to the betterment of humanity, and they sacrificed their innate good qualities to fulfill an aberrant sense of superiority, swayed by a distorted logic, which Tagore summed up in a letter from Russia: "For if no one was down below, no one was up above... the advance of civilization depends on keeping down the bulk of humanity and denying it its human rights".

Tagore's diatribe on nationalism, or his anti-nationalist sentiment, is perhaps the single most consistent political motif in all his writings: his essays, lectures, poems, plays and fiction. He began his systematic attack on the doctrine of nationalism long before the ideal gained its political and emotional legitimacy in modern society, or became, as Bill Ashcroft and his co-writers suggest, "the most implacably powerful force in twentieth century politics".

In a poem entitled "The Sunset of the Century," written on the last day of the nineteenth century, Tagore indicts nationalism as a source of war and carnage. In this poem, he depicts the political idea of the nation as a famished and ruthlessly rapacious creature that in its omnivorous greed is bent on destroying the world. In what is his first, and one of his most caustic attacks on nationalism, he writes:

> The last sun of the century sets amidst the blood-red clouds of the West and the whirlwind of hatred.
>
> The naked passion of the self-love of Nations, in its drunken delirium of greed, is dancing to the clash of steel and howling verses of vengeance.
>
> The hungry self of the Nation shall burst in a violence of fury from its shameless feeding.

For it has made the world its food.
And licking it, crunching it and swallowing it in big morsels...

(Nationalism 80, ll. 1-5)

This same view of nationalism as a diabolical force, or "a cruel epidemic of evil" (Nationalism 9) as he dubs it elsewhere—which also forms the core of his lectures on nationalism in 1916, and his novels, The Home and the World and Four Chapters, published respectively in 1915 and 1934—persists in his travel writings, especially in many of his letters sent from abroad.

However, since the letters are more intimate and informal, meant for an individual friend or family member, his message comes across in them more directly and forcefully than his other published works; they capture the poet's impromptu responses to events without any literary disguise. Moreover, the letters and his travel writings generally compliment his canonical works by giving a more complete picture of his ideas on empire and nation.

Tagore considered nationalism as a highly intoxicating and addictive sentiment that breeds radicalism and passionate excitement in people. Comparing nationalist zeal and religious fanaticism, in that they both mutilate the sense and sensibility of the individual and nations, in a letter from New York, dated 20 December 1920, he wrote: "Formalism in religion is like nationalism in politics: it breeds sectarian arrogance, mutual misunderstanding and a spirit of persecution" (Letters 85).

Tagore also accused nationalism of exclusivism and provincialism since it creates artificial walls between nations by enclosing each in a separate "geographical cage." It eventually leads individuals to think in a narrow either/or mode of fierce separateness between one nation and another, fostering aggressive national egoism and fatal rivalry amongst nations. In a letter from Stockholm, dated 27 May 1921, he explains:

> The nations love their own countries; and that national love has only given rise to hatred and suspicion of one another... When we hear "Bande Mataram" ["Hail to thee mother"—a nationalist slogan in India that became popular during the Swadeshi movement in Bengal, in 1905] from the housetops, we shout to our neighbors: "You are not our brothers"... Whatever may be its use for the present, it is like the house being set on fire simply for roasting the pig! Love of self, whether national or individual, can have no other destination except suicide. (Letters 143)

In another letter from New York, dated 8 February 1921, Tagore recounts how he himself witnessed the sinister effect of this dichotomous sentiment in the US, culminating in emotional and sometimes physical violence towards people who were deemed as "other." He gives the examples of the Asians, who were viewed with antipathy by the mainstream white community, and the blacks, who were "burnt alive, sometimes merely because they tried to exercise their right to vote, given to them by law".

Moreover, the Germans were "reviled," and the Russians were "deliberately misrepresented." In other words, Tagore asserts that for Americans to realise their national identity as a people, they had to constantly put themselves on a higher plane and calumniate others, or see their relationships with non-whites and non-Americans in a dichotomous light. They had to feed their individual and national egos through "a continual supply of hatred, contempt, jealousy and lies and lies".

Tagore was a holistic thinker, who believed in the multifaceted nature of the human being; "To me humanity is rich and large and many-sided", he wrote in a letter from New York, dated 14 January 1921. To operate efficaciously in society, any ideal would have to take into account this multiplicity in the human individual and bring wholesome nourishment for the whole being. This multiplicity included body, mind and soul, and for Tagore an ideal had to minister to each of these attributes so that each is brought to fullness.

Only then would the individual's inner unity and creative bond of wholeness be reinforced, steering the world towards a "grand harmony of all human races". Given this multilateral outlook, Tagore naturally perceived nationalism to be a unilateral and monolithic concept, utterly indifferent to the spiritual aspect of the human individual.

Nationalism required the individual and nation to sacrifice the spirit, or the higher ideal of humanity, at the altar of greed and gain, magnifying thereby, Tagore explains, "our vulgarity [and] cruelty...dethroning God, to put up [the] bloated self in its place". This forceful displacement of the sacred element of the soul with self-love is sacrilege to Tagore, and one that upsets man's moral balance by subjugating his inherent nobility and goodness to a worldly Maya.

Tagore was outraged by the idea of the nation in general but much of his criticism was directed against Gandhi's nationalist movement in particular. He had a great personal respect for Gandhi, but he could not accept the latter's political vision of Swadeshi and Swaraj for various reasons. He believed Gandhi's movement had no spiritual basis; it did not fulfill the Upanishadic principle that we all belong to One Self-Effulgent Brahman and that we should work towards realising that divine one identity of humanity by overcoming worldly temptations. Instead, his search for a separate identity for India helped frustrate the attainment of that Ultimate Reality by creating a world that is disunited and fractured.

In one of his letters from Chicago, Tagore painfully explains how Gandhi's nationalist program was more inclined towards the Buddhist philosophy of dukkha (misery) and nirvana, than the Hindu philosophy of Om (everlasting yes), anandam (blissful joy) and mukti. Nirvana calls on the individual to attain the truth of nothingness by following the negative path of destroying the self. Mukti, on the other hand, requires the self to reach out for Brahman through the positive path of purifying the soul of its worldly delusions and forgetfulness. This latter idea can be best understood in light of the following statement from *Mundaka Upanishad*:

> The individual self, deluded by forgetfulness of his identity with the divine Self, bewildered by his ego, grieves and is sad. But when he recognises the worshipful Lord as his own true Self, and beholds his glory, he grieves no more.... The Lord is the one life shining forth from every creature. Seeing him present in all, the wise man is humble, puts not himself forward. His delight is in the Self, his joy is in the Self, he serves the Lord in all. Such as he, indeed, are the true knowers of Brahman.

With his intrinsically peaceful and harmonious view of humanity and god, Tagore came to believe that Gandhi's Satyagraha movement, in spite of Gandhi's non-violent objectives, was generating excessive negative excitement among Indians, inflaming their hatred and vengefulness against the British. Such proliferation of emotional violence could not remedy India's problems, since what India needed was the wisdom of love, acceptance and tolerance and not a spirit of hostility and persecution. Hostility would only breed more hostility, pushing the country to the brink of destruction. Besides, as Tagore points out sharply, in a letter from London, "it is hateful to hate" (Letters 126)—a weltanschauung rooted in hatred can reap no positive outcome.

In another letter from Ardennes, France, dated 7 September 1920, he encourages his compatriots to disperse their negative sentiments for the sake of their self-respect and pride, "Stung by the insult of cruel injustice we try to repudiate Europe, but by doing so we insult ourselves. Let us have the dignity not to quarrel or retaliate; not to pay back smallness by being small ourselves". In the same letter, he further reminds his fellow Indians that their true mission should be to carry out their own duties wholeheartedly and not worry about the wrong doings of others. "Let us...set our house in order. Do not mind the waves of the sea, but mind the leaks in your vessel", he said.

The above comment brings us to the crux of Tagore's argument. He essentially believed that India ought to be more inward looking and soul-searching; that it should strive to redress its own overwhelming social problems before it could gain the moral authority to resist the injustices of the British. How could India rightfully stand up against an oppressive colonial power, when it had for centuries abused multitudes of its own people? India should first address the caste issue, which had taken a hypnotic hold on the mind of its people, creating a gigantic system of cold-blooded repression of the untouchables. It should also address the issues of poverty and gender discrimination, and work out a method to foster religious and racial harmony among its various groups.

If India could come to grips with its "burden of heterogeneity". and forge a horizontal relationship between its cross-sections of people, it would then become imperative for the British to quit India because of the moral superiority of the natives. Perhaps it would then also provide a positive lesson to the British and the rest of the world on how to live in fellowship and mutual harmony in a multi-racial and multi-religious milieu, without degenerating into physical or intellectual brutality.

Tagore believed that the real solution to India's problems was education and the enlivening of Indian minds, and not a "blind revolution" or the miracle of political freedom built upon the quicksand of social slavery. What India needed was a "thought impetus" similar to the one experienced by Europe during the Renaissance. If India could get proper education and induce the spirit of sacrifice in its people, then it could rise like a giant from its "dry sand-bed of dead customs". He was convinced that Gandhi could help India in this regard by kindling the fire of love and undertaking programs of cooperation among its people. He goaded Gandhi to invest his leadership genius to educating Indians and motivating them to social service, rather than exciting them with his nationalist call, which Tagore felt was not a constructive deed.

In a letter from Paris, dated 18 September 1920, he wrote in a solicitous tone, referring to Gandhi: "I shall be willing to sit at his feet and do his bidding if he commands me to cooperate with my countrymen in service and love. I refuse to waste my manhood in lighting fires of anger and spreading it from house to house".

Tagore rebuffed Gandhi's nationalist movement for another reason: he reckoned that like any other movement, it glorified an abstract Cause at the expense of the individual. In consequence, many individual lives were sacrificed foolishly at the altar of the Cause. As a poet, who valued the concrete over the abstract, and a humane thinker, who deemed every single life invaluable and sacred, this practice of perceiving the individual through the prism of a giant cause, reducing him/her to a phantom, was utterly unacceptable to him.

In a letter from Chicago to his friend Charles Andrews, dated 5 March 1921, Tagore complains how many Indian college students were taking up Gandhi's call to boycott the British education system and sacrificing their learning and future, without any alternative provision planned for them by the leaders. This negligence of the leaders would inflict serious injustice on the students, as their passionate response to the call would deprive them of a possible better future, which they could have otherwise accomplished through proper education.

Tagore expresses his fury in the letter at such unscrupulous victimisation of helpless youths for an ideal that, in itself, was ill advised and flawed—and a practice he saw was becoming rather too commonplace in the modern world. In a tone of mockery, mixed with lamentation, he writes, "I wish I were the little creature Jack whose one mission was to kill the giant abstraction which is claiming the sacrifice of the individuals all over the world under highly painted masks of delusion".

12

Tagore's Concept of One World

The anti-nationalitarian sentiment-that nationalism is a source of war and carnage; death, destruction and divisiveness, rather than international solidarity, that induces a larger and more expansive vision of the world-remains at the heart of Tagore's imagination in most of his writings: his letters, essays, lectures, poems, plays and fiction. He was always opposed to the nationalism of Realpolitik and hyper-nationalism that breathed meaning into Thucydides's ancient maxim that "large nations do what they wish, while small nations accept what they must" and that in which, as Radhakrishnan said, "self-interest is the end; brute force, the means; conscience is taboo".

Radical nationalism that acted as opiate of the people, making them irrational and fanatical, blind to the senses of truth and justice, and willing to both kill and die for it, perpetuating a logic of "lunacy" and war, instead of a cycle of freedom and peace, was an anathema to Tagore. He spurned it as "a cruel epidemic of evil... sweeping over the human world of the present age and eating into its moral fibre"; a terrible absurdity that is seeking to engulf humanity in a suicidal conflagration.

Tagore was a believer in an interactive, dialogic world, given to a deep sense of sympathy, generosity and mutuality, and in which nations would not be parochial, xenophobic and centripetal, or guided by mere selfishness and self-aggrandisement, but poised towards a morally and politically enlightened community of nations through the espousal of a centrifugal outlook, multilateral imagination, principal of universality and reciprocal recognitions. In this sense Tagore stands a precursor to many of the modern critics and philosophers of post/ trans-nationalism and globalism such as Frantz Fanon, Edward Said and Noam Chomsky.

Much like Chomsky, Tagore believed, to put it in Chomsky's words, that "'another world is possible' [by] seeking to create constructive alternatives of thought, actions and institutions," and by bringing "a measure of peace and justice and hope to the world". Tagore imagined of a commonwealth of nations in which no nation (or race) would deprive another "of its rightful place in the world festival" and every nation would "keep alight its own lamp of mind as its part of the illumination of the world".

Tagore was an avid advocate of inter-civilisational alliance; his vision was given to a symbiosis of the East and West. He was no doubt furious with the British cruelty and oppression in India during the colonial period, and felt that the West was often immersed in commercialism, "moral cannibalism", "political expediency", militarism and "war-madness", and was unduly full of contempt for the East; yet he never gave up hope for a possible union of the East and West, in which the East and the West would meet as equal partners in a creative engagement; "I believe in the true meeting of the East and the West", he affirmed in a letter to Charles Andrews.

In a letter to Foss Westcott, Tagore further wrote, "Believe me, nothing would give me greater happiness than to see the people of the West and the East march in a common crusade against all that robs the human spirit of its significance". Moreover, he took exception to Kipling's remark that the East and the West were too divergent and "'Never the twain shall meet" by affirming, much like in Emerson's spirit in his essay "Compensation," that the realisation of a unitary and stable world was contingent upon the meeting of these two opposing halves, which compensated one another:

> Earnestly I ask the poet of the western world to realise and sing... with all the great power of music which he has, that the East and West are ever in search of each other, and that they must meet not merely in the fullness of physical strength, but in fullness of truth; that the right hand, which wields the sword, has the need of the left, which holds the shield of safety. (Dutta 213)

Tagore's indictment of nationalism elicited furious criticisms from many of his contemporaries, especially in the West, with the Marxist critic, Georg Lukacs, and the English writer, D. H. Lawrence, leading the pack, making the duo strange bedfellows in their Tagore hatred. Lukacs, who found both Tagore and Gandhi counter-revolutionary, took the opportunity to pounce on Tagore, after the publication of his anti-nationalist, anti-revolutionary novel, The Home and the World.

In the characteristic tone of one who saw a Cause greater than a living, breathing human being, and to whom the abstract was more sanctified than the palpable, Lukacs condemned Tagore as "a wholly insignificant figure... [Who] survives by sticking scraps of the Upanishads and the Bhagavadgita into his works amid the sluggish flow of his tediousness".

Lawrence, on the other hand, felt outraged by what he called the "wretched worship-of-Tagore attitude" and admonished that Tagore was a "horribly decadent [figure] reverting to all forms of barbarism in all sorts of ugly ways." Lawrence further said, creating the same us/them, West/East hierarchical binary, which Tagore had found disagreeable in Kipling's imagination, "our European civilization stands [far higher] than the East, India, or Persia ever dreamed of".

Lawrence's arrogance and contempt in the above statement only ratified Tagore's claim that the chasm between the East and the West was created by the West's unwarranted contempt for the East, which in return generated hatred in the East against the West. His response to such contempt was, "The blindness of contempt is more hopeless than the blindness of ignorance; for contempt kills the light which ignorance merely leaves unignited".

Tagore urged the West to overcome its "logic of egoism", ignoble triumphalism, "forcible parasitism" and intentional ignorance, and seek to understand the East in a true spirit of creativity, fellowship and welfare of humanity. He reminded that the British belligerency and its singular passion for power and wealth during the colonial period turned the world into a cauldron of animosities; the way to conquer the world, Tagore said, was not war but active sympathy. In his novel The Home and the World, his protagonist, Nikhil, bursts out against the British atrocities in India as well as the atrocities perpetrated by the Indian nationalist terrorists:

> It was Buddha who conquered the world, not Alexander-this is untrue when stated in dry prose-oh when shall we be able to sing it? When shall all these most intimate truths of the universe overflow the pages of printed books and leap out in a sacred stream like the Ganges from the Gangotri? (134-35)

However, in spite of the derogatory remarks made by Lukacs and Lawrence, and the attempts to dismiss him as a sentimental alarmist by others, Tagore's assertive denunciation of the Nation proved prophetic with the outbreak of two world wars, costing millions of lives;

UK's war in Kenya in the 1950s, to quell the rebels against its colonial rule, costing 150,000 lives; the genocide in Bangladesh by the Pakistani junta in 1970, claiming a toll of three million lives, but most importantly, the nuclear arms race that pushed the world to the brink of destruction in the 1960s.

The Cuban missile crisis was the most dangerous moment in human history, Chomsky reminds us. In October 1962, during the height of the crisis, he explains, it was one Soviet submarine officer named Vasili Arkhipov who saved the world by blocking "an order to fire nuclear armed torpedoes on October 27... when the submarines were under attack by US destroyers". Thus, ironically, this world of pomp and finery, wealth and power, at its height of crisis, was left to the wisdom of one person; and had Arkhipov been as "insane" as some of the other nationalist chauvinists, the world would have almost surely been extinct now through a major nuclear warfare-if not the world, the Northern Hemisphere.

After humanity was plentifully gorged with the blood of some 50 million people, killed in violent circumstances in the twentieth century, mostly in wars that invoked the nation in one form or another, many had thought that peace and sanity would return to the world, especially since the Cold War was over. But that was not to be. As the world had barely crossed the portal of a new millennium, and stepped into the twenty-first century, it found itself again battered in torrents of blood and locked in a devil dance of destruction.

The "jihadists" (not only to the radical Islamists but also the ferocious jingoists, who seem equally enthusiastic in violence and to kill innocent civilians with utter abandon like the "terrorists") have struck again and the world has suffered colossal disasters. The horrendous events of 9-11 which caused "the most devastating instant human toll on record, outside of war"; America's military response to 9-11, defying world opinion, with massive coordinated bombings in Afghanistan, which turned "major urban concentrations [in the country] into 'ghost towns'"-a campaign, in which, the veteran Spanish journalist Miguel Angel Aguilar says, "we were trying to kill mosquitoes with bombs. Innocents were killed and democracy suffered and we are no safer";

America's "pre-emptive/preventive" war in Iraq, which Paul O'Neill painfully explains to Ron Suskind, America started hatching at the very first meeting of the current American president with the National Security Council, on "January 30, ten days after his inauguration" -such destructive events, which have changed the world, leaving humanity peering into the abyss of the future, have all been undertaken in the name of national safety and national security, whether it is the pan-Islamic religious nationalism of the militants or secular nationalism of the West.

However, we are not done yet, security of the homeland has not been achieved, as President Bush has thoughtfully declared, "There is no telling how many wars it will take to secure freedom in the homeland". Perhaps respite will come only when the "pious warlords" after all their calculated savagery and sacrifices to the "dark gods of war" will have successfully realised Bertrand Russell's sombre prediction about world peace:

> After ages during which the earth produced harmless trilobites and butterflies, evolution progressed to the point at which it has generated Neroes, Genghis Khans, and Hitlers. This, however, I believe is a passing nightmare; in time the earth will become again incapable of supporting life, and peace will return.

Nationalism and Tagore

Benedict Anderson defines the nation as "imagined

community" but acknowledges that it is "notoriously difficult to define, let alone to analyse" "Nation, nationality, nationalism". Hugh Seton-Watson maintains, "no 'scientific definition' of the nation can be devised". Ernst Gellner observes that nationalism is an 'invention,' 'fabrication': "Nationalism is not the awakening of nations to self-consciousness: it invents nations where they do not exist".

Despite its "mythical" quality, and the difficulties involved in defining it, the phenomenon still enjoys profound political and emotional legitimacy in modern society. Bill Ashcroft et al. affirm that in spite of "all its contentiousness, and the difficulty of theorising it adequately, remains the most implacably powerful force in twentieth century politics".

Nationalism as a political expression, with people sharing a common geographical boundary and some unifying cultural/political signifier is relatively new, although cultural nationalism has prevailed since the beginning of society. Anderson suggests that the nation as a political institution is the product of European Enlightenment and Industrial Revolution. He argues that the rise of nationalism in Western Europe was made possible by the decline, if not the death, of religious modes of thought, in the wake of the rationalist secularism of the Enlightenment, or the Age of Reason.

The guiding principles of this intellectual movement were the glorification of reason and faith in human dignity, both of which were sufficient to break down the old belief systems that gave centrality to the church and a theocentric worldview. Thus a more pragmatic and worldly socio-political system of nationalism emerged to suit the post-religious, secular world. Anderson explains, "What then was required was a secular transformation of fatality into continuity, contingency into meaning... few things were (are) better suited to this end than an idea of nation".

Ernest Gellner, on the other hand, attributes the emergence of nationalism to the rise of industrial-capitalism in the eighteenth and nineteenth centuries. The epochal shift of human society from pre-industrial to industrial economies, he argues, set up the conditions required for the creation of larger social units and economies that would be culturally "homogenous" and cooperative as workforce, thus paving the way for the formation of the more complex and intricate social organisation of the nation-state. Effectively, the expansion of the workforce and the market made the earlier pre-industrial, tribal societies and their structures both inadequate and obsolete.

Timothy Brennan examines the role of literature, especially the novel, in the formation of national consciousness during its early period: "the end of the eighteenth and the beginning of the nineteenth centuries". He maintains:

> It was the novel that historically accompanied the rise of nations by objectifying the 'one, yet many' of national life, and by mimicking the structures of the nation. . . . But it did more than that. Its manner of presentation allowed people to imagine the special community that the nation was.

Despite literature's such active complicity in the formation of the institution and the global acceptance of nationalism as the only legitimate form of political organisation, India's myriad-minded poet, Rabindranath Tagore-whom Bertrand Russell considered "worthy of the highest honour", and Ezra Pound deemed "greater than any of us" as a poet-shared not an iota of positive sentiment towards the ideology. His foremost objection came from its very nature and purpose as an institution. The very fact that it is a social institution, a mechanical organisation, modelled on certain utilitarian objectives in mind, made it unpalatable to Tagore, who was a champion of creation over construction, imagination over reason and the natural over the artificial and the man-made: "Construction is for a purpose, it expresses our wants; but creation is for itself, it expresses our very beings".

Tagore took the view that since nationalism emerged in the post-religious laboratory of industrial-capitalism, it was only an "organisation of politics and commerce", that brings "harvests of wealth", or "carnivals of materialism", by spreading tentacles of greed, selfishness, power and prosperity, or churning up the baser instincts of mankind, and sacrificing in the process "the moral man, the complete man . . . to make room for the political and commercial man, the man of limited purpose".

Nationalism, according to Tagore, is not "a spontaneous self-expression of man as social being," where human relationships are naturally regulated, "so that men can develop ideals of life in co-operation with one another", but rather a political and commercial union of a group of people, in which they congregate to maximise their profit, progress and power; it is "the organised self-interest of a people, where it is least human and least spiritual".

Tagore deemed nationalism a recurrent threat to humanity, because with its propensity for the material and the rational, it trampled over the human spirit and human emotion; it upset man's moral balance, "obscuring his human side under the shadow of soul-less organisation". Thus, Tagore called into question both the constructed aspect of nationalism, which stifled the innate and instinctive qualities of the human individual, and its overemphasis on the commercial and political aspects, at the expense of man's moral and spiritual qualities. Both of these limitations reduced nationalism to an incomplete, monolithic and unipolar ideology-essentially inadequate for human beings given to an inherent multiplicity and seeming contraries, that needed to be unified and synthesised, through a process of soulful negotiation and striking of an axial line between opposites, to create the whole and wholesome person.

Tagore also found the fetish of nationalism a source of war, hatred and mutual suspicion between nations. In The Home and the World, Nikhil, Tagore's alter ego in the novel, who is patriotic but wouldn't place nation above truth and conscience says, "I am willing to serve my country; but my worship I reserve for Right which is far greater than country. To worship my country as a god is to bring curse upon it". However, Nikhil's friend, Sandip, a charismatic but unconscionable nationalist, to whom any action in the name of the nation is right, no matter how far it may be from truth or justice, exclaims, "country's needs must be made into a god", and one must "set aside . . . conscience . . . by putting the country in its place".

Tagore saw this radical view of Sandip, in which the nation is apotheosised and placed above truth and conscience, as a recipe for disaster. It breeds exclusivism and dogmatism through the Hegelian dichotomous logic of self's fundamental hostility towards the other; thus every nation becomes narcissistic and considers the presence of another a threat to itself; waging war against other nations for its self-fulfilment and self-aggrandisement becomes a justifiable and even "holy" act. Tagore explains:

> The Nation, with all its paraphernalia of power and prosperity, its flags and pious hymns, its blasphemous prayers in the churches, and the literary mock thunders of its patriotic bragging, cannot hide the fact that the Nation is the greatest evil for the Nation, that all its precautions are against it, and any new birth of its fellow in the world

> is always followed in its mind by the dread of a new peril. (Nationalism 17-18)

Tagore argued that British colonialism found its justification in the ideology of nationalism, as the coloniser came to India and other rich pastures of the world to plunder and so further the prosperity of their own nation. They were never sincere in developing colonised countries/nations, as to convert their "hunting grounds" into "cultivated fields" would have been contrary to their national interest. Like predators, they thrived by victimising and violating other nations, and never felt deterred in their heinous actions by the principles of love, sympathy or universal fellowship.

The logic is simple but cruel, and is sustained by a privileging norm, that in order to have rich and powerful nations, some nations ought to be left poor and pregnable: "Because this civilization is the civilization of power, therefore it is exclusive, it is naturally unwilling to open its sources of power to those whom it has selected for its purposes for exploitation". By its very nature as an organisation, Tagore argued, nationalism could ill afford any altruism in this regard.

One might think that Tagore's critique of nationalism is a little lofty and far-fetched-"too pious" as Pound might have said; his arguments are layered in atavistic spiritualism and romantic idealism. However, much of what Tagore said is intellectually valid and some of it is borne out by contemporary post-colonial criticism. Critics concur that nation is a necessity, it has laboured on behalf of modernity, and it helps to bolster the present civilization; as a political organisation it befits the social and intellectual milieu of present-day society, but they hardly claim its moral authority or its beneficial role in the reinforcement of human virtue.

Critics also view the constructed aspect of nationalism as a weakness in the ideology. It is vulnerable to regressing into more natural social units of clan, tribe and race, or language and religious groups. Its very formative process introduces a self-deconstructing logic in it. The process of formation/invention further makes it a potent site of power discourse; although it is meant to stand for horizontal comradeship, exploitation and inequality remain a daily occurrence in its body, and the nation never speaks of the hopes and aspirations of its entire "imagined community."

In conceiving its overarching ideologies it often places the dominant group at the centre, pushing the minority population to the periphery. Thus, instead of a fraternity, it creates a new hierarchy and hegemony within its structure, and exposes the fracture between its rhetoric and reality. Fanon expresses this misgiving, when he says, "National consciousness, instead of being the all-embracing crystallization of the innermost hopes of the whole people [becomes] a crude and fragile travesty of what it might have been [when] the nation is passed over for the race, and the tribe is preferred to the state".

Several post-colonial critics agree with Tagore's view that nationalism begets a disquisition of intolerance and "othering." Ernest Gellner, Benedict Anderson and Tom Nairn have pointed out the irrationality, prejudice and hatred that nationalism generates, and Leela Gandhi speaks of its attendant racism and loathing, and the alacrity with which citizens are willing to both kill and die for the sake of the nation. In a letter to Yone Noguchi, a Japanese writer who had asked for Tagore's moral support for Japan's invasion of China in 1937, in the name of "saving China for Asia", Tagore roundly criticises Noguchi for his naive acceptance of the grotesque rhetoric meant to veil an adventure of greed:

> I was amused to read the recent statement of a Tokyo politician that the military alliance of Japan with Italy and Germany was made for 'highly spiritual and moral reasons' and 'had no materialistic considerations behind it.' Quite so. What is not so amusing is that writers and thinkers should echo such remarkable sentiments that translate military swagger into spiritual bravados. (Dutta 192-93)

Thomas Jefferson's observation on the world situation of his day sums up the hypocrisy behind such use of exalted language in war, most tellingly:

> We believe no more in Bonaparte's fighting for the liberties of the seas, than in Great Britain's fighting for the liberties of mankind. The object is the same, to draw to themselves the power, the wealth, and the resources of other nations.

Jefferson's point further helps bolster Tagore's claim that the discourse of nationalism overlaps with the discourse imperialism; the imperialist nations adopt the role of the Lacanian grand Other and seek to inscribe their authority unilaterally over the colonised nations; they are not impelled by the ideology of benevolence towards the colonised countries. Tagore describes them as aggressive people essentially driven by greed; who "go out of their way and spread their coat-tails in other peoples' thoroughfares, claiming indemnity when these are trodden upon".

According to Amy Cesaire, the imperial objective is to "thingify" the colonial subjects, and Fanon suggest that the colonisers are inherently bent upon not only plundering the wealth of the colonised nations but also to rob them of their culture: "By a kind of perverted logic, it turns the past of the oppressed people, and distorts, disfigures, and destroys it".

A classic example of this later instance was the introduction of English language in India in 1835 with the view of anglicising a group of Indians who would serve the colonial cause.

Tagore and Indian Nationalism

Tagore was opposed to the idea of the nation; he was even more fiercely opposed to India joining the bandwagon of nationalism. This would compromise India's history and identity as a culture and bring it under the shadow of the West. He warned:

> We, in India, must make up our minds that we cannot borrow other people's history, and that if we stifle our own we are committing suicide. When you borrow things that do not belong to your life, they only serve to crush your life. . . . I believe that it does India no good to compete with Western civilization in its own field.. . . India is no beggar of the West. (Soares 106)

Tagore was born in 1861, a period during which the nationalist movement in India against the British rule was crystallising and gaining momentum. In 1857, only four years before the poet was born, the first military uprising for self-rule broke out in India. In 1905, the Swadeshi movement started on Tagore's doorstep, as a response to the British policy of partitioning Bengal.

Although a political by temperament, Tagore at first was drawn to the movement and started giving lectures and writing patriotic songs with such fervour that Ezra Pound quipped, "Tagore has sung Bengal into a nation". But soon after, Tagore saw the movement turning violent with the nationalists agitating against innocent civilians who were indifferent to their cause, and especially the Muslims who were in favour of the partition for practical as well as political reasons.

A champion of non-violence or Ahimsa, Tagore found it difficult to accept the insanity of the nationalists in their burning of all foreign goods as a mark of non-cooperation, although it was hurting the poor in Bengal who found homemade products more expensive than foreign goods. He was further disheartened to see that many of the impassioned youths turned to the cuit of the bomb, hoping to liberate their motherland from the yoke of foreign tyranny by violence and terror. Thus, finally, Tagore withdrew from the movement, when a young Bengali radical, Khudiram Bose, hurled a bomb, killing two innocent British civilians, in 1908.

This sudden withdrawal of Tagore was seen as an act of betrayal by many of the nationalists, but nothing could alter his decision. He would not have anything to do with a movement that was hijacked by the Bengali Bhadroloks (elites) for their vested interest, and that saw the individual through the prism of a giant Cause. Tagore's response to his critics was fictionally articulated in both The Home and the World and Four Chapters.

In both the novels, Tagore dramatises how exploitation, violence and killing become ritual acts when the individual sacrifices his/her self to an abstraction, and nationalism is put on a pedestal, sacrificing righteousness and conscience; how the nationalist movements in Bengal and later, during Gandhi's Satyagraha movement, in India, often veered into terrorist movements because of the excessiveness of the nationalist leaders, and sometimes their tendency to abuse the movement for personal political gain, as, for example, do both Sandip and Indranath, respectively in The Home and the World and Four Chapters.

Both Sandip and Indranath, begin as charismatic nationalist figures, but gradually become self-obsessed and vainglorious in their cause, losing sight of their dharma of dispassionate, disinterested action (as advised by Krishna to Arjuna in The Bhagavad Gita), and use violence as a fetish for personal gain; thus their early optimism is replaced later by a sense of nada.

Tagore and Gandhi were on friendly terms, and in many ways Tagore was a precursor of Gandhi; it was Tagore who gave the title "Mahatma" (the great soul) to Gandhi, and in return Gandhi dubbed Tagore "Gurudev" (the venerable teacher) and greeted him as "poet of the world." Romain Rolland once described a meeting between Tagore and Gandhi as one between "a philosopher and an apostle, a St. Paul and a Plato". Yet Tagore and Gandhi never saw eye to eye on the way towards India's future, as Tagore stubbornly refused to support Gandhi's nationalist movement against the British rule.

Unlike Gandhi, Tagore believed that political freedom and attainment of a nationalist identity by driving the British out was not the right solution for India's problems; "I am not for thrusting off Western civilization and becoming segregated in our independence. Let us have a deep association", he said in his characteristic hopefulness. In a letter to an American lawyer Myron H. Phelps, he rhetorically stated, "Must we not have that greater vision of humanity which will impel us to shake off the fetters that shackle our individual life before we begin to dream of national freedom?".

Tagore took the view that what India needed was not a "blind revolution" or the "miracle of freedom [built] upon the quicksand of social slavery", "but steady purposeful education", or an evolution from within; "what India most needed was constructive work coming from within herself," he argued in "Nationalism in India". He believed that a "thought impetus" similar to the one experienced by Europe during the Renaissance that broke up "the feudal system and the tyrannical conventionalism of the Latin Church" was the right remedy for a country languishing on the "dry sand-bed of dead customs".

Tagore maintained that India's immediate problems were social and cultural and not political. India is the world in miniature, this is where the races and the religions have met; therefore she must constantly strive to resolve her "burden of heterogeneity," by evolving out of "these warring contradictions a great synthesis". First and foremost, India must address the caste issue.

The caste system has become too rigid and taken a hypnotic hold on the mind of the people; what was once meant to introduce social order by accommodating the various racial groups in India, has now become a gigantic system of cold-blooded repression. India ought to come out of this social stagnation by educating the people out of their trance; only when the immovable walls of society were removed, or made flexible, will India regain her vitality and dynamism as a society and find true freedom. What is the purpose of political freedom when the elites in society are exploiting the lower classes, especially the untouchables so ruthlessly?

In his short story, "Purification," he exposes the absurdity of Gandhi's Satyagraha movement and the hypocrisy of the Indian nationalists by showing how selfish and superficial the nationalists were in their quest for freedom; they were fervently opposed to the British oppression, but oppressed the poor as well as the untouchables themselves; they wanted dignity and respect but wouldn't allow the same to their less fortunate brethren.

Kalika, a young wife and a nationalist dogmatist, who badgers her husband, a moderate but sensitive person, for not being fervent enough, refuses to come to the aid of an old municipal sweeper, who is being assaulted by a group of orthodox Hindus for accidentally touching someone in the crowd, just because he is an untouchable. Such "mendicant politics" that fails to tear down the customary barriers between people, was of little worth to Tagore. His hope was that if India could establish equanimity between the various races and religious groups, through a basis of social co-operation and regeneration of the spirit, then she could hold herself as a model of unity for the rest of the world.

Tagore emphasises racial and religious unity persistently in his writings. In a beautiful hymn to India, entitled Bharat Tirtha ("The Indian Pilgrimage"), he urges all Indians to unite across race, class and religion, shedding their differences, to fulfil the noble destiny of their homeland, standing above the whirlwind of dusty politics:

> Come, O Aryans, come, non-Aryans, Hindus and Mussulmans-
>
> Come today, O Englishmen, come, Oh come, Christians!
>
> Come, O Brahmin, cleansing your mind
>
> Join hands with all-
>
> Come, O Downtrodden, let the burden
>
> Of every insult be forever dispelled.
>
> Make haste and come to Mother's coronation, the vessel auspicious
>
> Is yet to be filled
>
> With sacred water sanctified by the touch of all
>
> By the shore of the sea of Bharat's Great Humanity!

Tagore was of the view that such unity and plurality of consciousness could be achieved only through proper education of the people, eradication of poverty through modernisation and cultivation of freedom of thought and imagination; "Freedom of mind is needed for the reception of truth", he said. It was education, and not adulation for the Charka (the spinning wheel) that Gandhi suggested, which could liberate India from the tyranny of the past and the towering misery of unreasoned, unbridled orthodoxy.

When Gandhi chastised Tagore for his disregard for the Charka as well as Swaraj saying, "Every one must spin. Let Tagore spin like the others. Let him burn his foreign clothes; that is his duty today. God will take care of the morrow", Tagore respectfully replied, "The charka does not require anyone to think; one simply turns the wheel of the antiquated invention endlessly, using the minimum of judgment and stamina".

To break the spell of stasis through intellectual/ cultural revival and find freedom, India ought to keep itself open to the West and not become insular from the rest of the world through the appropriation of a provincial nationalism; "We of the Orient should learn from the Occident . . . to say that it is wrong to cooperate with the West is to encourage the worst form of provincialism and can produce nothing but intellectual indigence".

The West could in fact help liberate India from its "mind-forg'd manacles" and lift the dead weight of tradition from its soul through a constructive engagement and inducement of energy, strength, elasticity, tolerance, resolve and courage among its people-qualities that the West possessed but India lacked.

Tagore's vision of a free India-free from the fetters of materialism, nationalism as well as religious and racial orthodoxy-actively seeking a common destiny with the rest of mankind, constantly evolving towards a global society, is most ardently and expressly expressed in the following poem in Gitanjali, written in the form of a supplication:

> Where the mind is without fear and the head is held high;
>
> Where knowledge is free;
>
> Where the world has not been broken up into fragments
> by narrow domestic walls;
>
> Where words come from the depth of truth;

> Where tireless striving stretches its arms towards perfection;
>
> Where the clear stream of reason has not lost its way into the dreary desert sand of dead habit;
>
> Where the mind is led forward by thee into ever widening thought and action-
>
> Into that heaven of freedom, my Father, let my country awake. (27-28)

Tagore could perhaps be faulted for impracticality; his vision for India was too sublime and unrealisable in an imperfect world. His wish that the West could help India in her mission was also impracticable, especially since he knew that the West came to the subcontinent, as he recounted in his essay "East and West," "not with the imagination and sympathy to create and unite, but with a shock of passion-passion for power and wealth". West had its own axe to grind; in spite of their "superior force of character", they were not interested in the "nest-building of truth" but in money, machine and matter. Yet his transcendent thought provides a testament to his noble and beautiful mind, and strikes a cord in the moral person in each of us.

Moreover, the on-going violence in the subcontinent vindicates his position. India has since been broken up into three countries: India, Pakistan and Bangladesh; ten million people were made homeless in the aftermath of the independence of India and Pakistan in 1947, one million of which also lost their lives in inter-religious riots; two major wars have been fought in the subcontinent, with border skirmishes and threats of further wars, including a nuclear war, casting a shadow of desperation on the people; several riots have also broken out between the Hindus and the Muslims, claiming thousands of lives. India still remains a poor country, with political corruption rife, and plights of the downtrodden a daily reality.

Tagore's prediction that joining the bandwagon of nationalism would make India a beggar of the West has also come true. Although India is a free country now (ironically broken up into three fragments), the appropriation of nationalist ideology has erased the sense of India's difference as a society, capable of standing on its own; forging of links with the West on unequal terms (since India has merely copied the Western thoughts and has nothing to offer of her own) has allowed neo-colonialist controls to operate over the country both explicitly and implicitly, spelling political and cultural doom for its people.

Finally, India's assumption of a separate identity by driving the British out has also dealt a blow to the possible realisation of Tagore's vision for "one world," at least for the time being, since anti-colonial nationalism also carries the seeds of provincialism and cultural particularism.

13

Concept of Quality Education

In ancient and medieval systems, education was a privilege which usually went with elites, and by itself conveyed quality or distinction. The legend of Eklavya, which figures in the Indian epic, the Mahabharata, illustrates the association between education and elites with cruel precision. In this story, a tribal boy is openly denied the opportunity to learn archery from a famous teacher who was appointed to train the local princes. Refusing to be discouraged, the tribal boy attains mastery by selfpractice, in the symbolic presence of a clay idol of the famous teacher. When this secret self-training is found out one day, the teacher asks the boy to cut off his right thumb and give it as a ritual gift. This way, the teacher reinstates the social order which allowed only the royal sons to receive archery instruction of the highest quality.

Modernity has disturbed the hierarchical principle of the distribution of educational opportunities. The pervasive impact of modernisation continues to unfold worldwide; the unfolding has not ended even in the fully industrialised societies where universalization of literacy and basic education started in the 19th century, in response to the needs of industrialization and the socio-political and cultural dynamics it had triggered. One major dimension of the impact is the question of quality:

how to conceptualize and maintain it so that it becomes a universal privilege during childhood. Clearly, the question is linked to the ideal of protecting childhood as an experience from the distressful and highly reproductive commonplaces of the human condition, such as the inequalities and injustices of different kinds.

For the industrially advanced or, in that sense, developed societies, the quality of education during childhood has presented the challenge of 'social efficiency', a term used by Dewey in his classic, Democracy and Education to convey a high rate of participation and communication. Despite the availability of economic resources, the developed world can hardly be said to have achieved the goal of nullifying the association between quality and status.

In most parts of the late-industrialising world, particularly in the regions affected by the political economy of colonialism, the tension between quality and equality remains a strong obstacle to social and policy change. The late J.P. Naik, the architect of modern educational planning in India, nicely captured this tension in the sub-title of his Tagore lectures delivered in 1975. Referring to the contrary pulls working on educational policy in the shape of demands and resistance, he called equality, quality and quantity an 'elusive triangle'.

Concern for Quality

Concern for quality has remained vague and poorly anchored in social theory. The processes and imperatives associated with global competitiveness in the face of rapid technological change and financial uncertainty have taken their toll on children's right to grow up and be educated in a protective ethos. The problems are not entirely new, but seem greatly compounded by the use of the market as the sole reference point for judging the worth of an idea or policy.

Since knowledge and training are so critical as factors in the current political economy, education at every level is being called upon to be market-oriented and market-worthy. This situation has created the apprehension that the concept of education itself may be in a state of crisis. The late Basil Bernstein, one of the most influential sociologists of education in the 20th century, explained the crisis by referring to the lengthening shadow of marketing managers:

> The principles of the market and its managers are more and more the managers of the policy and practices of education. Market relevance is becoming the key orientating criterion for the selection of discourses, their relation to each other, their forms and their research. This movement has profound implications from the primary school to the university. This can be seen in the stress on basic measurable skills at the primary level, vocational courses and specialisations at the secondary level, spurious decentralisation, and the new instruments of state control over higher education and research.
>
> (Bernstein, 1996, p87)

Bernstein's concerns give us a quick sense of the scale at which we need to worry about quality in the context of education, and to warn us how wrong it would be to limit our concerns and discussion to the developing countries alone. The current concern for quality has its immediate origins in the idea of globalisation, particularly in the uncertainties associated with it. There is no consensus on what globalisation constitutes, what it implies for education, and what its future might be.

Moreover, the discourse of globalisation has been changing with unexpected speed. The bold, often romantic pronouncements made in the immediate aftermath of the collapse of the Soviet Union have been replaced by more cautious remarks. The competition among nation-states for resources, both natural and human, has exacerbated, along with an increase in aggression and violence. The relationship between economic growth, employment and well being, between knowledge and opportunities, and between prosperity and security has become vague if not inscrutable.

More disturbingly, it has become unclear whether modernity-with its emphasis on reason, individuality and democracy-is a viable ideal for more than a small fraction of humanity. The uncertainties, the volatility, and the stress of competitiveness associated with globalisation are reflected in the manner in which quality is being defined and applied in the context of education.

Commoditization of knowledge and the perception of the student as a product are not new: these were implied in the linking of institutionalised education with the industrial economy. Similarly, the idea of education as a means of human resource development is not new. These perceptions of the role of education are integral aspects of modernisation under capitalism. What is new is the extreme pressure under which the value-system of modernity has come under advanced capitalism.

The role of education as an aspect of the culture of modernity-with is emphasis on equality, dignity of the individual, and room for social justice-has faced unprecedented stress during the recent phase of global history. The concept of 'globalisation' does not offer much help to make sense of this recent history; at best, it highlights the issues we need to study hard and attend to in the real world. Some of the issues have a direct relevance to education, especially to distinguishing education of a certain quality from one which signifies no more than token access to a service provided by the state or a non-government agency.

Perhaps the two most important issues we need to probe are the relationship between education and work, and between education and culture. The first deserves our concern because the new processes of production and economic management do not warrant the customary linking of education with a stable opportunity to work for a career and self -development. As Smith discusses, the idea of work as a source of satisfaction and dignity is not relevant to the emerging corporate culture of production.

Franklin perceives the roots of this development in the social formations of technology. A renowned physicist, Franklin makes a strong plea for revisiting the debates on the social character of technological choices as a way to overcome the economic and moral dilemmas of our times. She also distinguishes between 'growth' and 'product' models of learning, and finds the former to be of higher value.

The second key issue that globalisation has brought to the fore is the relationship between education and culture. In theoretical terms, it is a subset of the relationship between modernisation and culture. As Dube points out, early theorists and planners of modernisation neglected culture, with the consequence that assertion of ethnic identities grew under the nose of modern institutions.

Localism, in this sense, is as manifest today as globalism, and modernity seems rather inadequate for making an appeal for reason in either sphere. As a means of disseminating the skills of reasoning, education continues to offer the promise of modernity, but on the condition that sustained security will be available. Education signifies for many a desperate means of coping with the intensely competitive, highly insecure global situation.

Recent Phenomena

That, precisely, is the core of many current attempts to

define and apply the idea of 'quality' in the context of education. Cross-national comparative studies of student achievement are not a recent phenomena, but the purpose of such exercises has changed, from academic to practical. The most ambitious exercise of this kind currently underway is the Programme for International Student Assessment (PISA) started in 1997 by the OECD on the basis of shared, policy-driven interests of member countries and a few others.

The PISA studies aim at enabling national policy-makers to compare the performance of their education systems with that of other countries. This explicitly practical orientation of PISA studies, which distinguishes them from earlier and ongoing work of the International Association for the Evaluation of Educational Achievement (IEA), can be seen as a response to the association discussed above between globalisation and the inevitability of intense economic competition among nation-states.

The PISA framework defines 'quality' in terms of students' academic achievement at age 15 and the factors which explain achievement scores. Three broad curricular spheres are the focus of assessment: rending, mathematics and science. However, problem-solving skills which have cross-disciplinary origins and application are also covered and some attention is being paid to student background and home environment.

'Quality' is also the concern of the Latin American Laboratory set up in 1994 as a network of national systems. The largest study undertaken by it so far focused on grade 3 and 4 children of primary schools in Latin America and the Caribbean, Home-related factors and pedagogical process were also taken into account in this study which attempted to conceptualise an 'ideal' school by analysing teachers' perception of their profession and earnings, the involvement of parents in schoolrelated matters, and the classroom ethos.

The Latin American Laboratory, thus, takes a wider view of quality, linking it not merely with outcomes or student performance, but to some extent, with the values reflected in the school environment. Taken together, PISA and Latin America Laboratory studies encourage us to characterise quality as an attribute reflected in the learner as a product of an educational system. These studies add a few to the parameters developed earlier under the IEA studies.

One of the latest IEA concerns is the assessment of children's achievement in civic education, an area related to the cultural anxieties aroused by globalisation. The issue of culture-sensitivity has also been raised in the context of language testing at the primary level in French-speaking African countries under a post-Jomtien initiative. The post-Jomtien discourse of quality uses it as a criterion for judging the depth of access-related claims made by governments. Bloom and Cohen claim that 'in many areas, official statistics disguise fundamenal flaws and...reveal little about the quality of education.'

School effectiveness and a holistic framework of education have been presented as alternatives to measurable-outcome view of quality. This usage of quality often carries a moral overtone, reminding us that the expansion of access refers to the children, especially girls, of marginalised and oppressed groups. The system's ability to educate them depends on the new strategies it adopts. Several reports perceive this exigency in terms of 'inclusion' -a term that directly suggests a responsibility to reshape a system which has so far functioned as an instrument of exclusion, in an economic as well as cultural sense.

The association of 'quality' with the inclusive capacity of a system becomes all the more relevant when we notice the parallel growth of privatisation. The policies followed in many developing as well as developed countries since the early 1980s have encouraged privatisation of education at all levels. Privately run institutions thrive on the popular assumption that whatever is not under state control must be of some quality.

The popularity and power of this assumption can be estimated from the endorsement it has received from India's Supreme Court in an important judgment concerning minority rights. Sadly, we have hardly any studies comparing state schools with privately managed schools in matters like quality of infrastructure, the performance and capacities of teachers, and the involvements of parents. This is surprising in view of the awareness of the possibility that unrecognised private schools may be siphoning off the children, especially boys, of the marginally better-off strata of rural society in many parts of India.

Theoretical Caution

This brief discussion of recent studies suggests that 'globalisation'-with its paradoxes, contradictions and insecurities-may have provided us with a valuable opportunity for addressing an elusive concept. The need to think about it has been there for a long time, but the circumstances pushing us to do so were less universal earlier. The temptation to judge the quality of education as we might judge the quality of, say, a factory, a hotel or a car, is strong. Not only is the market discourse of quality currently in high fashion; it is also compelling, to the extent that it relates to the images of the good life pervading all spheres of what we might call the global civilization of modernity.

The overwhelming presence of market metaphors in our times requires what Taylor calls 'epistemological precautions' in the use of quality-control as a metaphor for educational reform. Without such precautions, we can easily miss the consequences that outcometesting may have for classroom teaching and curriculum development. The view of teaching as an outcome-oriented activity could squander the hard work done over decades in certain countries to popularize the constructivist paradigm of education which is derived from Piaget's theory of knowledge. The culture of management has also weakened the humanistic models of curriculum design, and has led to behaviourist revivalism.

The point is not so much to challenge the claim that the market represents the modern reality-perhaps it would be futile to refute such a claim-but rather to expand the scope of quality-related concerns. In an attempt to do this, Malkova points out that the anxieties triggered by the competitive environment of today's technocratic society ought to include certain concerns which cannot be allayed within a technocratic paradigm of educational reform, which focuses on children's achievement in science and mathematics. These other concerns refer to the wider context of childhood, mental health and peace. The definition of quality proposed by her refers quality as "a system of socially determined parameters of the level of knowledge, skills, habits and values that must be reached by school levers".

We can derive a similar perspective from the Indian philosopher J. Krishnamurti. In a dialogue on education and world peace, he perceives the competitive, highly individualistic and nationalistic education given today as a threat to peace at all levels-personal, social and global. Peace may be an important precondition for the reform of education in view of the contradiction Stephens underlines in his analysis of the quality of primary education in developing countries:

> The situation of primary education in most developing countries is not good. In many countries poverty, child malnutrition and ill-health are advancing again after decades of steady retreat. And, although the reasons are many and complex, overshadowing all is the stark fact that the governments of the developing world as a whole have now reached the point of devoting half of their total annual expenditures to the maintenance of the military and the servicing of debt...
>
> (Stephens, 1991; p223)

Stephens links quality in education with the quality of decisionmaking and reminds us, following Bowles, that decision making in the educational system is 'a sensitive barometer of power relations in society.' This kind of awareness of the social foundations of education may well be the main missing element in the current research and debates on quality.

The senior American educator Seymour B. Sarason draws upon Dewey's presidential address to the American Psychological Association a century ago where he made two points: one, education and its problems must be conceptualised and embedded in the social sciences, or else the inadequacies of education will not be understood; and two, the fruits of research and theory-building must be made known to teachers and other practitioners.

Applied as criteria, Dewey's points reveal the roots of the confusion we see in the contemporary literature on quality improvement and in the efforts to transform the grim reality. Sarason also makes the plea that we should learn to view the system of education as a whole, not in terms of its specialised parts, but as a structure of interrelated parts.

The analysis of education in the lateindustrialising countries by Dore offers fine evidence of the advantage of taking such a systemic view. By juxtaposing the relative role of the school and higher level institutions with economic growth and employment data, Dore has been able to put forward the powerful thesis that the quality of school education cannot be improved unless the urge for qualification-gathering relents.

Framework

As we attempt to develop an encompassing framework of quality, we should remember that the issue of quality is as old as education itself. As a tool of comparison, it was always available to those concerned about the ways in which education might be given or used.

In the Republic, Plato uses the phrase 'better and more complete education', suggesting that there is education of different levels of quality, not merely different kinds of education. Similarly, the Buddha's discourse indicates the significance of correctness in the choice of knowledge and ways of teaching it, for an incorrect choice could be dangerous. This idea impels us to include aims and assumption in our framework for conceptualising quality in education.

In his classic work on curriculum research and development, the late Lawrence Stenhouse located the central problem of education in the appreciation of its relation to culture. As a means of widening the scope of our communicational universe, Stenhouse argues, education directly affects human relations, both in terms of individuals and groups. Education enhances our freedom and creativity inasmuch as it ushers us into culture-our own as well as others'-as a system to think with.

Distinguishing three processes in school education-namely, training, instruction, and induction- Stenhouse says that "education as induction into knowledge is successful to the extent that it makes the behavioural outcomes of the student unpredictable". Stenhouse argues that the outcomes-approach to the assessment of quality weakens our appreciation of the teacher's role and capacities as a judge of quality; it also forces us to take an instrumental, and necessarily trivialising, view of knowledge. At a time when we see people frantically assembling indicators of quality in order to carry out large-scale achievement surveys, we can hope to profit greatly, both in terms of direction and ideas, by revisiting Stenhouse.

India's Educational Experience

India's experience in education over the second half of the 20th century is a useful resource available to us for studying the issue of quality. As a case study of improvement in the quality of education, India is particularly interesting because of the democratic character of its struggle against colonial role and the sustenance of democratic governance afterward, in the face of bewildering internal and external difficulties. India also offers a unique philosophical resource in this context.

The political leadership of Gandhi and the intellectual leadership of Tagore made significant contributions to the success of India's anti-colonial struggle and development. Both Gandhi and Tagore were deeply interested in educational change, and they launched exciting ventures in educational reform. Discussions of India's educational system tend to focus on its endemic problems and the contradictions it faces in relation to the social structure. This familiar trend is easy to understand, given India's unimpressive achievement in literacy and primary education.

The familiar portrayal of India's educational reality arouses no curiosity about the energies put into innovative reform. For this reason, our discussion of

India's educational experience starts with two stories of major attempts made to improve the quality of education; namely, the programme of Basic Education (BE) undertaken in the first decade of independence and the Hoshangabad Science Teaching Programme (HSTP), which started in the early 1970's and closed as recently as 2002.

Nai Talim

BE was inspired by Mahatma Gandhi's proposal for nai talim (literally, new education), first announced in 1937, a decade before India won its independence from colonial rule. Adopted as state policy after independence and Gandhi's assassination, BE entered into a full-scale, stringent testing of its key ideas.

The most important among these ideas was the incorporation of manual work or handson experience of a productive craft in the core curriculum of primary schools. This was a radical idea, not only in pedagogic terms, but, and far more crucially, in social terms too, given the caste framework of Indian society which legitimises derision for manual work by linking it with the lower castes and others stigmatised by exclusion from the hierarchy of castes.

The other important ideas were integration of the knowledge given under different subjects with the learning of handicrafts and the use of the child's mother-tongue as the medium of instruction. All of these ideas contradicted the curriculum and pedagogic practices entrenched since colonial days, some drawing strength from older cultural beliefs about learning. BE challenged rote learning, the dominance of the prescribed textbook as a pedagogic tool, and the practice of examining by asking children to regurgitate memorised facts. It met stiff resistance from not only teachers who were trained in traditional didactics, but also from politicians, bureaucrats and publishers of textbooks.

The critics of BE invoked structural issues like parity of basic and nonbasic schools, the difficulties of stretching basic education upwards to the secondary grades which were oriented towards a public examination of memorising and writing skills. A great deal of regional variation was characteristic of BE, and that was perfectly consistent with its philosophy, but India's educational planners failed to foresee a rapid erosion of faith in Gandhi's philosophy even as India entered the turbulent decade of the 1960s in which it faced two wars with its neighbours, two successive years of famine, the death of two prime ministers (one of whom is rightly known as the builder of modern India), and a historic break-up of the Congress Party under whose leadership India had won independence.

No single factor can explain why BE was abandoned as a policy. However, its best achievements do underline the importance of political and ideological support for any educational innovation. In terms of quality and commitment, the implementation of BE varied a great deal, an important factor being the contribution of voluntary or non-government institutions. BE triggered fresh thinking on curriculum development and teacher training, though the dearth of good 'basic trained' teachers remained a chronic problem. A dent was made, in many regions and institutions, in the old system of 'normal school' training, and attention was paid to the challenge of bridging the gap between intellectual and manual work.

The realisation that the hands-on experience of making or doing something serves multiple developmental purposes in children's lives had revolutionary potential in a society accustomed to regarding manual work with upper-caste contempt. This was Gandhi's subtle formula for bringing about a change in attitudes. It worked so long as there was a conducive ethos to uphold its functioning. Such an ethos existed in many parts of India in the decade following independence, apparently as a residue of the headier ethos produced by the struggle for independence under Gandhi's leadership.

The state too felt a moral responsibility to keep Gandhi's legacy alive by giving it an ideological support in the face of widespread scepticism and resistance. In the mid-1960s, when the state's positive bias gave way to pressures favouring mechanistic modernisation of agricultural productivity, enthusiasm for BE dried up. In its memory, a slot of 'work experience' was carved into the old-style, textbook-based curriculum of secondary classes. With no responsibility left to provide any hands-on experience, the primary school returned to being what it had been.

Bal Vaigyanik

Our second story of innovation, the HSTP was initiated in the early 1970s by two voluntary agencies, namely Kishore Bharati and the Friend's Rural Centre; later on, it became the responsibility of Eklavya. The well-entrenched tradition of voluntary work in India has seldom meddled with state-run schools. Things are changing now, but traditionally voluntary institutions have shown indifference to the state system. HSTP presents the lone instance since independence wherein a voluntary initiative made a radical large-scale intervention in state schools.

The scale of this intervention was narrow at the beginning: 8 rural middle schools (with Grades VI to VIII, corresponding roughly to ages 11 to 13) of Hoshangabad district of Madhya Pradesh (MP); but this number rapidly increased from the late 1970s onwards, reaching the figure of 1000 schools spread over several adjoining districts in the course of the next decade. HSTP had three dimensions:

i) Preparation of new, experiment-based textbooks with kits, both reflecting the immediate, rural milieu in choice of topics to be studied and the design of equipment and lessons;

ii) Training of existing government school teachers of science in the new methods which focussed on children's own discovery of ideas, explanation, and new questions; virtually prohibiting old-style teaching without hands-on experience;

iii) Designing of new assessment techniques, replacing the memory-based examination taken at the end of the year.

Undertaking these tasks in collaboration with the government was the key challenge. The HSTP pulled off this unique feat in India's educational history with exemplary liaison-management, but also because its legitimacy was impressively tied to the status of some of India's best known institutions of higher learning in science and technology. In all aspects of decision-making and execution, HSTP was closely assisted by members of the faculty of prestigious national institutions like Tata Institute of Fundamental Research, Indian Institute of Technology, and a core group of the Departments of Physics and Chemistry at the University of Delhi, apart from several individual teachers of the colleges and universities based in MP.

The mobilisation of institutional support with the help of the University Grants Commission (UGC) was also unique. It was a dream come true, exactly as it had been envisaged by India's most ambitious document on educational reform, i.e. the report of the Kothari commission (1964-66) entitled Education and National

Development (NCERT, 1971). HSTP demonstrated that university faculty and school teachers could work together for improvement in the quality of children's classroom experience.

We can recognise three broad lessons in the innovative attempts we have briefly studied; one, the socio-political ethos has a decisive role in sustaining innovative effort; two, institutions of higher learning can play a major part in the reform of school education; and three, voluntary or non-government institutions are an important resource for new ideas and methods. Both stories of innovation remind us how tenacious a challenge the 'system' or the status quo presents.

BE and HSTP were aimed at changing the social character of school learning and thereby improving the quality-of education available to rural children. Social barriers of caste, class and gender have long been known to impede the progress of education in rural India. These barriers act in complex ways, affecting curriculum policy as well as the daily life of the school. BE and HSTP attempted to transcend the interplay of such negative forces, one by anchoring a new curriculum in the radical perspective of Gandhi, and the other by insisting that a theoretical understanding of the epistemology of science must guide the teaching of school science.

Larger Picture

For a country of India's size and complexity two brief case studies can hardly suffice, in an illustrative sense, to encapsulate what the process of change constitutes. We must remain cautious and prepared to appreciate the scale of the task involved in reforming a vast system so as to equip it better to meet an elusive goal. That goal was enunciated in the Constitution of India as the construction of a liberal society based on democracy and social justice. The Constitution presented a transformative vision of governance and it named education as an important means of realising that vision.

Universalising literacy and elementary education was an inevitable responsibility attached to the fulfillment of the vision. When we review the second half of 20th century from the perspective of the Indian Constitution, we are forced to recognise the extraordinary challenges that democracy has had to face, but we are also struck by the formidable difficulties that education, as a means of serving and strengthening democracy, has presented to the state.

Any attempt to obtain an overview of India's performance in education is likely to be constrained by the multiplicity of factors affecting our judgement. In the mid-1970s, J.P. Naik, to whom a reference was made earlier, attempted to present an overview. He was better qualified than anyone else one can think of to undertake such an exercise, given his key role as a participant in decision-making and his socially committed perspective. His assessment of India's educational performance in the first quarter-century of its independence was the following:

> (T)he pursuit of quality has often linked itself with privilege and become inimical to that of quantity; the pursuit of quantity, in its turn, has often led to a deterioration of standards, and the pursuit of equality, in its turn, has often led to a deterioration of standards, and the pursuit of equality has often found to the inimical to that of quality, and has been frequently hampered by the very inequalities in society which it was intended to remove. We have tried to reconcile the inevitable conflicts with little result. . .
>
> Has the pursuit of these goals of equality, quality and quantity in education made any impact on the social structure and rendered it less stratified and hierarchical or more egalitarian? The answer probably is that the impact

> of education on the basic features of the social structure has been rather limited.
>
> (Naik, 1975, p. 4)

The question whether education has served a transformative role in relation to the social order and the values underpinning it has inspired considerable scholarship in the recent decades, but the answer has remained elusive and ambivalent. In the mid-1980s, the government initiated a national debate on education by releasing a document titled The Challenge of Education. This document portrayed a picture of stagnation in elementary education, both in terms of the system's reach and quality. Indeed, the slowing down of the growth of enrolment is perceived as a consequence of poor quality, and both these tendencies are discussed in the context of the widening of economic and social divide between the poor and the elites.

The 1986 National Policy of Education (NPE) promised the upgradation of school facilities and the application of child-centred methods among the steps to be taken for enhancing retention and improving quality. The policy continues to be in operation-having survived a period of considerable political and cultural anxiety-but many significant changes have occurred in the arrangements through which the system works. At the beginning of the 1990s a newly elected central government decided to overcome an acute fiscal crisis by opting for structural adjustment and social safety net policies which brought external financial resources-both loan and aid-for improving the quality of elementary education and universalising its reach.

New approaches and procedures were developed in successive, rapidly covered stages. These included administrative decentralisation, creation of local-level structures for planning, decision making and monitoring, and the involvement of non-government organisations. A massive drive to improve school buildings, reorganise the curriculum and recruit and train teachers at the local level was launched.

The outcomes of these strategies are not yet fully understood, and many of them are being currently debated even as the effort to conserve the visible gains made in the first phase of externally-supported District Primary Education Programme (DPEP). Measures like para-teachers have permitted certain states to increase the number of schools (or alternative structures) quite radically during a period of financial crunch. Para-teachers are locally recruited; they receive a far lower salary than regular teachers, their training is short, and their services are vulnerable.

School teaching is regarded in India as a low-status occupation; its status has now plummeted further. The efficacy of new arrangements like para-teachers and monitoring by the community need to be debated and researched. In curricular debates, an ideological thrust, favouring religio-cultural nationalism, has surfaced and, this development too has been all but ignored in quality-related discussions, which have focused mainly on the learner achievement under the new arrangements associated with DPEP.

As far as the government is concerned, it has assumed the legitimacy of these arrangements, taking advantage of the recent amendment made in the constitution which confers on all children of 6-14 years a fundamental right to receive education through a school or its alternative. In any case, the NPE had already equated non-formal education with formal schooling as a valid instrument of universalisation of elementary education.

Traditionally, the Indian system has depended on the use of public or centralised examination as a means to evaluate students and to select the ones who can proceed further. The examinations taken at the end of grade X and XII are characterised by high rates of failure, which is seen as a sign of rigour and quality. The national average of success rates in these two examinations are less than 50% for grade X, and less than 60% for grade XII. In many states, children appear for district-level centralised examination at grade V and VIII levels, but there is no national-level database about the results of these examinations.

An important feature of the 1990s is the conduct of large-scale surveys of children's learning achievement made under the auspices of DPEP. These surveys have been carried out mostly in accordance with a curricular document which outlines minimum levels of learning (NCERT, 1990) in each subject.

The minimalist idea is consistent with, and to a great extent constitutes a response to, the demand for accountability made over the recent years in projects funded by external agencies. Such a demand has inadvertently promoted the outcome-oriented approach in teacher training and the preparation of curriculum material like textbooks. Under the rudimentary conditions of most Indian schools, such an approach tends to showcase and prioritise attendance figures and test-scores, often at the expense of the teacher's commitment to children and confidence to be honest.

14

Vision of Neo-universalism

Tagore, a multifaceted genius, a darling of versatility, was the most respected name in the literary-cultural world during his lifetime, in both the East and West. He was not only the first Asian to receive the Nobel Prize for Literature 'but also only the second writer in English to receive it'.

Fondly dubbed 'Gurudev' (venerable teacher) by Mahatma Gandhi (whose title 'Mahatma,' or 'the great soul' was suitably given by Tagore) and 'eagle-sized lark' by Romain Rolland, his exquisite poetic power and gifted musical sensibility made him the author of the national anthems of three countries - Bangladesh, Sri Lanka and India - a feat still unmatched in history. He was knighted by King George V of England in 1915 (which he renounced in protest of the heinous massacre at Jalianwalla Bagh, Amritsar in 1919) and awarded an honorary doctorate by Oxford in 1940, for which Oxford had to travel to the poet's doorstep because of his ill health.

When Tagore was alive, he played on the heartstrings of many with his wizard fingers and breathtaking creativity. On reading Tagore's Gitanjali, a volume of poetry that earned him the Nobel Prize for Literature, W.B. Yeats was so moved by the 'simplicity' and 'abundance' of his work that he instantaneously hailed Tagore as founder of a 'new Indian Renaissance,' and said in an extraordinary tribute to the poet:

> [The poems of] Rabindranath Tagore have stirred my blood as nothing has for years ...These lyrics ...display in their thought a world I have dreamed all my life ... Rabindranath Tagore ...is so abundant, so spontaneous, so daring in his passion, so full of surprise, because he is doing something which has never seemed strange, unnatural, or in need of defence. These verses will not die in little well-printed books upon ladies' tables ...or be carried about by students at the university to be laid aside when the work of life begins, but as the generations pass, travellers will hum them on the highway and men rowing upon rivers. Lovers, while they await one another, shall find, in murmuring them, this love of God a magic gulf wherein their own more bitter passion may bathe and renew its youth.

Tagore's reputation far exceeded the boundary of the literary-cultural world. He was in the company of the likes of Russell, Einstein, Mussolini and Gandhi, and they all held him in the highest esteem. Albert Schweitzer called him 'the Goethe of India',and Romain Rolland described a meeting between him and Gandhi as a 'meeting between...a St. Paul and a Plato'. So why has Tagore's reputation suffered since his death? Why is the poet who was considered a literary titan in his time, a supreme symbol of India's culture and spirit, now so widely neglected? Is it because of some change of taste in poetry? As Tagore has aptly said, 'poetry is...a matter of taste'. Or is it because Tagore was too provincial a poet to retain a universal appeal after his death?

Perhaps the reasons are not so much poetical but ideological and philosophical, for Tagore was a poet-philosopher and the world simply chose not to tread the path that he sought to pave. Tagore's vision of universal human unity, of 'living bonds in society'; of 'spontaneous expression of man as a social being'; of 'wholeness and wholesomeness of human ideals', proved too good for a world that believed in the 'bondage of the dust,' the tyranny of matter, machine and money, and in the fetish of nationalism. According to Tagore, such 'ideals' replace the true identity of the self with a blend of corporate identity, rooted not in truth, beauty, sympathy or moral welfare of mankind but in a 'spirit of conflict and conquest' and a whirlwind of greed, jealousy and suspicion, reducing mankind, Tagore poignantly suggests, to 'a pack of predatory creatures' or 'band of robbers'.

Critics are often apologetic when discussing Tagore, as though it is for some inherent weakness that he is neglected now; for instance, his lack of a proper understanding of the world, or his overlay mystical tone, which suggests a blindness to the realities of life. But such apologies are unnecessary - and Tagore is never in 'need of defence,' as Yeats rightfully said- since he stood for the totality of life, for the physical as well as the spiritual; for the real and the ideal; and for the values of truth, compassion and justice that the world will reckon its own, as soon as it chooses to break the current hypnotic allure of money and materialism, and rise from the dungeon of illusion.

Given the present crisis in the world, in which nations, fiercely locked in a devil-dance of destruction, are perpetuating cycles of retribution and retaliation, and hollow hysteria between fanatics of nation and fanatics of religion is taking its toll on innocent civilians everywhere, Tagore's alternative vision based on peace, harmony and the spiritual unity of humankind has become more relevant than ever. What the world needs at this juncture of widespread agitation and unrest is Tagore's healing message and the restoration of his blissful, paradisiacal imagination, imbued with teachings of simplicity, self-restraint and ahimsa, or nonviolence. Remembering

Tagore's advice in the 1915 lecture, "Nationalism in the West," which was delivered as the West was engrossed in the savage bloodbath of World War I, may help to instil some sense as our planet grapples afresh with the global ramifications of recent disastrous events that opened the doors to a new pandemonium:

> Be more good, more just, more true in your relation to man, control your greed, make your life wholesome in its simplicity and let your consciousness of the divine in humanity be more perfect in its expression.

Tagore's vision of human unity and equality, and his critique of modern civilisation, with its twin principles of materialism and nationalism, is recurrent in all his works. His vision emerges most explicitly and powerfully, however, in several of his lectures and addresses, including "My Life," "My School," "My Religion," "Civilisation and Progress," "Construction versus Creation," "Nationalism in India," "Nationalism in Japan," "Nationalism in the West," "International Relations," "The Voices of Humanity," and "The Realisation of the Infinite," as well as in his novels The Home and the World (Ghare Baire) and Four Chapters (Char Adhyay), the poems of Gitanjali and "The Sunset of the Century." In each of these works, Tagore most engagingly and energetically investigates what has gone wrong with the world and where the remedy lies.

Tagore was opposed to modern civilisation for its lack of completeness; its fragmented and fragmenting nature; its undue bias towards the physical, the intellectual and the practical; its predilection for the material rather than the moral progress of humankind; and its celebration of bloodless policies and canned, constructed ideas, in lieu of a fearless striving for truth, creativity and imagination. Modern civilisation, Tagore believed, is built on the law of necessity rather than the law of truth; the law of might instead of the law of right; and of self-interest and success, rather than perfection in humanity. In "Civilisation and Progress," he explains,

> Civilisation cannot merely be a growing totality of happenings that by chance have assumed a particular shape and tendency which we consider to be excellent. It must be the expression of some guiding moral force which we have evolved in our society for the object of attaining perfection ...A civilisation remains healthy and strong as long as it contains in its centre some creative ideal that binds its members in a rhythm of relationship. It is a relationship which is beautiful and not merely utilitarian. When the creative ideal which is dharma gives place to some overmastering passion, then this civilisation bursts into conflagration.

In other words, for its absence of a moral centre, this civilisation is, to Tagore, a civilisation of adhrama, in which, as he explains using a quote from the Upanishads, 'man prospers, gains what appears desirable, conquers enemies, but perishes at the root'. It both shoots out of and caters to the baser instincts of the individual and has nothing to do with that innate spiritual power that ennobles us and brings us together as one large family living in the reality and unity of one ineffable God. Thus, progress, as it is understood in the modern civilisation, is nothing but a millstone on the human spirit, bringing with it dehumanisation, despiritualisation, deformity and doom.

Tagore was essentially a religious thinker and he always upheld the primacy of the soul. In "My Religion," he emphasised, 'Man's religion is his innermost truth... One's religion is at the source of one's being'. However, he was not religious in the traditional sense and was least concerned with the practices of the communal religion he belonged to i.e. Hinduism. Rather, he was influenced by the teachings of the Upanishads and, like the English Romantics and American Transcendentalists before him, came to believe in its pantheistic teachings. In this regard, his first-hand influence was his father, a leading member of a religious movement called the Brahmo Samajwho, Tagore explains, believed in 'a strict monotheism based upon the teachings of the Upanishads'.

The Upanishadic God is, paradoxically, both transcendent and immanent; both present and absent in His creation. He is a Personality who does not dissociate Himself fully from His creation but recurrently manifests Himself in all created objects, making this world a 'living expression of the spirit'. In Svetasatara Upanishad, for example, God is described thus:

> O Brahman Supreme!
> Formless art thou, and yet
> (Though the reason none knows)
> Thou bringest forth many forms;
> Thou bringest them forth, and then
> Withdrawest them to thyself.
> Fill us with thoughts of thee!
> Thou art the fire,
> Thou art the sun,
> Thou art the air,
> Thou art the moon,
> Thou art the starry firmament:
> Thou art the waters - thou,
> The creator of all.

God is also present in every human heart: 'Self-luminous is Brahman, ever present in the hearts of all... In him exists all that is'.

The Upanishadic faith in a living God, a 'deep abiding creative force' as Tagore describes it - a force that expresses itself in the living objects of the world, including human begins - runs through all of his works and forms the cornerstone of his visvovod, or vision of universal human unity. His argument is simple: since God dwells in every human heart, we are innately inseparable, and to realise God we must therefore overcome the visible differences between us as individuals and learn to treat one another - in spite of caste, creed and race - with love and utmost respect. In "My Life," Tagore explains:

> In the night we stumble over things and become acutely conscious of their individual separateness, but the day reveals the great unity which embraces them. And the man, whose inner vision is bathed in an illumination of his consciousness, at once realises the spiritual unity reigning supreme over all differences of race, and his mind no longer awkwardly stumbles over individual facts of separateness in the human world, accepting them as final; he realises that peace is in the inner harmony which dwells in truth, and in any outer adjustments; that beauty carries an eternal assurance of our spiritual relationship to reality, which waits for its perfection in the response of our love.

In "International Relations," a lecture delivered in Japan, in 1923, he further affirms that:

> The Kingdom of Heaven is here on this earth. It is there, where we realise our best relations with our fellow-beings, where there is no mutual suspicion and misunderstanding - there is the Kingdom of Heaven, in the spirit of comradeship and love.

Tagore's pantheistic and anthropocentric world view is exquisitely dramatised, in the following poem, through a series of dialogues between God and His devotee, which he used as an epigraph to his essay "My Religion":

> In the deep of the night, the man averse to worldly pleasures said:
>
> 'I shall leave home to seek my desired God.

> Who is it that has kept me here, tied?'
> God said, 'It is I,' but the man paid no heed.
> Clasping the sleeping infant to her breast
> the loving wife lay at one end of the bed in deep slumber.
> The man said, 'what are you all - the trickery of illusion?'
> 'It is I,' said God. No one paid any heed.
> Leaving his bed the man called 'Where are Thou, my Lord?'
> God said, 'I am here!' Still His words were not heard.
> The child cried out in his sleep hugging his mother;
> God said, 'Turn back.' But His words were lost.
> God heaved a sigh and said, 'Alas! Deserting me,
> whither goes my devotee to find me?'

This view of a divine presence in the human individual, which forms the basis of universal unity, contains clear overtones of Emerson. Like Tagore, Emerson, as mentioned earlier, was also much influenced by the teachings of the Upanishads. In "The American Scholar," for example, Emerson comments:

> The old fable covers a doctrine ever new and sublime; that there is one Man, - present to all particular men only partially, or through one faculty; and that you must take the whole society to find the whole man. Man is not a farmer, or a professor, or an engineer, but he is all. Man is priest, and scholar, and statesman, and producer, and soldier ...man is one ...It is one soul which animates all men.

To both Emerson and Tagore, soul was at the centre as well as the circumference of life; soul, in their view, is what makes us wholesome and whole; and, as they saw it, the remedy to human deformity in modern society, in its carnival of materialism and perpetual pursuit of wealth, was, as Emerson put it, 'first, soul, and second soul, and evermore, soul'.To both, the doctrine of the soul was anything but outmoded or ancient. To Emerson it was 'ever new,' and so to Tagore, who announced affirmatively in "My Life," 'The impertinence of material things is extremely old. The revelation of spirit in man is truly modern: I am on its side, for I am modern'.

The Isha Upanishad says, 'To darkness are they doomed who worship only the body, and to greater darkness they who worship only the spirit'. In the Katha Upanishad it is stated, 'What is within us is also without. What is without is also within. He who sees difference between what is within and what is without goes evermore from death to death'.

Tagore inherited this Upanishadic 'double consciousness,' which calls for a recurrent synthesis of body and soul, physical and spiritual, mind and matter. As he maintains in "Construction versus Creation," 'Life is a continual process of synthesis'. In spite of his cardinal faith in the cult of the soul, he was not disdainful of the material and practical side of life. He knew that body and spirit, visible and invisible, within and without are interdependent for their mutual realisation - they are one and the same, and one is not without the other.

Like Emerson, he believed that 'Human life is made up of two elements, power and form, and proportion must be invariably kept if we have it sweet and sound';and, like Whitman, he was an 'arbiter of the diverse'who sought to knit "the old knot of contrariety". In "My Religion," Tagore comments, 'I am not in favour of rejecting anything, for I am only complete with the inclusion of everything. I want to accept all excluding nothing, / for it is I, my friend, that waits outside to meet me!'. This is his inclusive, multilateral ideology; he was realistic enough not to look for the soul outside the body, or for God outside nature and the world. In "Voice of Humanity," he explains:

> I do not cry down the material world. I fully realise that this is the nurse and the cradle of the Spirit. By achieving the Infinite in the heart of the material world you have made this world more generous than it ever was.

The poem that was quoted earlier ("In the deep of the night..."), also testifies to this view, where God urges that his devotee need not seek Him outside the daily realities of life but in the midst of everyday happenings. He should attend to his crying child and his lonely, affectionate wife in order to realise God and his own self; only by attending to the practical affairs of life and bestowing love upon his family can he pacify his thirst for God.

Contrary to Tagore's inclusivism and multilateralism, balance and equilibrium, modern civilisation, he suggests, thrives on a partial and unilateral outlook. It is totally indignant of the moral and the spiritual side of life, of beauty and truth, of love and sympathy, of 'the music of soul' and the great rhythm of 'symphony' that lies 'at the very heart of the world'. It aspires solely and shamelessly to a life of material fulfilment and bodily comfort. Instead of goodness, it champions greed; instead of self-sacrifice, self-aggrandisement; instead of giving, possessing; instead of spiritual human unity, collective worldliness; instead of moral freedom, material bondage; instead of magnanimity, vindictiveness; instead of being, becoming.

It replaces feelings, spontaneity and imagination with a bloodless, mechanical logic, based on the principles of usefulness and need. It looks upon the world like a grammarian who is singularly absorbed in the functional side of language in the study of a poem, instead of appreciating the full poem in its rhythm, harmony and meaning. Its interest ranges between the human stomach and the human head, leaving out the heart where the soul dwells, giving rise to a culture of mere production and consumption, buying and selling, pomp and pageantry, with no peace, understanding and amity in sight for the human race.

If civilisation is a site of contention for Tagore, so is the nation, which he considers as the main institutional/ political machinery through which the current materialistic and capitalistic civilisation manifests and fulfils itself. Tagore was born at a time when nationalist movement in India against the British Raj was gaining ground.

The Sepoy Mutiny of 1857, which was the first organised uprising by the Indian soldiers against their colonisers, took place only four years before the poet was born. In 1905, the Swadeshi movement broke out at the very door steps of the poet, when the British, in keeping with their policy of divide and rule, partitioned Bengal, an Indian province inhabited by the same Bengali speaking people for centuries, into two: East Bengal (presently Bangladesh) and West Bengal.

Initially, Tagore was infuriated by the British injustice and insanity in this action, and became actively involved in the Swadeshi movement, writing patriotic songs to unite and inspire the people against British oppression, with such fury that Ezra Pound quipped, 'Tagore has sung Bengal into a nation'. Soon after, he withdrew from the movement, never to have anything to do with nationalism again, except to launch a systematic diatribe against it in a series of lectures and essays, most prominently, "Nationalism in India," "Nationalism in Japan" and "Nationalism in the West." His departure from the Swadeshi movement of 1905 made him vulnerable to wild criticisms from many of his contemporaries and compatriots, to which Tagore responded through his novel The Home and the World, published in 1915 - a political allegory that dramatises the writer's pacifist, universalist ideology vis-à-vis the nationalism of Realpolitik, in which Radhakrishnan poignantly capsulised, 'self-interest is the end; brute force, the means; conscience is taboo'. Even Gandhi's repeated urgings, during his Satyagraha movements that eventually brought independence to India, in 1947, from cruel and conniving British rule, failed to persuade Tagore to return to the fold of nationalism or reinstate his faith in the idea of the nation.

Nationalism is no doubt a deeply ingrained idea in the modern imagination. Anderson suggests that it is 'the most universally legitimate value in the political life of our time'. Bill Ashcroft et al. are of the view that in spite of 'all its contentiousness, and the difficulty of theorising it adequately, [nation/nationalism] remains the most implacably powerful force in twentieth century politics'. Despite its dominance and universal acceptance as a political institution, the idea of the nation is of course relatively new. In 1882, when Tagore was still a young writer, the French Orientalist, Ernest Renan, in an address at Sorbonne, "What is a Nation?," felt it necessary to explain the origins of the idea to his audience because of its relative obscurity:

> Nations...are something fairly new in history. Antiquity was unfamiliar with them; Egypt, China and ancient Chaldea were in no way nations. They were flocks led by a Son of the Sun or by a Son of Heaven. Neither in Egypt nor in China were there citizens as such. Classical antiquity had republics, municipal kingdoms, confederates of local republics and empires, yet it can hardly be said to have had nations in our understanding of the term.

So, what is the nation? How and when did it come about? What are Tagore's objections to it? How justified is he in his fury against the nation? Why did he consider it a 'menace' to mankind and spurn it as 'a cruel epidemic of evil...sweeping over the human world of the present age and eating into its moral fibre'? Why did he castigate it as a source of human diminishment, war and carnage, as he did with utmost ferocity in "The Sunset of the Century," a poem written on the last day of the nineteenth century, even before he was drawn into the Swadeshi movement of 1905 and subsequently withdraw from it as a result of a growing sense of frustration and disillusionment? Here are the opening lines of the poem as a preview to the intensity of Tagore's outrage against nationalism:

> The last sun of the century sets amidst the blood-red clouds of the West and the whirlwind of hatred.
>
> The naked passion of the self-love of Nations, in its drunken delirium of greed, is dancing to the clash of steel and howling verses of vengeance.
>
> The hungry self of the Nation shall burst in a violence of fury from its own shameless feeding.
>
> For it has made the world its food.

Nation is a socio-cultural-political formation - an 'imagined community,' as Benedict Anderson has described it - of a group of people, living within a certain geographical boundary, with either a unifying cultural signifier, such as language, as in the case of linguistic nationalism of Europe, or certain shared collective values and overarching ideologies, but no inherently homogenising signifier/s as, for example, in 'Creole nationalism.'

As an institution, it is of European origin and its provenance can be traced in European political and social heritage. Critics suggest that the nation is a product of the European Enlightenment and the Industrial Revolution. Benedict Anderson argues that the rise of nationalism in Western Europe was made possible by the decline, if not the death, of religious modes of thought, in the wake of the rationalist secularism of Enlightenment, or the Age of

Reason. The guiding principles of this intellectual movement were the glorification of reason and faith in human dignity, both of which were instrumental in breaking down old belief systems, which gave centrality to the church and the ocentric worldview, and gave rise to a more pragmatic and worldly socio-political system of the nation, that would suit the new post-religious, secular world, or the godless expanse of what Anderson describes as 'homogenous empty time'. Anderson explains, 'What was then required, was a secular transformation of fatality into continuity, contingency into meaning ...few things were better suited to this end than an idea of the nation'.

Ernst Gellner attributes the emergence of nationalism to the rise of industrialism, or capitalist economies, in the eighteenth and nineteenth centuries. The epochal shift of human society from pre-industrial to industrial economies, he argues, set up the conditions required for the creation of larger social units and economies that would also be culturally 'homogenous' and cooperative as a workforce, thus paving the way for the formation of the more complex and intricate social organisation of the nation-state. Effectively, the expansion of the workforce and the market made the earlier pre-industrial, tribal societies and their structures both inadequate and redundant.

Tagore's objections to nation/nationalism lie in its very nature and purpose as an institution. The fact that it is a social construction, a mechanical organisation, modelled with certain utilitarian objectives in mind, made it unpalatable to Tagore, who always valued creation over construction, imagination over reason, 'expression' over want, natural and organic over the man-made and contrived. In Tagore's view, 'Construction is for a purpose, it expresses our wants; but creation is for itself, it expresses our very beings'. He believed that the nation as a formation, based on needs and wants rather than truth and love, could not contribute much to man's moral fulfilment or to the dignity of human beings. To Tagore, race was a more natural, and therefore acceptable, social unit than the nation and he envisioned a world where races would live together in amity, keeping their 'distinct characteristics but all attached to the stem of humanity by the bond of love'.

Tagore was of the view that since nationalism emerged in the post-religious laboratory of industrial-capitalism, it is but an 'organisation of politics and commerce', that brings 'harvests of wealth' by spreading tentacles of greed, selfishness, power and prosperity, and sacrificing in the process, 'the moral man, the complete man...to make room for the political and the commercial man, the man of limited purpose'.

Nationalism, Tagore expressed, is not 'a spontaneous selfexpression of man as social being,' where human relationships are naturally regulated, 'so that men can develop ideals of life in co-operation with one another', but rather a political and commercial union of a group of people, in which they come together to maximise their profit, progress and power. Tagore dismissed nationalism as 'the organised self-interest of a people, where it is least human and least spiritual'. He saw it as a recurrent threat to humanity because it trampled over the human spirit and 'upset man's moral balance, obscuring his human side under the shadow of soul-less organisation'.

Tagore also found the fetish nationalism a source of war, hatred, mutual suspicion between nations and militarism. As Sandip argues in The Home and the World, 'country's needs must be made into a god' and one must 'set aside...conscience...by putting the country in its place'. This deification of the nation, where it is made to occupy the place of god and conscience, breeds exclusivism, fanaticism, cultural particularism, paranoia and xenophobia, thus every nation considering another a threat to its existence and waging war against it for selffulfilment and self-aggrandisement, a justifiable act. Tagore explains:

> The Nation, with all its paraphernalia of power and prosperity, its flags and pious hymns, its blasphemous prayers in the churches, and the literary mock thunders of its patriotic bragging, cannot hide the fact that the Nation is the greatest evil for the Nation, that all its precautions are against it, and any new birth of its fellow in the world is always followed in its mind by the dread of a new peril.

Tagore argued that British colonialism also found its justification in the ideology of the nation as the British came to India and other rich pastures of the world only to plunder and so prosper their own nation. They were never interested in developing the countries of occupation, as it would contribute little to their national cause to turn their 'hunting grounds' into 'cultivated fields'. Like predators, they thrived by victimising and looting other nations and never felt deterred by love, sympathy, fellowship, or humanity in perpetrating heinous crimes for the sake of their nation.

In other words, in Tagore's view, there is an inherent discourse of victimisation/othering in the discourse of nationalism - in order to have rich and powerful nations, some nations ought be left poor and pregnable: 'Because this civilisation is the civilisation of power, therefore it is exclusive, it is naturally unwilling to open its sources of power to those whom it has selected for its purposes of exploitation'.

Of course, Tagore's critique of nationalism might seem a little lofty and farfetched - 'too pious,' as Pound might have said- but much of it is intellectually valid and some of it is borne out by contemporary post-colonial criticism. Critics, for example, hardly ascribe the nation with any moral authority but emphasise its practical necessity, its legitimacy on the ground that it has laboured on behalf of modernity, an outcome of the overlapping discourses of Reason, Modernity and History that serves as an underpinning to modern civilisation.

In the view of Leela Gandhi, 'nationalism is the only form of political organisation which is appropriate to the social and intellectual condition of the modern world'. She does not, however, suggest how beneficial it is from a human point of view, how much it contributes to the moral and spiritual fulfilment of human beings. Interestingly, that does not seem to be part of the contemporary discourse, something that Tagore was so preoccupied with; modern discourse is monocular in its acceptance of progress, civilisation and modernity as a material and intellectual process only, and not both material and moral, or intellectual as well as spiritual - precisely the criticism that Tagore, a multilateral thinker, directed at the current unilineal civilisation.

Critics also view the constructed aspect of nationalism as a weakness in the ideology. They believe that nations are profoundly unstable formations and are always likely to regress into more natural social units of clan, tribe, and race, or language and religious groups; that this structural vulnerability, or self-deconstructing discourse, is the inevitable consequence of its being a social construction.

The process of formation/invention of the nation further makes it a potent site of power discourse, as the signifiers of homogeneity/overarching ideologies in creating the myth of nationhood almost always fail to represent the diversity of the actual national community that they profess to represent, and express and consolidate instead the interests of the dominant group/s of people, thus creating a new hierarchy, hegemony, domination and exclusion within the structures of the nation. Fanon describes this as one of the principle dangers of nationalism, especially in the post-colonial societies, where nationalism is a derivative discourse and is often faced with additional problems:

> National consciousness, instead of being the all-embracing crystallisation of the innermost hopes of the whole people ...[becomes] a crude and fragile travesty of what it might have been ...[when] the nation is passed over for the race, and the tribe is preferred to the state.

Critics furthermore concur with Tagore's arguments that nationalism breeds xenophobia and violence, and contains a discourse of binarism, which perpetuates the process of victimising and othering of nations by one another. It is simply horrifying to see the gruesome violence and number of deaths that have taken place in recent times in the name of the nation, whether in Chechnya, Russia, Afghanistan or the USA, and the alacrity with which citizens are willing both to kill and to die for the sake of their nations.

In some instances, the fanaticism and irrationality that nationalism generates is no less than the religious fanaticism that preoccupies some people in the underdeveloped parts of the world, countries that are not yet considered part of the elite league of nations, and where, in some instances, so-called civilisation and modernity have not yet travelled. Gellner, Anderson and Tom Nairn have pointed out the irrationality, prejudice, hatred, sentimentality, collective egoism and aggression that nationalism generates, and Leela Gandhi explains it in the following words:

> East or West, we are now aware of the xenophobia, racism and loathing which attends the rhetoric of [national/cultural] particularism. Nationalism has become the

> popular pretext for contemporary disquisitions of intolerance, separating Croatians and Serbians, Greeks and Macedonians, Estonians and Russians, Slovaks and Czechs, Armenians and Azerbaijanis, Israelis and Palestinians, Hindus and Muslims.

Were Gandhi to write her book more recently, she might have included in her list the new strained relationships that have evolved in the wake of the most tragic and repugnant events of 9/11 and the Bali massacre; and as the monstrous, menacing, satanic figure of neo-imperialism emerges from the spiritus mundi and threatens to engulf the world in a suicidal conflagration.

Tagore is astute in equating the imperial discourse with the discourse of nationalism and asserting the process of othering colonised nations by the Lacanian grande-autre, the great Other, or the colonising Other, to fulfil its imperial ego. A nation can construct itself only by constructing its others in such a way as to confirm its own reality. Thus every nation is given to an inherent discourse of self and other, each finding its identity by positing itself against the other, thereby making each potentially an enemy of the other. This vindicates Tagore's statement, quoted earlier, 'that the Nation is the greatest evil for the Nation, that all its precautions are against it, and any new birth of its fellow in the world is always followed in its mind by the dread of a new peril'.

If nations are given to a binary relationship, so are the coloniser and the colonised. The business of creating an empire is a business of creating the enemy, of drawing the opposition that must exist, in order that the empire might define itself against those it colonises/excludes/marginalises. A colonising nation can never be benevolent to the colonised nation - it is there to ascribe its authority on the 'mastered' subjects through a discourse of power, and plunder them of their wealth and culture, like 'predatory creatures,' using Tagore's phrases, prowling through 'its hunting grounds,' which they would never like to convert 'into cultivated fields'. As Amy Césaire starkly put it 'colonisation = "thingification"'. Or as Fanon has more elaborately stated:

> Colonialism is not satisfied merely with holding a people in its grip and emptying the native's brain of all form and content. By a kind of perverted logic, it turns the past of the oppressed people, and distorts, disfigures, and destroys it.

Tagore was intensely opposed to India joining the bandwagon of nationalism. It would compromise India's history and identity as a culture and bring her under the shadow of the West. In "Nationalism in India," Tagore cautioned:

> We, in India, must make up our minds that we cannot borrow other people's history, and that if we stifle our own we are committing suicide. When you borrow things that do not belong to your life, they only serve to crush your life ...I believe that it does India no good to compete with Western civilisation in its own field ...India is no beggar of the West.

Tagore's warnings have come true because although India has attained freedom from the British Raj by appropriating the coloniser's own political discourse, thus using the master's tools to dismantle the master's house, it has ironically made the country follow the destiny that the West has thrust on her. The incorporation of the Western model of nationalism has erased the sense of difference of India as a society, capable of standing on its own, and created linkages that now allow neo-colonialist controls to operate over her both explicitly and implicitly, thus effectively reducing her to a 'beggar of the West.'

Tagore's lectures on nationalism drew many angry responses, even from those of kindred spirit, such as D.H. Lawrence, who spitefully declared Tagore, 'horribly decadent and reverting to all forms of barbarisms in all sorts of ugly ways' and denounced the 'wretched worship-of-Tagore attitude' as 'disgusting'. However, not all were offended; not everyone misunderstood him. The French Nobel Laureate, Romain Rolland, greeted him in a salubrious personal letter:

> The reading of Nationalism has been a great joy for me; for I entirely agree with your thoughts, and I love them even more now that I have heard them expressed by you with this noble and harmonious wisdom which, being your own, is so dear to us ...

Tagore's animosity to nationalism should not make us think that he was not patriotic or that he was anti-West. He believed in a symbiosis of the East and West, a 'deep association' or a living relationship between the two cultures; a creative unity that was possible only when the East had discovered its soul and its separate identity. Moreover, his profound love for Bengal and India is manifest in his many immortal songs and poems. His love and intensity for the land transcended the bounds of a narrow, selfish and self-aggrandising nationalism and carried such depth, generosity and broadness that his compositions were adopted as national anthems in three countries.

Despite the fervour, Tagore never allowed his love for his country to stand in the way of his love for truth, justice and humanity - he was not given to a national consciousness but a world-consciousness, a visvovod in which every country would keep alight its own lamp of mind as its part in the illumination of the world. As Nikhil says in The Home and the World, 'I am willing to serve my country; but my worship I reserve for Right which is far greater than my country. To worship my country as a god is to bring a curse upon it'. And as Atin says to Ela in Four Chapters:

> The patriotism of those who have no faith in that which is above patriotism is like a crocodile's back used as a ferry to cross the river ... That the life of the country can be saved by killing its soul, is the monstrously false doctrine that nationalists all over the world are bellowing forth stridently. My heart groans to give it effective contradictions ...

And, indeed, effective contradictions Tagore gave all through his life, through his paradisiacal imagination that envisioned a world of love, equality, honesty, bravery and spiritual unity of all mankind - of sympathy and fellowship across race, religion and gender - the world of sattva (light), to put it in a phrase from The Bhagavad Gita, rising from its current tamasik (dark) state, that the present humanity, infatuated with greed, wealth and power may not choose to tread, but it is there for them to choose when they rise from their long and horrific moral slumber.

15

Tagore on Peace Education

Tagore, Sir Rabindranath, Indian author and guru, b. Calcutta. Tagore came from a wealthy Bengali family. He went abroad in 1877 to study law in England but soon returned to India. For a time he managed his father's estates and became involved with the Indian nationalist movement, writing propaganda. His characteristic later style combines natural descriptions with religious and philosophical speculation. Tagore drew on the classical literature of India, especially the ancient Sanskrit scriptures and the writings of Kalidasa. His prodigious output includes approximately 50 dramas, 100 books of verse, 40 volumes of novels and shorter fiction, and books of essays and philosophy.

In his devotion to peace, Tagore denounced nationalism and violence. He sought to instill in human beings a sense of their unity; he was severely critical of the Indian caste system. His most important philosophical work is *Sadhana: The Realisation of Life*, which echoes the fundamental ideas inherent in sacred Hindu writings. His dramas are filled with lyricism and philosophy, while his poems deal with amorous, mystical, and fabulous themes. In India his appeal was nearly universal. A man of striking appearance, Tagore came to be regarded with the reverence due an ancient teacher. He wrote in Bengali but translated much of his work into English. It attracted attention in the West, and he was awarded the 1913 Nobel Prize in Literature, especially for his collection of poetry, *Gitanjali*. His *Janaganamana* (*Thou Art the Ruler of All Minds*) was adopted as the Indian national anthem

Rabindranath Tagore, Asia's first Nobel Laureate, was born into a prominent Calcutta family known for its socio-religious and cultural innovations during the 19th Bengal Renaissance. The profound social and cultural involvement of his family would later play a strong role in the formulation of Rabindranath's educational priorities. His grandfather Dwarkanath was involved in supporting medical facilities, educational institutions and the arts, and he fought for religious and social reform and the establishment of a free press. His father was also a leader in social and religious reform, who encouraged a multi-cultural exchange in the family mansion Jorasanko. Within the joint family, Rabindranath's thirteen brothers and sisters were mathematicians, journalists, novelists, musicians, artists. His cousins, who shared the family mansion, were leaders in theatre, science and a new art movement.

The tremendous excitement and cultural richness of his extended family permitted young Rabindranath to absorb and learn subconsciously at his own pace, giving him a dynamic open model of education, which he later tried to recreate in his school at Santiniketan. Not surprisingly, he found his outside formal schooling to be inferior and boring and, after a brief exposure to several schools, he refused to attend school. The only degrees he ever received were honorary ones bestowed late in life.

His experiences at Jorasanko provided him with a lifelong conviction concerning the importance of freedom in education. He also realised in a profound manner the importance of the arts for developing empathy and sensitivity, and the necessity for an intimate relationship with one's cultural and natural environment. In participating in the cosmopolitan activities of the family, he came to reject narrowness in general, and in particular, any form of narrowness that separated human being from human being. He saw education as a vehicle for appreciating the richest aspects of other cultures, while maintaining one's own cultural specificity. As he wrote:

> I was brought up in an atmosphere of aspiration, for the expansion of the human spirit. We in our home sought freedom of power in our language, freedom of imagination in our literature, freedom of soul in our religious creeds and that of mind in our social environment. Such an opportunity has given me confidence in the power of education which is one with life and only which can give us real freedom, the highest that is claimed for man, his freedom of moral communion in the human world.... I try to assert in my words and works that education has its only meaning and object in freedom–freedom from ignorance about the laws of the universe, and freedom from passion and prejudice in our communication with the human world. In my institution I have attempted to create an atmosphere of naturalness in our relationship with strangers, and the spirit of hospitality which is the first virtue in men that made civilisation possible.
>
> I invited thinkers and scholars from foreign lands to let our boys know how easy it is to realise our common fellowship, when we deal with those who are great, and that it is the puny who with their petty vanities set up barriers between man and man.

As well as growing up in a household that was the meeting place for leading artists and intellectuals from India and the West, Rabindranath had a further experience which was unusual for someone of his upbringing. In the 1890s, he was put in charge of the family's rural properties in East Bengal. His first experiments in adult education were carried out there as he gradually became aware of the acute material and cultural poverty that permeated the villages, as well as the great divide between the uneducated rural areas and the city elites. His experiences made him determined to do something about rural uplift, and later at Santiniketan, students and teachers were involved with literacy training and social work and the promotion of cooperative schemes.

As an alternative to the existing forms of education, he started a small school at Santiniketan in 1901 that developed into a university and rural reconstruction centre, where he tried to develop an alternative model of education that stemmed from his own learning experiences.

Rabindranath composed his first poem at age eight, and by the end of his life, had written over twenty-five volumes of poetry, fifteen plays, ninety short stories, eleven novels, thirteen volumes of essays, initiated and edited various journals, prepared Bengali textbooks, kept up a correspondence involving thousands of letters, composed over two thousand songs; and—after the age of seventy—created more than two thousand pictures and sketches. He dedicated forty years of his life to his educational institution at Santiniketan, West Bengal. Rabindranath's school contained a children's school as well as a university known as Visva-Bharati and a rural education Centre known as Sriniketan.

Rabindranath's Key Ideas

Rabindranath did not write a central educational treatise, and his ideas must be gleaned through his various writings and educational experiments at Santiniketan In general, he envisioned an education that was deeply rooted in one's immediate surroundings but connected to the cultures of the wider world, predicated upon pleasurable learning and individualised to the personality of the child. He felt that a curriculum should revolve organically around nature with classes held in the open air under the trees to provide for a spontaneous appreciation of the fluidity of the plant and animal kingdoms, and seasonal changes. Children sat on hand-woven mats beneath the trees, which they were allowed to climb and run beneath between classes.

Nature walks and excursions were a part of the curriculum and students were encouraged to follow the life cycles of insects, birds and plants. Class schedules were made flexible to allow for shifts in the weather or special attention to natural phenomena, and seasonal festivals were created for the children by Tagore. In an essay entitled "A Poet's School," he emphasizes the importance of an empathetic sense of interconnectedness with the surrounding world:

> We have come to this world to accept it, not merely to know it. We may become powerful by knowledge, but we attain fullness by sympathy. The highest education is that which does not merely give us information but makes our life in harmony with all existence. But we find that this education of sympathy is not only systematically ignored in schools, but it is severely repressed. From our very childhood habits are formed and knowledge is imparted in such a manner that our life is weaned away from nature and our mind and the world are set in opposition from the beginning of our days. Thus the greatest of educations for which we came prepared is neglected, and we are made to lose our world to find a bagful of information instead. We rob the child of his earth to teach him geography, of language to teach him grammar. His hunger is for the Epic, but he is supplied with chronicles of facts and dates...Child-nature protests against such calamity with all its power of suffering, subdued at last into silence by punishment.

In Tagore's philosophy of education, the aesthetic development of the senses was as important as the intellectual—if not more so—and music, literature, art, dance and drama were given great prominence in the daily life of the school. This was particularly so after the first decade of the school. Drawing on his home life at Jorasanko, Rabindranath tried to create an atmosphere in which the arts would become instinctive. One of the first areas to be emphasized was music. Rabindranath writes that in his adolescence, a 'cascade of musical emotion' gushed forth day after day at Jorasanko. 'We felt we would try to test everything,' he writes, 'and no achievement seemed impossible...We wrote, we sang, we acted, we poured ourselves out on every side.'

In keeping with his theory of subconscious learning, Rabindranath never talked or wrote down to the students, but rather involved them with whatever he was writing or composing. The students were allowed access to the room where he read his new writings to teachers and critics, and they were encouraged to read out their own writings in special literary evenings. In teaching also he believed in presenting difficult levels of literature, which the students might not fully grasp, but which would stimulate them. The writing and publishing of periodicals had always been an important aspect of Jorasanko life, and students at Santiniketan were encouraged to create their own publications and put out several illustrated magazines. The children were encouraged to follow their ideas in painting and drawing and to draw inspiration from the many visiting artists and writers.

Most of Rabindranath's dramas were written at Santiniketan and the students took part in both the performing and production sides. He writes how well the students were able to enter into the spirit of the dramas and perform their roles, which required subtle understanding and sympathy without special training.

As Rabindranath began conceiving of Visva-Bharati as a national centre for the arts, he encouraged artists such as Nandalal Bose to take up residence at Santiniketan and to devote themselves full-time to promoting a national form of art. Without music and the fine arts, he wrote, a nation lacks its highest means of national self-expression and the people remain inarticulate. Tagore was one of the first to support and bring together different forms of Indian dance. He helped revive folk dances and introduced dance forms from other parts of India, such as Manipuri, Kathak and Kathakali. He also supported modern dance and was one of the first to recognise the talents of Uday Sankar, who was invited to perform at Santiniketan.

The meeting-ground of cultures, as Rabindranath envisioned it at Visva-Bharati, should be a learning centre where conflicting interests are minimized, where individuals work together in a common pursuit of truth and realise 'that artists in all parts of the world have created forms of beauty, scientists discovered secrets of the universe, philosophers solved the problems of existence, saints made the truth of the spiritual world organic in their own lives, not merely for some particular race to which they belonged, but for all mankind.'

To encourage mutuality, Rabindranath invited artists and scholars from other parts of India and the world to live together at Santiniketan on a daily basis to share their cultures with Visva-Bharati. The Constitution designated Visva-Bharati as an Indian, Eastern and Global cultural centre whose goals were:

- To study the mind of Man in its realisation of different aspects of truth from diverse points of view.
- To bring into more intimate relation with one another through patient study and research, the different cultures of the East on the basis of their underlying unity.
- To approach the West from the standpoint of such a unity of the life and thought of Asia.
- To seek to realise in a common fellowship of study the meeting of East and West and thus ultimately to

strengthen the fundamental conditions of world peace through the free communication of ideas between the two hemispheres.

And with such Ideals in view to provide at Santiniketan a centre of culture where research into the study of the religion, literature, history, science and art of Hindu, Buddhist, Jain, Zoroastrian, Islamic, Sikh, Christian and other civilisations may be pursued along with the culture of the West, with that simplicity of externals which is necessary for true spiritual realisation, in amity, good-fellowship and co-operation between the thinkers and scholars of both Eastern and Western countries, free from all antagonisms of race, nationality, creed or caste and in the name of the One Supreme Being who is Shantam, Shivam, Advaitam.

In terms of curriculum, he advocated a different emphasis in teaching. Rather than studying national cultures for the wars won and cultural dominance imposed, he advocated a teaching system that analysed history and culture for the progress that had been made in breaking down social and religious barriers. Such an approach emphasized the innovations that had been made in integrating individuals of diverse backgrounds into a larger framework, and in devising the economic policies which emphasized social justice and narrowed the gap between rich and poor. Art would be studied for its role in furthering the aesthetic imagination and expressing universal themes.

It should be noted that Rabindranath in his own person was a living icon of the type of mutuality and creative exchange that he advocated. His vision of culture was not a static one, but one that advocated new cultural fusions, and he fought for a world where multiple voices were encouraged to interact with one another and to reconcile differences within an overriding commitment to peace and mutual interconnectedness. His generous personality and his striving to break down barriers of all sorts gives us a model for the way multiculturalism can exist within a single human personality, and the type of individual which the educational process should be aspiring towards.

Tagore's educational efforts were ground-breaking in many areas. He was one of the first in India to argue for a humane educational system that was in touch with the environment and aimed at overall development of the personality. Santiniketan became a model for vernacular instruction and the development of Bengali textbooks; as well, it offered one of the earliest coeducational programmes in South Asia. The establishment of Visva-Bharati and Sriniketan led to pioneering efforts in many directions, including models for distinctively Indian higher education and mass education, as well as pan-Asian and global cultural exchange.

One characteristic that sets Rabindranath's educational theory apart is his approach to education as a poet. At Santiniketan, he stated, his goal was to create a poem 'in a medium other than words.' It was this poetic vision that enabled him to fashion a scheme of education which was all inclusive, and to devise a unique programme for education in nature and creative self-expression in a learning climate congenial to global cultural exchange.

Rabindranath Tagore, by his efforts and achievements, is part of a global network of pioneering educators, such as Rousseau, Pestalozzi, Froebel, Montessori and Dewey—and in the contemporary context, Malcolm Knowles—who have striven to create non-authoritarian learning systems appropriate to their respective surroundings. In a poem that expresses Tagore's goals for international education, he writes:

Where the mind is without fear and the head is held high,

Where knowledge is free;

Where the world has not been broken up into fragments by narrow domestic walls;

Where words come out from the depth of truth;

Where tireless striving stretches its arms towards perfection;

Where the clear stream of reason has not lost its way into the dreary desert sand of dead habit;

Where the mind is led forward by thee into ever-widening thought and action-- into that heaven of freedom, my Father, Let my country awake.

Conversation between Tagore and Einstein

Tagore and Einstein met through a common friend, Dr. Mendel. Tagore visited Einstein at his residence at Kaputh in the suburbs of Berlin on July 14, 1930, and Einstein returned the call and visited Tagore at the Mendel home. Both conversations were recorded and the above photograph was taken. The July 14 conversation is reproduced here, and was originally published in The Religion of Man.

Tagore: I was discussing with Dr. Mendel today the new mathematical discoveries which tell us that in the realm of infinitesimal atoms chance has its play; the drama of existence is not absolutely predestined in character.

Einstein: The facts that make science tend toward this view do not say good-bye to causality.

Tagore: Maybe not, yet it appears that the idea of causality is not in the elements, but that some other force builds up with them an organised universe.

Einstein: One tries to understand in the higher plane how the order is. The order is there, where the big elements combine and guide existence, but in the minute elements this order is not perceptible.

Tagore: Thus duality is in the depths of existence, the contradiction of free impulse and the directive will which works upon it and evolves an orderly scheme of things.

Einstein: Modern physics would not say they are contradictory. Clouds look as one from a distance, but if you see them nearby, they show themselves as disorderly drops of water.

Tagore: I find a parallel in human psychology. Our passions and desires are unruly, but our character subdues these elements into a harmonious whole. Does something similar to this happen in the physical world? Are the elements rebellious, dynamic with individual impulse? And is there a principle in the physical world which dominates them and puts them into an orderly organisation?

Einstein: Even the elements are not without statistical order; elements of radium will always maintain their specific order, now and ever onward, just as they have done all along. There is, then, a statistical order in the elements.

Tagore: Otherwise, the drama of existence would be too desultory. It is the constant harmony of chance and determination which makes it eternally new and living.

Einstein: I believe that whatever we do or live for has its causality; it is good, however, that we cannot see through to it.

Tagore: There is in human affairs an element of elasticity also, some freedom within a small range which is for the expression of our personality. It is like the musical system in India, which is not so rigidly fixed as western music. Our composers give a certain definite outline, a system of melody and rhythmic arrangement, and within a certain limit the player can improvise upon it. He must be one with the law of that particular melody, and then he can give spontaneous expression to his musical feeling within the prescribed regulation. We praise the composer for his genius in creating a foundation along with a superstructure of melodies, but we expect from the player his own skill in the creation of variations of melodic flourish and ornamentation. In creation we follow the central law of existence, but if we do not cut ourselves adrift from it, we can have sufficient freedom within the limits of our personality for the fullest self-expression.

Einstein: That is possible only when there is a strong artistic tradition in music to guide the people's mind. In Europe, music has come too far away from popular art and popular feeling and has become something like a secret art with conventions and traditions of its own.

Tagore: You have to be absolutely obedient to this too complicated music. In India, the measure of a singer's freedom is in his own creative personality. He can sing the composer's song as his own, if he has the power creatively to assert himself in his interpretation of the general law of the melody which he is given to interpret.

Einstein: It requires a very high standard of art to realise fully the great idea in the original music, so that one can make variations upon it. In our country, the variations are often prescribed.

Tagore: If in our conduct we can follow the law of goodness, we can have real liberty of self-expression. The principle of conduct is there, but the character which makes it true and individual is our own creation. In our music there is a duality of freedom and prescribed order.

Einstein: Are the words of a song also free? I mean to say, is the singer at liberty to add his own words to the song which he is singing?

Tagore: Yes. In Bengal we have a kind of song-kirtan, we call it-which gives freedom to the singer to introduce parenthetical comments, phrases not in the original song. This occasions great enthusiasm, since the audience is constantly thrilled by some beautiful, spontaneous sentiment added by the singer.

Einstein: Is the metrical form quite severe?

Tagore: Yes, quite. You cannot exceed the limits of versification; the singer in all his variations must keep the rhythm and the time, which is fixed. In European music you have a comparative liberty with time, but not with melody.

Einstein: Can the Indian music be sung without words? Can one understand a song without words?

Tagore: Yes, we have songs with unmeaning words, sounds which just help to act as carriers of the notes. In North India, music is an independent art, not the interpretation of words and thoughts, as in Bengal. The music is very intricate and subtle and is a complete world of melody by itself.

Einstein: Is it not polyphonic?

Tagore: Instruments are used, not for harmony, but for keeping time and adding to the volume and depth. Has melody suffered in your music by the imposition of harmony?

Einstein: Sometimes it does suffer very much. Sometimes the harmony swallows up the melody altogether.

Tagore: Melody and harmony are like lines and colours in pictures. A simple linear picture may be completely beautiful; the introduction of color may make it vague and insignificant. Yet color may, by combination with lines, create great pictures, so long as it does not smother and destroy their value.

Einstein: It is a beautiful comparison; line is also much older than color. It seems that your melody is much richer in structure than ours. Japanese music also seems to be so.

Tagore: It is difficult to analyse the effect of eastern and western music on our minds. I am deeply moved by the western music; I feel that it is great, that it is vast in its structure and grand in its composition. Our own music touches me more deeply by its fundamental lyrical appeal. European music is epic in character; it has a broad background and is Gothic in its structure.

Einstein: This is a question we Europeans cannot properly answer, we are so used to our own music. We want to know whether our own music is a conventional or a fundamental human feeling, whether to feel consonance

	and dissonance is natural, or a convention which we accept.
Tagore:	Somehow the piano confounds me. The violin pleases me much more.
Einstein:	It would be interesting to study the effects of European music on an Indian who had never heard it when he was young.
Tagore:	Once I asked an English musician to analyse for me some classical music, and explain to me what elements make for the beauty of the piece.
Einstein:	The difficulty is that the really good music, whether of the East or of the West, cannot be analysed.
Tagore:	Yes, and what deeply affects the hearer is beyond himself.
Einstein:	The same uncertainty will always be there about everything fundamental in our experience, in our reaction to art, whether in Europe or in Asia. Even the red flower I see before me on your table may not be the same to you and me.
Tagore:	And yet there is always going on the process of reconciliation between them, the individual taste conforming to the universal standard.

SANTINIKETAN —TAGORE'S ABODE OF PEACE

In 1862, Maharshi Devendranath Tagore, while on a boat journey to Raipur, came across a landscape with red laterite and meadows of lush green paddy fields. An orchard of chhatim trees and date palms specially captivated him. Here he planted more saplings and built a small house. He called his home Santiniketan (abode of peace). Santiniketan became a spiritual centre where people from all religions were invited to join for meditation and prayers.

On December 22 1901, Devendranath's son, Rabindranath Tagore started a school at Santiniketan named Brahmacharyasrama modelled on the lines of the ancient gurukul system. Later it was renamed Visva Bharati, it's symbolic meaning being defined by Tagore as "where the world makes a home in a nest". The aim of this educational institute was the quest for truth, blending the methods of learning of the East and West. Visva Bharati is now more than a hundred years old, one of the most prestigious universities of India with degree courses in humanities, social science, science, fine arts, music, performing arts, education, agricultural science and rural reconstruction. It has retained its traditional ambience but has also evolved with the changing times. Visva Bharati University is a reflection of the cultural heritage.

Santiniketan is in the Birbhum District of Bengal, famed for the Baul singers, the wandering minstrels of Bengal who sing songs of love and devotion on the ektara. The sprawling Visva Bharati University campus is amidst verdant green. School students in orange uniforms can be seen studying under the cool shade of trees, formal classes are held outdoors, just as Tagore had intended it to be. India's first Nobel Laureate, Tagore had dropped out from school, as he felt claustrophobic within the four walls of the classroom. He felt that students should be close to nature. Tagore was not a mere dreamer, he was a visionary with the will power to translate them to reality. Visva Bharati University is proof of that.

Some notable places of historical and cultural interest are Santiniketan Griha—the building where most poems of Gitanjali were composed, the Upasana Griha—a deityless Belgium glass temple, the Amra Kunja (mangrove) where spring festivals are held, Dinantika—the tea club where teachers and staff would gather for a chat and Tin Pahar—where the infant Tagore had once made three hillocks of pebbles.

The Rabindra Museum, inaugurated by Pandit Jawaharlal Nehru in 1961 has manuscripts, letters, paintings and gifts presented by various dignitaries of foreign countries; Tagore's hand written letter refusing to accept Knighthood, his Nobel Prize medallion and citation, and personal items of the poet. In the video parlour Tagore's voice can be heard.

Santiniketan was previously called Bhubandanga (named after Bhuban Dakat, a local dacoit), and owned by the Tagore family. Rabindranath's father, Maharshi Debendranath Tagore, found it very peaceful and renamed it Santiniketan, which means abode (*niketan*) of peace (*shanti*). It was here that Rabindranath Tagore started Patha Bhavana, the school of his ideals, whose central premise was that learning in a natural environment would be more enjoyable and fruitful. After he received the Nobel Prize, the school was expanded into a university. Many world famous teachers have become associated with it. Indira Gandhi, Satyajit Ray, and Amartya Sen are among its more illustrious students,

Kala Bhavana, the art college of Santiniketan, is still considered one of the best art colleges in the world. Other institutions here include Vidya Bhavana; the Institute of Humanities, Shiksha Bhavana; the Institute of Science, Sangit Bhavana; Institute of Dance, Drama and Music, Vinaya Bhavana; Institute of Education, Rabindra Bhavana, Institute of Tagore Studies and Research, Palli-Samgathana Vibhaga; Institute of Rural Reconstruction, and Palli Shiksha Bhavana; Institute of Agricultural Sciences.

There are also other centres, affiliated to major institutions such as Nippon Bhavana, the Indira Gandhi

Centre for National Integration, Rural Extension Centre, Silpa Sadana; Centre for Rural Craft, Technology and Design, Palli-Charcha Kendra; Centre for Social Studies and Rural Development, Centre for Biotechnology, Centre for Mathematics Education, Centre for Environmental Studies, Computer Centre and Indira Gandhi Centre for National Integration. As well as Patha-Bhavana, there are two schools for kindergarten level education; Mrinalini Ananda Pathsala, Santosh Pathsala; a school for primary and secondary education known as Shiksha Satra, and a school of higher secondary education known as Uttar-Shiksha Sadana. Santiniketan is also home to Amartya Sen, the 1998 Nobel Prize winner in Economics.

Numerous social and cultural events taking place through out the year, have become part and parcel of Santiniketan. These include - Basanta Utsav, Barsha Mangal, Sharodutsav, Nandan Mela, Poush Mela, Magh Mela, Rabindra Jayanti to name a few. Of these, the *Poush Mela* deserves special mention, this being a major tourist attraction. It is a 3-day fair (Bengali, *mela* means a fair),starting on the seventh day of the Bengali month *Poush (usually,* last week of December). It fetches not just tourists, but also artisans, folk singers, dancers, and the traditional Baul from the neighbourhood.

Santiniketan has changed considerably since the days of Tagore. Although Visva-Bharati University still plays an active role, Santiniketan has become a haven for India's nouveau riche, and large houses have been built on what used to be barren, khoai (desert) and condominiums are becoming commonplace. But travel beyond the outskirts of the ever-expanding "small town" and one is soon back in village India.

The idyllic existence envisioned by Tagore in Santiniketan is rapidly disappearing, but it still maintains a "college town" feel, with many large shade-covered open spaces on campus where students can congregate.

The student population remains international in origin, as does the faculty, and some of the best thinkers and intellectuals in India remember their college life in Santiniketan with fondness.

The calm & peaceful University township has today become a haven for the urban rich with intentions beyond cultural. Sometime around the late eighties Shantiniketan became a playground of the rich intellectuals of Bengal. Some of the best known contemporary Bangalee Poets and lyricists built their houses in the outskirts...the trend began a 'land-rush' thereby converting most of the serene khoai and the green fields into a modern day urban jungle.

A famous ex-student recently made a comment in UK on this..."Shantiniketan today has more outsiders with different purpose than what Tagore had originally envisioned"...I don think he is wrong. Its fashionable among upmarket Bangalees today to have a house in Shantiniketan. The land prices have swollen way beyond the common man's reach. The support system lies in shambles, the ecosystem is soon to be affected (if not already), Shantiniketan needs some serious thinking in terms of its ability to sustain ecologically

Peace Education for Sustainable Development

'The world could be transformed and peace would reign if the basis of Education is knowledge wielded by love and value for sustainable development'. Education is the single most important means for empowerment and sustained improvement in all well being. Sustainable development is a basic Human Right and unless this target is reached with the potent tool of Education the purpose of Education would remain unfulfilled.

Education for Sustainable development is a dynamic undertaking where every person has a chance to benefit from Educational opportunities and learn the life style, behaviour and values necessary to create a sustainable future. If Sustainable development has to move into reality, the world, both, developed and developing must move towards a new world order in which 'Peace' must be in the agenda. In the words of Betty Reardon Peace Education would provide knowledge to be applicable to the problems of reforming and restructuring the present conflicting and violent human society to make it peaceful, unified and violence-free.

Confronting issues like HIV/AIDS, illeteracy, war, ethenic violence, violation of Human rights and militancy are addressed separately and some of the issues are treated as separate components for sensitisation and imparting Education to the learners. The best approach would be to club some of the sensitive issues under one heading to be called 'Peace Education'. An attempt is made in this paper to throw light on the impediments leading to Peace Education and to develop a culture of peace by using Education as the potent tool with reference to Higher education.

The 21st century society is the knowledge, information and education society. Higher education is called upon to make a key contribution for opening up of and highlighting new pathways to a better future for the society, to the individuals and to give better shape and direction to the future. The development of capacities to explore the future and to anticipate this deserves the full attention of Higher education.

The missiõn of HE is therefore to see that the new society merges with our own smoothly and this requires active participation of all concerned in solving the major Global, National Regional and Local problems comprising poverty illiteracy, social insecurity, breach of peace, degradation of the environment, rise of militancy, corruption, extortions, violations of Human rights, communal and ethnic violence as well as threats and wars. Higher education must highlight these sensitive issues and lead the mission for an end to all these and sow the seeds of peace and harmony. The UNESCO's comprehensive document on 'Higher Education for 21st. century visualises the Universities to have multidisciplinary approach for the path finding mission.

Objectives of Higher Education

Sir Ashotosh Mukherjee described the meaning and purpose of HE years back in 1922 in his Convocation address at Calcutta University that, 'to my mind, the University is a great store house of learning, A great bureau of standards, a great workshop of knowledge a great laboratory for the training of men of thought as well as men of action. The University is thus the instrument of the state for the conservation of knowledge, for the discovery of knowledge, for the distribution of knowledge and above all for the creation of knowledge makers."

Education is a basic component of human development, its interface with the sustainable development is established. Education is the single most important means for empowerment and sustained improvement in all well being Sustainable development is a basic Human right and unless this target is reached with Education as a tool, the purpose of HE would remain unfulfilled. The link between the two must be forged into a closer bond to empower the people.

Education for sustainable development is a dynamic understanding that envisions a world where every person has a chance to benefit from educational opportunities and to learn the life style, behaviour and values necessary to create a sustainable future.

The UN Earth Summit-the conference on Environment and Development (UNCED) held in 1992

June at Rio De Jenerio came out with the manifesto called 'Agenda 21'or Rio Declaration in which the concept of sustainable development was first spelt out. The principles set forth cover economic, social political, environment and Pacific concerns of human existence as a whole.

Sustainability when looked from social sphere would mean an egalitarian community that ensures an equal sharing of resources and opportunities for sustained human welfare. If sustainable development has to move from wishful thinking and slogan mongering into a reality, the world both developed and developing must move towards a new world order in which peace in the world must be in the agenda

Peace Education

Peace education is a broader discipline. Disarment education, Environment education, Human right education, International education are associated with Peace education.' Peace education deals with conflicts arising out of aggression or war situations and also arising out of injustice, exploitations and violation of Human rights'.

Peace education creates a culture of peace, helping to build a non violent and just society and is essential for survival of human beings on this earth. Robert Aspeshgh in his write up on' Peace education stated that "Peace education is feasible in a violent world because there is a societal and educational necessity of Peace education. The societal necessity of Peace education focuses the need of insight to be given to Global issues and to bring changes accordingly and the people in general needs to be educated in order to be aware of the fact that the Global society should be made more peaceful.

The main objective of peace education is to sensitise the learners towards the problems arising on the Globe and to play a positive and effective role. The objective of sensitisation would be the instrumental in struggling for social justice and other social problems at Global, National and Regional level. Peace education would arise the dawn of 'Peace culture." Once this culture is learnt it would help in minimizing and eradicating the social ills like poverty, exploitation, oppression, violence and wars.

In the words of Betty Reardon, the purpose of Peace education is to provide knowledge to be applicable to the problems of reforming/restructuring present Human society to make it more just and less violent. UNESCO calls for a 'comprehensive system of education and training for all groups of people at all levels and forms of education. Education for Peace and sustainable development needs to be holistic and participatory; focusing on Peace and non violence, Human rights, democracy, tolerance, international and intercultural understanding as well as cultural and linguistic diversity"

Educational programmes can make great efforts at achieving Peace through formal, non formal and informal education. Ginsberg Et Al. stated that schools and Universities can function towards educating students for cultivating the seeds of Peace. Curriculum and pedagogy to be followed at all levels of education can encourage development of Peace and international understanding.

India has a past history of promoting Peace, International understanding, tolerance and self restraint. which are evident from the Vedas, Puranas and Upanishads. The ancient Indian Rishis visualised the Earth as a Global village. They visualised it as "vasudaiva kutumbakam'- meaning The whole word is a family. Swami Vivekananda,the illustrious apostle of Sri Rama Krishna whose great mission was to preach unto mankind their divinity and how to make it manifest in every moment of life.

Swami highlighted the ultimate aim of education to establish internal Peace and security by strengthening the spiritual foundations of different Nations. He preached tolerance in religion and education which essentially lead to Peace. He preached the Universal Brotherhood of man.

Srimanta Shanker Dev of Assam not only propagated the new "Vaishanavism" in Assam but consolidated the foundation of the Assamese culture, music literature and unified the people of diverse caste and community. He preached the principle of equality, compassion, love and brotherhood and boldly asserted in the Kirtan Ghosa the need of giving everyone equal status and dignity in the society.

Swami Chinmayananda was an ascetic of modern India who worked for over four decades spreading the Vedantic message of Peace and happiness to the classes and masses around the Globe. The thoughts and actions for promoting Peace by outstanding personalities like Mahatma Gandhi, Md. Iqbal, Rabindra Nath Tagore and Bishnu Prasad Rava captivated the world's attention. Living spiritual leaders of India like Sri Satya Sai Baba, Sri Sri Ravi Shankar of Art of Living are the apostle of peace and harmony.

Our Indian President APJ Abdul Kalam linked Nation's prosperity with peace. He referred the message received from a Buddhist Monk in a statement that, 'If you want peace, remove 'I' and 'Me'. When you remove I and Me, You remove Ego. When you remove Ego, you remove hatred. When you remove hatred you have Peace.

Peace to prevail Peace education is significant and would be possible by sowing in the minds of the Learners and the people in general the seeds of Spirituality, Human rights knowledge, Human values and by Learning to live as well as to dismantle the present conflict and violence culture.

Culture of Violence

The UN Human Development report noted the Armed conflicts, Civil wars, Gurilla wars, Ethnic violences, Separatists movements are bringing untold miseries and tragic deaths to our own brothers and sisters living all over the Globe. Terrorism has now acquired Global dimensions and has become a challenge for the world. Terrorist activities in Bangladesh, India, Afghanistan, Cambodia are just a few picked up Nations subjected to blood shed and deaths.

A report from Geneva, Oct'2002 as reported in Hindu (Daily publication) stated that violence kills more than 1.6 million people every year. In addition to deaths millions are left injured and suffer from physical, sexual, reproductive and mental health problems.

In the year 2006 86 people have been killed in military related incidents.

Table 1

Sl	Civilians	Security/F	Terrorists	Total
Jan'06	5	1	2	8
Feb'06	10	1	1	12
March'06	3	0	0	3
April'06	4	0	3	7
May'06	1	1	0	2
June'06	13	6	5	24
July'06	7	0	3	10
Aug'06	5	7	8	20
Total	48	16	22	86

India's North-Eastern region which was once undivided Peaceful Assam is now in the grip of violence and terrorists activities A number of cultural and social effects of militarisation and leading to loss of Human resources for development has taken place. The Government is spending enormously on maintaining Law and order resulting in tardy development of the state. Exploitations, sexual violence and so many horrified effects has intensified sustainable development.

Therefore for sustainable development it has become essential to understand, realise and get sensitised about the horrifying effects of war, conflicts, militancies at all levels of life. The UNESCO in its preamble has stated, 'Since war begins in the minds of man, it is in the minds of man that defence of Peace must be constructed'. Human beings are involved in both war and Peace, knowledge, understanding, critical thinking and kindness and therefore stands as the most potential instrument for tuning the mind sets of the learners at all levels of Education particularly at Higher level.

Teachers at the micro level should be sensitised to shun physical violence, assaults, corporal punishments at the Institutions. The learners at all levels must be taught to say 'No' to wars/conflicts/violence so that education for sustainable development becomes possible on the Globe. Learners must be made to understand that to build a 'Humane society' a social order is essential where violence, exploitations and inequality has no place in the Institutions.

The new vision of curriculum in HE should therefore envisage education for mutual understanding, tolerance, peace, harmony, international, cooperation, coexistence, and appreciation to develop the spirit of unity in diversity, equality of gender and removal of social barriers. Through course contents of syllabus in HE the internalisation of values of love, compassion, generosity, empathy spirituality, gratitude and non violence are possible resulting in learning to live in peace and harmony.

The NCERT has taken a positive strategy in this regard through syllabus at school level. If sustainable development has to be translated into action the restructuring of syllabus/course contents in HE is the need of the hour. HE needs an agenda to be adopted in tangible steps to follow the path of sustainable development.

Human Rights Awareness

'All human beings are born free and equal in dignity and right'. These words are included in the Article 1 of Universal Declaration of HRs and is the theme and basic of all fundamental rights of each and every democratic constitution and declaration. The doctrine of Universal declaration of Human rights rests on ancient injustice perpetrated on poor and helpless in the social structure.

The HR violations and Human assertions for dignity and freedom has now become very much visible. HR violations leading to impeachment of peace is visible from the rapid growth of Nationalism, racism, xenophobia, sexism and religious intolerance.

The world conference on HR and the Vienna Declarations stated that HRE, training and public awareness has become essential for the promotion and achievement of stable and harmonious relations amongst all communities for fostering mutual understanding tolerance and peace The major task in the area of HRE was taken by UNESCO at the General conference in 1974 by bringing out UNESCO's recommendations concerning education for International understanding, cooperation, peace and education relating to HR and fundamental freedom.

The need is arising is now to mould the minds of the young and adult learners the vision of a world that is 'Human centred' and genuinely democratic where all human beings living on this planet are from the same family guided by the universal principles of democracy and equality.

The decade of 1990s witnessed a series of Global conferences and most of these conferences highlighted issues relating to HRs particularly those affecting sectors like women and children and issues like Health, Population Habitat and Environment. The 1993 world conference on HR at Vienna led to significant results such as the establishment of the office of the High commissioner for HR and the adoption of the UN decade for HRE. At the National level the Vienna conference helped to establish HR Institutions as well as adoption of HR action plans in several countries in Asia-Pacificregions.

HR education should be imparted through Civic education Moral education Religious education and Gender studies. Along with theoretical studies the learners should have hands on practice in the affairs of the family, society, state and in the National level.

The NCERT stated that 'HRE is not an independent area in the school curriculum but its various aspect and discussion have been integrated in the curriculum of various school subjects and educational materials particularly text books based on them. This suggestion is also applicable in case of Higher education as HRE makes an essential contribution to the maintenance and promotion of peace as well as to socio ecomic progress. Therefore through course contents HRE and teachings should be based on the principles underlying Universal Declaration of HR.'.

Spiritual Development

Spiritualism lies in looking at life and the world through the eyes of the soul. It is to identify the self with all the beings. Where there is total identification of objects and persons involved, the realisation of this concept is the essence of spiritualism. Spiritualism is person's 'whole' process which is based on values that are eternal.

The average human beings in today's world gives a great deal of thought and applies a great amount of energy to attain material welfare. Not withstanding even success in this endeavour there is much unhappiness, discontent and misery pervading the lives of people. it is the result of unbalanced application of efforts. The human existence consists of both material and spiritual aspects and both are equally important for harmonious development of human beings. Our ancient fore fathers neglected the material existence and generally lived in sickness and poverty. In this world today majority of human beings neglect spiritual life and this is resulting in horror and sufferings. Therefore along with advancements spiritual attainments through spiritual education has become essential.

The learners at all levels should be taught to view the world as a whole. It is beautifully said in Bhagavad Gita-"Sarvabhu tastham atmanamsarvabhutani"-ie, he who holds the self in all the beings and all beings in the self'. This is how spiritualism wants us to see things. Life and body becomes for us only an outer chamber. This education is spiritual education.

In reality spiritual education helps in understanding the 'truth' which is overlooked in our present educational system at all levels. Now 'Specialist education has bypassed Spiritual education and this is failing to produce the real man and the failure to cultivate inner peace of mind leading to peacelessness.

Spiritual leaders and Peace educators all over the world have talked about 'inner dimensions and sources of peaceful values and practices" needing equal cultivation in the mind of learners. Most of the teachings of spiritual leaders, saints or sages stated the strategies for developing inner equilibrium and tranquillity through meditation and contemplation and to use the teachings for holistic process of spiritual growth..

Faiths and spirituality traditions educate the followers to cultivate inner peace and thereby adopt life styles based on interpersonal relationships, justice, nonviolence, respect love and kindness for all beings living on this planet. The reflection on creating inner peace as an essential theme for educating the learners to develop a culture of Peace suggests that a holistic paradigm of ESD should not be isolated from the ideas, principles, spiritual knowledge and wisdom found in all cultures, faiths and civilisation.

What is essential now for the learners at all levels particularly at Higher level to develop better concentration, positive thinking and inner peace and these can be developed through 'Raj yoga' as introduced by 'Brahma Kumari Iswaria Vishwavidyalaya' of India. The power of concentration can be achieved through the practice of easy Rajyoga. Raj yoga is nothing but the establishment of the connection of the soul with the source-the supreme soul-the source of all values. Through connection with one eternal and unlimited source of power human being's 'reservoir' overflows with silent strength. As the rays of light concentrated through the lens can burn a paper so the waste thoughts and negative dispositions can be burnt by concentrating the mind on the supreme soul which is the source of all values.

When a young adult emerges from his/her Alma mater it is important that he/she should acquire the qualification to facilitate financially rewarding employment and it is also equally important for him/her to prepare for meeting the various social challenges and stresses and expectations of life in the family, community Nation and the Globe as a whole. Therefore HE needs to play the pertinent role through education to teach cultures integrity, values and other skills and dimensions which would make the learners better man and woman to contribute qualitatively for developing a better world where Peace and other values can survive.

Learners should be made to understand and develop 'the four aspects of spiritual education-Love, Knowledge, Power and Beauty. These four attributes will spontaneously express themselves in our being. The psychic will be the vehicle of true and pure love, the mind that of infallible knowledge, the vital will manifest invincible power and the body will be the expression of a perfect beauty and perfect harmony'.

Developing Peace Culture

Today's society is a Knowledge society. Generation of knowledge, storage and retrieval of knowledge, dissemination of knowledge are the main functions of an Educational system particularly in HE. Education output concentrate on teaching situations and learning required skills. This focuses the holistic purpose of education which rests on intellectual, physical, emotional and other aspects of the learners and the overriding purpose of all these is to prepare the learners to prepare them to learn to live together.

The HE must make the learners more open minded and receptive to new ideas and challenges. The liberating power of education is of great relevance to the society. The HE system must produce products (students) of positive outlook inspired with sprit of service as well as values, ethics, attitudes and knowledge to constitute the social capital necessary to construct healthy societies and socially binding cultures.

Education is considered also as social necessity and it socialises the individuals in the society where learning and sharing takes place Education must promote learning to the present and future society. Dr. S.Radhakrishnan, the first president of independent India rightly commented, "It is essential for us not to live apart but to live together, understanding one another, knowing one another's fear and anxieties, aspirations and thoughts'.

"Learning-The treasure within" highlights the four pillars of learning and the third pillar which is most important is-Learning to live together.

'Let us work together

Think together

Achieve together

With no hatred to each other.'

This is most important to all particularly to the learners to learn to live together on this planet. In order to survive on this planet peacefully every one must learn to live in harmony and in a violence free environment. Differences in race, caste, colour, creed, language, customs, traditions and cultures exist and to learn to live amidst these differences should be a wonderful and unique experiences for all.

To help the learners to learn to live together, the present Educational policy in India needs to be reviewed and made systematic where the social aspects of education must have a place in the curriculum. In the Educational Institutions particularly HE the curriculum should aim at contents to develop in the learners not only the desirable behaviour but attribute to the moral, cultural and ethnic aspects

What is more effective to the learners to learn to live together in the Institutions is the 'Role' of teachers. Teachers are the best "Role models' to the learning community and through their attitudes, behaviour, democratic administration and interactions would build the desirable and congenial ambience to learn to live together. The learners must be made to understand that differences and diversities are opportunities to know each other. The Institutions must help the learners to participate more in community works, extension works and co curricular activities so that they learn to live and work amidst diversities.

In regards to 'Learning to live together' the cardinal relationship between learners and teachers should be maintained. Through dissemination of knowledge the learners must learn to respect and protect their relationship which is important to promote the frame work for appropriate behaviour. Teacher education for Peace and sustainable development needs to be included in the Teacher education curriculum for moulding pupils who can find a difference in the Institutions and learn to live in peace and harmony.

It is from the Institutions that learners learn to behave in appropriate ways. The training of Teachers and Administrators towards democratic interactions must be one of the leading agenda of Teacher education programmes. It is also important to translate into action what is learnt in the Institutions to carry to the homes media, communities and other informal agencies so as to learn to live together.

For Learning to live together the role of Education must be activated, awareness strategies to be adopted and to develop strategies at all levels of education so that the learners can learn to live together in this beautiful world.

Swami Vivekananda said, 'We want that Education by which character is formed, strength is increased, the intellect is expanded and by which one can stand on one's own feet'. To him the end and aim of all education, all training should be man making. The end and aim of training is to make the man grow. The training by which the correct and expression of will are brought under control and made fruitful is called Education". Swami's thinking reflects the eternal and universal values which is important for all to learn in order to live in the culturally pluralistic society.

Today science and technology are dominating the curriculum. Human values and universal values are given less importance which is accountable for large scale of criminalisation, dehumanisation, exploitation, environmental degradation wars, conflicts and violences. But today's world could be transformed and peace would reign if the basis of education is knowledge wielded by love and values for sustainable development.

The National policy of Education 1986 has pointed out the crisis of values in all aspects of life and recommended a special thrust on inculcation of values at all stages of education The Programme of action document 1992 dealt with value education as 'broad cultural education leading to removal of superstition, religion, fanatism and all other narrow loyalities. The POA stressed the importance of positive approach in which the roots of Indian culture have to be highlighted along with the development of scientific temper, unity and National integrity having a spiritual focus ".

Education for a peaceful and sustainable Global community must emphasis the crucial role of value formation through its pedagogical process. Peace education and sustainable development should be explicit about the preferred values like compassion, justice, equity, gender fairness, caring for life, non violence, integrity and sharing. In the Educational system the inculcation of values depends upon enthusiasm and commitment of Teachers, Management and Government. The curriculum framers should keep in mind that values permeate in all works and activities of educational system and in the Institutions it should be like a 'Guardian angle'.

In the HE system, strategies for inculcation of values should be through routine co-curricular activities and through curriculum course contents. Teachers should go through the curriculum and text books of the respective subjects and find out situations which normally evoke value questions and they should try to internalise the importance of all the values in life through discussions, role play, problem solving and assignments.

Learners at Higher level of learning have strong idealistic impulses and the urge to improve the world. Hence this is an appropriate stage in life of learners to utilise and channelise youthful energies in the right directions. Therefore at the HE level practical experiences need to be combined with academic inputs.

The University Grants Commission made several recommendations for the Universities to act upon in this regard. As education is the most effective tool for transforming younger generation the light of values must be lit by the educational institutions and for this during the Teacher education programmes, the teachers should be made clear the concept of value, inculcation of values and to get aware of the different methods and techniques, formal or informal, direct or indirect keeping in view the various physiological and psychological development of students for promoting Human values.

The learners at Higher level of education are generally adolescents and youths undergoing changes in the thinkings and emotions. The objective of inculcating ethical and social values is to develop positive personalities at this crucial stage of adolescence and youth.

Peace education at Higher level can be inculcated through core and applied programmes as well as through extension programmes. Higher education should adopt the ideal of better worldliness, pursuing universal knowledge and develop the physical, mental (intellectual and aesthetic) spiritual faculties of man to secure the wisdom so as to make right and correct decisions to live in peace and harmony on this planet. The ideal of better worldliness should become the goal of human life and the education system should be geared to meet this objective. The curriculum of HE should be the core of the educational system around which educational edifice is built. The curriculum contents should be built around the specific purposes for which the educational provisions are made and they should be made explicit to the learners and the society.

HE develops and nurtures values. It is important that special efforts must be made to preserve and promote educational values like thirst for knowledge, critical thinkings, search for truth and more important is to inculcate Universal Human values such as peace, tolerance, love patriotism, non violence through education. Such an education will have everlasting effect on achieving sustainable development.

At a time when pertinent issues like AIDS, Global education, Illeteracy, Population education, HR education are considered to be separate components, the approach would be to integrate these areas under one area of Learning called Peace education for sustainable development.

Bibliography

Bose, Buddhadeva, "Rabindranath Tagore and Bengali Prose," in *A Centenary Volume: Rabindranath Tagore*, 1861–1961, Sahitya Akademi, 1961.

Chakravorty, B. C., *Rabindranath Tagore: His Mind and Art*, Young India Publications, 1971.

D.M. Gupta, *Essays on Rabindranath Tagore*, edited by T.R. Sharma, Ghaziabad : Vimal Prakashan, 1987

Dutta, Krishna, *Rabindranath Tagore : The Myriad-Minded Man*, London: Bloomsbury, 1995.

Dyson, Ketaki Kushari, *In Your Blossoming Flower-Garden : Rabindranath Tagore and Victoria Ocampo*, New Delhi : Sahitya Akademi, 1988

Ghose, Sisirkumar, *The Later Poems of Tagore*, London, 1961

Hesse, Hermann, "Hermann Hesse on Tagore," in *Later Poems of Rabindranath Tagore*, translated by Aurobindo Bose, Peter Owen, 1974, p. 7, originally published in 1957.

Krishna Dutta and Andrew Robinson, *Rabindranath Tagore*, The Myriad-Minded Man, 1995.

Krishna Kripalani, Rabindranath Tagore: A Biography, 2nd rev. ed. (1980); and

Mary M. Lago, *Tagore's life and writings*, Rabindranath Tagore (1976);

Radhakrishnan, Sarvapalli, *The Philosophy of Rabindranath Tagore*, London : Macmillan, 1918

Ramananda Chatterjee, *The Golden Book of Tagore: A Homage to Rabindranath Tagore*, From India and the World, in Celebration of His Seventieth Birthday, Calcutta : The Golde Book Committee, 1931

Rothenstein, William, *Six Portraits of Rabindranath Tagore*, London, 1915

Roy, Basanta Koomar, *Rabindranath Tagore : The Man and His Poetry*, New York, 1915

Sinha, Sasadhar, *Social thinking of Rabindranath Tagore,* London, 1962

Thompson, Edward John, *Rabindranath Tagore : Poet and Dramatist,* London : Oxford University Press, 1948

Verma, Rajendra, *Rabindranath Tagore : Prophet Against Totalitarianism,* London, 1964

Index